Outpost

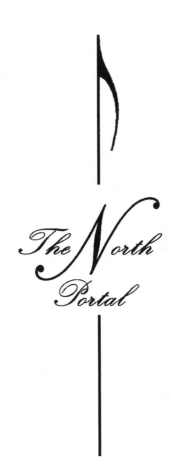

The North Portal

Dr. Dottie Graham

The cover design is based on original artwork
by Patricia Clancy.

Outpost Gypsy Tree: The North Portal was edited
by Paula Schlauch.

DEDICATION

To My Grandchildren
Anja, Christian, Chad, Brandon, Michael, Hunter, Skyller
And their generation.

Outpost Gypsy Tree by Dr. Dottie Graham is an adventurous journey into another dimension where holograms, angelic beings and teens unite to prepare for their mission. This book is an enchanting page-turner of beautiful descriptions, suspense and mystery. It captured me from the first sentence to the last page. I missed it when I was finished.

Dr. Clara Willard Boyle, RN, HTCP, CSTI, VRT

This is a story of courageous journeys and hair-raising adventures for a small group of teens who desire peace, love and brotherhood in their world. They are charged with the task to restore the Earth's North Portal which hovers over Ireland, and return it to its original pristine state. Upon being transported to Outpost Gypsy Tree, their studies revolve around an ancient Neolithic structure 5,000 years in their far distant past and a journey to that ancient world. An adventurous read into the universal laws of nature and physics.

Debbie Woodell, HTCP

You will be captured by the web Dr. Dottie Graham weaves, linking time and space, with the tangible earth and the energetic worlds as her present day teenage 'light travelers' pursue their quest over 5000 years ago. Vivid descriptions, believable characters, and a fantastic journey with suspense filled adventure convey this tale of hope realized by young adults on a true mission of love and peace. You'll join me anxiously awaiting the next mission.

MAC, HTCP

CONTENTS

CONTENTS

ACKNOWLEDGMENTS

This first in the series of Outpost Gypsy Tree Books has been a part of my daily life for the past fifteen years. So many people, too numerous to name, have been there for me as I opened to the realization of 'the writer' living and growing within me. You know who you are, and I thank you for believing in me and for feeding my writer's soul along the way. A very special thank you goes to my dear husband, John, who patiently watched and supported from the sidelines. To my precious children Leigh, Ted and Stacie, whose playful, impish nature, even as adults, inspires me. To my seven grandchildren whom I adore, this book is dedicated to you and your generation. To my dear friend Elaine who has been there for me since the first chapter was conceived. Special acknowledgement goes to my dear Paula without whose guidance, encouragement, editing and belief in my journey, the publication of this book would have been impossible. And to my dear muse, Yadkins who has guided me through it all: thank you for your ever present inspiration and wisdom.

PROLOGUE

Zero hour had arrived. The first chink of sunlight streamed through the roof box. It slowly made its way down the passageway and illuminated the ancient triple spiral carving in the stone womb. With her eyes fixed upon the pinnacle of the three-foot high obelisk before her, Drew Megan Campbell slowly rubbed a small white quartz stone between her hands. As Eittod had instructed her, she held the stone just inches above the tip of the obelisk's pinnacle. She sucked in a deep, nervous breath; her heart pounded hard against her ribs; her face was tense, flushed. After all, this was what she was born to do; it was her task and hers alone, her great-grandfather had said. Drew had to trust, even though she did not yet know the outcome of her next action. Her fellow light travelers' eyes were transfixed upon her. Their fate rested in her hands. As the triangular notch on the underside of the small quartz touched the capstone, three things happened in rapid succession: brilliant aquamarine lights flashed throughout the stone chamber blinding them; the earth began to tremble; and the heavy, scraping sounds of moving rocks deafened them. *It can't end like this, we've come too far,* Drew thought, bracing herself as the ground below her feet shifted. Locking eyes with

Patrick, they both instantly knew it just couldn't end like this! The others stared at Drew with concerned eyes as the earth below their feet moved downward. It was as if the ancient chamber was devouring them whole. They reached for each others' hands and gripped tight. The stone chamber began to descend like a modern-day elevator, but there was no light board indicating the number of floors below or above nor piped-in soothing music. Rather, ear-splitting scraping and groaning sounds of ancient heavy rocks vibrated through their bodies, rattling their bones and clattering their teeth. The aquamarine flashes became more intense, more tangible, surrounding them as if holding them all safely in place. An avalanche of thoughts spilled through their heads but no one made a sound. It was all happening in slow motion, freezing them speechless. Drew could feel their fear, hear their thoughts. Telepathically, she reminded them of her kinship with Patrick, hence this can't be the end. Drew's life flashed before her.

CHAPTER ONE:
The Campbell Family Myth

The earth glistened. Rapidly falling snow stuck against the icy window panes of the small cottage, as if peering through to witness the birth. "It's a girl," announced Doc O'Malley in his strong Irish brogue over the welcomed squall. "And she's a beauty and appears rock solid healthy too, Meg! Hear those strong lungs?"

Sighs of amazement and relief filled the dimly lit bedroom as Doc gently placed the newborn on Meg's chest for inspection.

"Congratulations! What a gift! Oh, my heavens! What a gift! And about time! Have you and Tom picked out a name yet, Meg?" Doc questioned excitedly.

Exhausted from her labor, the grateful mother softly sobbed as her tears washed onto the little one cradled tightly in her arms. Her husband caressed them both. Finally, a living child to fill their lives; they had lost so many. This time no names had been chosen – it seemed so fruitless. And yet, here she was!

Tom Campbell looked up from his wife's radiant face. "No Doc, no name yet, but I am sure we'll have a worthy Irish name soon enough. Grand will see to that!"

Meg and Tom watched anxiously as Nurse Kerry checked the new arrival from head to toe, then gave Doc O'Malley the thumbs up. Relief filled their faces. Nurse Kerry was a stout, middle aged woman with a gentle, kind face, who had been by Meg's side through all the disappointments of miscarriages and a stillborn. Once cleaned and bundled, she lovingly placed the newborn back into Meg's outstretched arms, arms that had ached for this moment for so long.

Meg and Tom were now in their mid-thirties. Meg was thin and fair-skinned with copper-colored hair. Tom, on the other hand, was olive-skinned and extremely muscular, with curly sandy brown locks.

"A miracle! That's what this is, a miracle – straight from heaven," Tom said as he buried his face into the infant's blankets. "Oh, she smells so sweet, Meg! I never realized babies smelt this good."

"You just wait 'til that tummy starts rumbling, then see how good she smells, Tom Campbell," injected Nurse Kerry with a hardy chuckle. The room filled with joyful laughter. A good dose of laughter was what they all needed; it had been a long, difficult night.

After a strong cup of morning brew, which consisted of coffee, Irish whiskey, brown sugar and heavy cream, Doc O'Malley pulled on his boots. Next, he wrapped his plaid scarf around his face and neck.

"Meg gave you a fine Valentine gift, Tom," said Doc. "Hard to top a present like that," he chuckled. Putting on his coat and cap, he bid Tom congratulations again as he made his way toward the kitchen door.

"Here's your bag, Doc, can't forget that," said Tom as he handed the physician his medical bag.

Doc O'Malley had been the Campbell family physician for as long as Tom could remember.

"I'd forget my head sometimes if the good lord hadn't attached it," joked Doc.

"Can you believe this weather, Tom? It's been a long time since Ireland's had a snowstorm like this. Your little one picked a mighty raw night to be born, and on St. Valentine's Day to boot," he said as he peered through the icy window pane.

"Kerry will take good care of your ladies. And she's brought some of her fresh home-baked brown bread and a fine hearty stew to warm you all for supper. And, Tom, you need to get some rest, too," he said, placing a hand on Tom's shoulder.

As Doc made his way out the door and down the back garden path leaving deep footprints in the mounting fresh snow, he called back. "You'd best let Grand know she's here. He'll want to have a look at his brand new great-granddaughter." The weather consumed him.

As Tom waved and turned from the door, Grand appeared in the kitchen. "Heard O'Malley shouting, how'd it go this time?" he asked, his voice weak and raspy.

"We need a name Grand; she's a healthy baby girl!" Tom announced. Tears leaked from their eyes as Grand feebly embraced him. "Come see for yourself! She's a beauty, Grand. And both Doc and Nurse Kerry checked her out, and said she's sound and healthy." Tom eagerly led Grand to Meg's side.

Grand gazed down at the soft pink bundle in Meg's arms. Taking a seat next to the bed, he stared at the bundle for a long time, speechless, caressing her little hands in his. Meg opened the blankets to give him a better look at his newest descendant. Her skin was soft, smooth and pink; her little legs were pulled up tight to her tummy, and a small watermelon seed-shaped birthmark showed on her left knee. Fine wisps of copper-colored curls peeked out from under her cap. And according to Meg, there were bright green eyes beneath those lightly lashed lids. Grand couldn't take his eyes from her; he gently touched a fingertip to the birthmark that graced her knee and smiled. Tears welled up in his pouched green eyes.

"Good job, Meg," he finally said in his weak voice, still not taking his gaze from the tiny form wiggling before him. "You're as beautiful as I had remembered you'd be; you've been a long time coming, young lady," Grand softly whispered in her little ear. "Remember me?" he asked.

Grand seemed mesmerized and so far away in his thoughts; tears slid slowly along the deep wrinkles in his old, weathered face. Then cocking his head to one side as if in another time and space, "Drew, that's her name!" commanded Grand, startling Tom, Meg and the infant. "Drew! It's a good Celtic name – means courageous. And that's what she'll need, courage, for what lies ahead for this little lass." His voice was strangely strong. His whole body trembled.

Concerned at his warning words, the new parents looked at each other, then back at Grand. This was a time for joy and celebration – not superstitious warnings. Grand was in his early nineties now and still embraced the old Irish myths and legends, including the legendary Campbell Family Myth.

"Drew Megan Campbell," Tom said, breaking the seriousness of Grand's words. "I like it!" he continued with excitement in his voice as if he had just realized he was a father at last. "What do you think, Meg?"

"Does she have to have my name?" Meg questioned.

"Of course she does!" said Tom. "If she has a courageous life to live," he continued exuberantly, "then she'll need the strength of the strong mother who gave her breath. So, Drew Megan Campbell it is!"

They all laughed, hugged and shed tears of joy and thanksgiving for the blessing bestowed upon them that snowy, February 14th morning.

As daylight surrendered into evening, Grand knocked on Meg and Tom's bedroom door. "Come in Grand!" their voices coming in whispers. Drew slept undisturbed in her cradle as Grand slowly moved into the dimly lit room. He seemed strange somehow, distant. Neither Tom nor Meg was able to put a word to it – just strange, trance-like even – his face was soft, sober and luminous.

"You okay?" queried Tom. Both Tom and Meg were concerned. Grand's health had been failing for months, but the excitement of a new baby coming seemed to have given him cause to live a bit longer.

Grand didn't answer. He slowly pulled a chair nearer the old cradle and sat with his back to Meg and Tom. He quietly stared at Drew. Again, tears washed down his pale cheeks. Slowly reaching into his shirt pocket, he withdrew a small quartz stone with a triple spiral design carved into its center and placed it on Drew's tiny left hand, wrapping her little fingers around its one edge. The flat stone was more than double the size of her tiny fist. Placing his aged, trembling hand on hers, he softly whispered, "The myth says the stone will know its rightful master – it has chosen you, dear child; the task is now laid upon you, Drew Megan Campbell."

A brilliant flash of aquamarine light rose from the cradle as Tom and Meg watched in stunned disbelief. Was the old Campbell Family Myth true?

By morning Grand had passed, a slight smile on his peaceful cold face; his entrusted charge was now fulfilled.

CHAPTER TWO:
The Paintings

Drew eased up onto her tip toes, stretched her slender body toward the blue sky and breathed in the delicious morning air; there was a slight breeze carrying the sweet smell of Ireland's wild meadow flowers to her senses. Her eyes drank in the lush green of the hillside overlooking the bend of the Boyne River. She missed the sounds of the whooper swans, but knew they would return in the fall. Until then she would muse at the grunting sounds of the mute swans as they flew overhead toward the river. This was Drew Megan Campbell's world – the only world she had ever known. Here in this place she was loved, protected, nurtured and fulfilled. She wished everyone in the world could be as safe and loved as she.

Yearnings for any other world had never entered her mind or heart, but her world as she knew it, was about to change.

"How strange, how very strange, yet how beautiful!" she said aloud to herself as she laid out her art supplies on the weathered back garden table. Her father waved from the other side of the garden. "Top of the morning, my little artist." Drew waved back absentmindedly, caught up in her wonderment. She had painted the familiar Irish landscape many times, but today there was a very different landscape wafting in her head.

At only fifteen, Drew was already an accomplished artist in her own right. Within the past year, she had had her work exhibited in a solo showing at her local library, and several award pieces now hung in a teen exhibition twenty miles away in the nation's capital of Dublin.

Drew loved watercolors; for her the transparency of the paints washed away the ugliness of the world, and only its true beauty shone through. Painting gave her a sense of peace, wholeness, connection – feelings that she wished truly existed in the hearts of all people all over the world. She rarely watched the news or read the newspaper because world affairs saddened her so. She wished that she could change it all for the better somehow. But what chance would a fifteen-year-old girl have against all the darkness in the world?

This particular morning as Drew's brushes washed across the canvas pad, a very strange and enormous, yet beautiful tree emerged. Its large, shiny green foliage was wrapped with thread-like vines of colorful beads. Sparkling bangles of gold, silver and crystal hung from its limbs, glistening. And glass balls of intricate designs were sprinkled throughout its massive branches, giving the beholder the sense that if touched, the branches would make a most enchanting vibrational sound.

"My goodness, Drew, that's an amazing tree," said her mother as she pushed open the back kitchen screen door a few hours later. "Your imagination's working overtime this morning."

Caught in the experience, Drew was unaware of Meg's presence. It was as if Drew was actually standing right in front of the large tree, mesmerized by its beauty. Puzzled, Meg shrugged and made her way to the garden to join Tom.

As the days passed, Drew painted in her every spare moment, each of her paintings more intriguing than the last: a wide meadow with a crystal blue river winding through; a forest encampment; stone archways etched with mysterious languages, shapes and symbols; and pathways that seemed to go nowhere. And the faces – oh such beautiful and unusual faces, faces she felt she knew. But how and from where?

Her mind was reeling – her daydreams so vivid. What was happening? she wondered. Where was all this coming from? She felt so alive, so joyous. Sometimes she would paint throughout the night as the endless, enticing images held her captive.

Drew's parents watched and worried as the weeks passed. Her obsession with this new, inner world was now playing out into her everyday real world. Witnessing her paintings, Meg and Tom feared that the time was drawing near for their precious daughter's walk with destiny – a destiny laid upon Drew by her great-grandfather on the day of her birth. They had hoped and prayed that the task would pass her by. They believed that if Drew were not aware of the myth, it would never come to pass. But these paintings, these faces! Was the Campbell Family Myth closing in on them in spite of their precautions?

Their only comfort was the love and gentleness they could see in the eyes of the many faces Drew painted: an olive-skinned gleeful youth with an elongated head, a kind-faced matronly woman in jeans and an older gentleman with compassionate eyes and a multicolored body. Meg and Tom sensed that whoever these people were, they would protect Drew and teach her how to survive in the mysterious new world she was being drawn to through her paintings.

With her father's help, Drew took down most of the other paintings from her bedroom walls and replaced them with the new wonderland she had created on canvas: the large colorful tree, the forest encampment, the wildflower strewn meadow, the carved stone archways and the amazing faces.

Her bedroom was full of all that she held dear, not an inch of space was wasted. A large floor to ceiling mirror with its many decorative hooks held her Irish dance awards, tiaras and wigs. Brass wall hooks displayed well-worn ghillies, and jig shoes of all sizes hung by their laces – shoes long-since outgrown, but still cherished. At the base of the large mirror, a scarred wooden platform, built by her dad for her dance practice, covered half the floor. As is typical for a teenage girl, Drew's dresser drawers were stuffed to the brim and overflowing with treasures, bobbles and clothes. White cotton poodle socks crawled out of a woven basket beside her Irish sleigh bed. Her nightstand was strewn with CD's of her favorite pop/rock artist, Irish dance music and a photo of her beloved great-grandfather, Grand.

On the other side of the room stood an old wooden easel, splattered with a collage of colors, that once belonged to her great-grandmother, Nana. Paint boxes and glass jars containing brushes of all shapes and sizes were stuffed on the large window seat, along with messy stacks of art paper and canvas pads waiting to be caressed by her paints. Cherished photos hung from the ceiling on varied lengths of brightly-colored satin ribbons – old wonderful black and whites of Grand and Nana, neither of whom had she ever known, but to whom she felt dearness. There were wedding photos of Mum and Dad, an array of childhood, school, dance and art show photos. And there were family holiday snapshots and photos of friends. Her favorite photo was one of her dad nervously holding her on the day she was born. She always teased him that there was more blanket than baby in his arms.

For this vibrant, green eyed, copper-colored curly haired lass, life was a fast-paced mixture of family, school, dance and painting. Drew was a master of all she pursued and she loved it. Yet she felt a strange new sense of herself emerging – one she knew little about. It was unnerving, yet exciting all at the same time.

One summer evening as she painted, Drew glimpsed herself walking in the forest encampment she had painted; she saw herself under the stone archways talking with other teens as wide-eyed as she. And she saw herself standing in front of the large, decorated tree waiting for permission to venture inside. The amazing faces she had come to know through her art began to speak with her in her head.

"Hello, Drew. I am Bezen of Early Earth and this is my son, Mingo," said the kind-faced lady in jeans as the tall young man nodded his elongated head at her. "We anxiously awaited your arrival," she finished.

The elderly gentleman with the colorful body introduced himself as Eittod of Tulsun Minor. As his deep echoing voice vibrated into her senses, his crystal blue eyes drew her into his world.

Throughout that night, Drew experienced her two artistic outlets working in tandem as they never had before – painting and dancing in feverous movements – as if she were plugged into the giant tree's energy source; she glowed and reveled in it.

Oblivious to the old grandfather clock in the downstairs sitting room striking three, Drew was in a reverie. Her hands flew back and forth across the canvas, frenzy-like. Her dancing feet matched the swift tempo of her brush strokes. Sweaty copper curls matted to her brow and neck, her face apple red. She was in another world far away from her beloved Ireland. Her fanciful musing reached its crescendo and then fell away as quickly as it had come. Drew collapsed across her bed into a deep sleep – finally unplugged.

Breakfast came and went without her, and then lunch time appeared, but still no Drew. Meg and Tom were very aware of her late night painting and dancing sessions, and tried not to interfere with her pleasure. Her art work had certainly moved to a new level; amazing new brush techniques and more vibrant paint mixes were appearing in her work. By mid-afternoon, Meg eased upstairs and quietly opened Drew's bedroom door. She was spread diagonally across the duvet, face down, still in her clothes of the day before. Her mother slipped into the room to take a peek at the new painting on the easel, being careful not to disturb any of the debris strewn about the floor. When Meg reached the easel, the truth of what Drew was experiencing tore deep into her. Tears raced down Meg's face. Panic riveted into every fiber of her being. She fought to hold back the fast-coming screams as she left the room, closing the door quietly behind her.

With a hand clasped tightly to her mouth, Meg ran down the steps, through the house, and out into the back garden beckoning Tom. The back kitchen screen door screeched as it flapped on its hinges behind her.

"Drew knows, Tom! She knows!" Meg screamed through her sobs. "It's on her easel along with some writing. She knows, Tom! Somehow she knows. Come quickly, Tom, Drew knows!" Meg waved her hands frantically in the air motioning for Tom to come. Her feet were pounding the earth as she ran in place at the edge of the garden, her apron flapping in the warm afternoon breeze.

Tom hurried from his knees. "Take hold of yourself, Meg!" he called, making his way to her across the garden, brushing dirt from his pants as he went.

"For heaven's sake, what's all this about? Drew knows what?" asked Tom, watching Meg continuing her manic-like movements.

"Meg, calm down!" he begged as he reached out taking hold of her. He hadn't seen Meg this unraveled in fifteen years.

"Her painting!" she gasped, looking for answers in Tom's face. "Last night Drew painted the carved stone Grand had given her, along with some writing."

"How could that be?" he recoiled. "Drew has never seen it, *never*, Meg! You *know* that!" His eyes darted to the far end of the garden. "How could she know? It's safe, Meg. Hidden, I tell you, hidden. We both know that!"

Meg shrugged, "I don't know, Tom. I don't know, but it's on her canvas." Meg's arms were again in motion, pounding her fists together in desperation.

"What does the writing say?" he questioned, his heart now pounding hard against his ribs.

"Oh, I don't know, Tom. I was so upset over the painting of the stone that I didn't even take time to read it. Come see for yourself. She's still asleep. Come! Come quickly!" gasped Meg, her body quivering, her face blood-red, her breathing labored.

"Meg, you need to calm down," pleaded Tom, taking hold of her fists and pulling them to his chest. "We'll do this together," he said calmly. "We'll take care of it. We always have, but you need to catch your breath and calm down," he stressed.

Meg leaned her sweaty wet face into him.

"It will be okay, Meg, you'll see. Please calm down," he begged, now gently stroking her matted red hair. Meg's breathing slowed to soft sobs as Tom gently held her, concern etched on his pallid face.

"Now, let's go take a look at that painting together," he said in a compassionate, reassuring tone.

Still quivering, Meg turned, threw open the screen door and made her way through the back kitchen to the staircase, Tom at her heels.

As they reached Drew's room, they paused, looking into each other's eyes for comfort and support. They were not known to pry into their daughter's affairs or private things. Although Drew was only fifteen, a strong bond of trust existed between them. But this situation was very different. This was something Meg and Tom had feared for fifteen years – something they couldn't understand or ignore. This was something they had to stop. But how?

As they entered Drew's room, Meg blotted her steady stream of tears with a corner of her apron as Tom moved quietly to the easel. Once there, his eyes confirmed his fears. Stunned by the sight of the quartz stone, Tom slowly read the writing on the canvas pad. Not believing what he had just read, he read it again. Turning to Meg, he motioned her forward, pointing to the invitation Drew had written in watercolor.

Her heart still pounding, Meg read the message.

Dear One:

Your silent pleas for peace in your world have been heard, and today, your pure and loving heart has answered the call of Eittod. Thank you!

You, Drew Megan Campbell, are invited to travel to Outpost Gypsy Tree for your instructions and assignment, whenever you so choose to depart. There is no need to pack, except for your stone; all needs will be met on this end. You will be moving out of the illusion of time, so you will not lose a moment of your linear time. Your parents, Meg and Tom, know of a task laid upon you by your great-grandfather, Grand, on the day of your birth. Their knowledge of the depth of the task before you is limited, but they can share what they know before your departure. All other questions that you may have will be answered upon your arrival. Whenever you desire to return to your precise split second in time, the departure passwords will be given to you. Remember, you have free will and your choices are always honored. When and if you are ready to travel, simply repeat the following transport passwords out loud.

"A peaceful, loving world is what I seek within my heart,
And I am willing to clear the way for it to happen.
I am part of the solution.
I am the solution!
I am chosen.
Eittod, this is Drew Megan Campbell.
Hear my petition for transport to Outpost Gypsy Tree!
NOW!"

Honorably yours,
Eittod of Tulsun Minor
Ambassador to the Regions Authority
Outpost Gypsy Tree

The nightmare Meg thought she and Tom had buried long ago stared defiantly into their faces. They were dumbstruck.

CHAPTER THREE:
The Triple Spiral Stone

Drew stirred. Her body slowly came back to life as she stretched each limb of her five-foot seven-inch frame, one limb at a time as if taking inventory of their function. As she lifted her head from the duvet, she realized someone was standing beside her bed. She quickly turned to see her parents looking down at her with concerned, tear-filled eyes. Alarmed, Drew leapt to her feet, stumbling on debris scattered about the wooden flooring.

"Oh, bummy!" she shouted kicking debris helter-skelter. "What's wrong? Who died?" she asked with alarm in her voice. "Mum! Dad! What's happened?"

Both reached out to hold her. Jumping back from their embrace, Drew hit hard against her nightstand and the youthful photo of her great-grandfather, Grand, hit the wall and crashed to the floor in pieces.

"Tell me what's going on!" she demanded. "You're scaring me!"

"Your painting, Drew, the one on the easel. We need to talk," said Tom in a soft, loving voice.

Drew gave them a reproachful look. "My painting?" she said. "My painting has you both in this state?"

Still not allowing them to touch her, she carefully stepped past the fragments of broken glass, and kicked her way through the debris to the paint-splattered easel. Drew's face softened as her eyes met the canvas pad. "I painted this?" she whispered in disbelief.

Painted on the canvas was a small, flat white quartz stone with a triple spiral symbol carved into its center; the spirals glowed with an aquamarine radiance that seemed to reach beyond the painting itself. She placed her left hand on the image of the stone and closed her eyes. Immediately, her head was full of an amazing panorama: a flat-top mound set on an elongated ridge, its walls and dome constructed of what appeared to be water-rolled quartz pebbles, and beyond, a flowing river. There were fruit trees abound, and livestock and whooper swans roamed the grassy hillside. Drew knew this structure and the triple spiral symbol, and knew them well.

Her eyes flew open. "I just saw Newgrange! I don't understand. This has to do with Newgrange?" She turned to her parents with a questioning look. "When I touched the stone on my painting, I saw an image of Newgrange so clearly, but not as it looks today. Livestock roamed the hillside and there was no visitor's center. I don't understand what's happening."

Newgrange, the most famous historic monument in all of Ireland, is said to be an Irish passagetomb constructed around 3200 BCE. According to archeologists, the structure is older than Egypt's Great Pyramid, older than Britain's Stonehenge, and located just miles from the Campbell Family homestead.

"Read the message, Drewkins, and then we'll talk," said Tom in the same soft, loving tone. Tom was doing his best to stay calm and focused for Drew's sake. Meg just nodded in agreement, still unable to speak. Her body trembled to its core.

Drew slowly turned to read the message, and then whispered, "Bring my stone? What stone?" Then finished, *"Honorably yours, Eittod of Tulsun Minor, Ambassador to the Regions Authority, Outpost Gypsy Tree?"*

Dazed, she stared at the painting, reading and re-reading the message, then reached to touch the name *Eittod*.

"This name seems so familiar. I've heard it before, but where?" she asked herself aloud. She slowly turned. Her eyes scanned the paintings on her bedroom walls and came to rest on one of an elderly gentleman with a colorful body.

As if a light bulb had been turned on over her head, Drew turned toward her parents. "Is this what I've been painting, a place called Outpost Gypsy Tree?" she questioned.

"All this time I've been connected with this place, with its people, and now I am invited to travel there? It's real? And – and…you know something about this?"

Meg and Tom nodded and slowly moved toward Drew, carefully stepping around the debris.

"Why haven't you said something? All these weeks – and you've not said a word. What's going on?" Questions tumbled out of Drew's mouth, like marbles spilling from a leather pouch turned on end. Confusion and apprehension took command of her face.

"Why don't you shower and dress, Drew," said Meg, finding her voice at last. "I'll fix you something to eat, and we'll talk. Okay?" she finished, gently and reassuringly reaching for Drew.

"Mum, my world has just been turned upside down and all you can say is 'take a shower, Drew?'" Again, Drew recoiled from Meg's reach.

"I need some answers, and I need them now!" Drew shouted. "What do you both know about this place, and what does this stone have to do with me? And where is it?" she demanded, pointing to the canvas.

Drew was always respectful of her parents and their wishes, but confusion and fear gripped her.

"I know you're upset and scared, Drewkins, and you have every right to be," whispered Tom.

He always called her by her baby name whenever he was concerned or to comfort her. It made her feel safe, protected and loved.

"You know we love you and will always help you and protect you," he said as he slowly reached out to her.

Trembling, Drew reached for his hand. "I'm scared, Dad. I am really scared." She glanced around her room at the faces she had painted. Drew could again hear their voices and somehow knew their names.

"What's happening to me, Dad? Am I going crazy?" Tears began to stream down her fair-skinned cheeks. "We need to call Doc O'Malley. I need his help. I fear I am mad."

"No! No! No! Nothing like that, dear," said Meg quickly. "Doc can't help with this."

Meg and Tom wrapped their arms around Drew and held her tight. This was a special family, one where honor, respect, encouragement and love flowed freely. Meg kissed Drew on the cheek and stroked her face with her finger tips, brushing away the tears that were fast coming.

"I need you to help me understand what's happening and why?" cried Drew looking into her parents' eyes. "No more secrets, please. No more secrets."

"We will, dear," Meg reassured her, "We will."

"Your mother and I will share the little that we know about what's happening and about the stone. I promise!" Tom said. "We should have been honest with you from the beginning. We know that now. Please, Drewkins, take a nice hot shower while your Mum fixes you something to eat," he smiled. "Then we'll talk. We'll answer your questions as best we can."

Drew nodded and slowly turned back to the easel for another read.

As Drew bathed and dressed, excitement began to build within her, drowning out some of her fear. "Could this all be real or am I just caught in a dream that I can't wake from?" she asked aloud.

Drew tossed it around in her head trying to make some kind of sense of it all. Standing in front of her mirror, she was quite aware of Outpost Gypsy Tree and its people surrounding her from her walls. The message from Eittod played out in her head – *Your silent pleas for peace in your world have been heard....*" Like glimpsing a dream, she began to recall their voices, their messages.

"This is a real place and these are real people, and I am invited to go there," she whispered, "but why me? No wonder Mum and Dad are acting this way. What could they know?" she asked herself as her wet copper curls glistened in the afternoon sunlight reflecting in her mirror.

Finally, Drew's nose lead her to the kitchen where a fine Irish breakfast of fried eggs, pork rashers covered with her mother's special seasoning, brown bread and tea was waiting for her at three o'clock in the afternoon. Meg and Tom were seated at the kitchen table smiling up at her.

The Campbell family was financially stable, but with little to spare for frills. For Meg and Tom, Drew's needs took first priority: her academics, her dance and art classes, and the clothing and supplies necessary to support these activities. Tom was a tradesman who kept a good size garden going in the summer months. Meg loved staying at home, and gave her support to the family finances by canning their fresh fruits and vegetables for the winter, and with the small income from her in-house cake and pastry business. Townspeople would tell her, "It's not officially a birthday without a Meg Campbell birthday creation." Creativity seemed to run rampant in the Campbell family.

Drew did her part by tutoring part-time after school and was her Dad's summer produce door-to-door huckster for which he gave her a percentage.

Their small, blue-trimmed white limestone cottage had been in the Campbell family for many generations. Tom, his father, grandfather, great-grandfather and great-great-grandfather before him were all born in the same room as Drew. Tom's trade kept the old house in very good repair knowing that someday it would belong to Drew if she chose it to be.

As Drew ate, Tom shared the little that he knew of the Campbell Family Myth and the sequence of events on that snowy Valentine's Day fifteen years ago. He told how he and his father had never put much stock in the myth – both of the opinion that it was just an old man's musing. Grand did love to tell stories, and the Campbell Family Myth was the whopper of them all in their minds!

"I guess the story was a bit far-fetched for your grandfather and me," said Tom. "Supposedly, a beautiful young Tuatha dé Danann goddess came out of Newgrange and passed the stone and the myth on to the Campbell family for safekeeping. I believe David Campbell was the one who started the myth back in the seventeen hundreds. Anyway, the goddess then walked back into the womb of the mound and was never seen again. It was assumed, according to mythology, that she was reborn into the other world."

Tom shared that Nana had believed the myth to be true and that Grand would be the last to pass the stone on. That in his lifetime the 'rightful master of the stone,' as Grand called it, would be born, and his task to pass it on would be fulfilled.

Hanging on Tom's every word, Drew absent-mindedly spread a knob of butter on her brown bread. Meg nervously glanced from one face to the other, gripping Tom's hand tightly.

"Around nightfall," he continued, "Grand knocked on our bedroom door. When he entered, he looked strange – trance-like even. I spoke to him, but he didn't respond. You were asleep in your cradle, Drew – the one you have all your dolls setting in, in the sitting room."

Drew nodded with a weak smile. Having finished her meal, she moved her chair closer to her mother for comfort. Meg put her arm around Drew's shoulders as they continued to listen to Tom's story.

"Anyhow," Tom continued, clearing his throat. "Grand pulled a chair up close to your cradle and after a few minutes whispered, *'It is said that the stone will know its rightful master – it has chosen you dear child; the task is now laid upon you, Drew Megan Campbell.'* Then a brilliant flash of aquamarine light rose from your cradle. Your mother and I watched in numbed disbelief, realizing that the myth was indeed true and that you – our *only* living child – were given this burden to carry," he sighed. Tom placed his right fist on the table and began to rub it with his other hand, nervously shifting his body in his chair as he spoke.

"I rushed to your cradle and saw to my great sorrow that the Campbell Family stone had been laid on your tiny left hand – the very same stone that you painted during the night, Drew," he said, tears sliding down his cheeks and onto the table cloth below.

"We begged for Grand to undo whatever he had done, but he said that it was impossible. He said the stone had chosen you, and his entrusted charge was now fulfilled. Grand died that very night, Drew!"

"But what about the myth, Dad?" asked Drew.

"All your mother and I know about the myth is that whoever is chosen 'master of the stone' will travel beyond our world, at great risk, in search of peace for mankind. That's all I know or remember knowing. I should have listened to Grand's stories all those years. I was judgmental, foolish and fearful. And then Grand was gone along with all the answers to questions I never asked," Tom finished, his voice now weak.

"But, the stone, Dad, where is the stone?" Drew questioned, now slowly getting to her feet.

Tom laid the back of his right fist on the table in front of her and slowly opened it. There in his outstretched hand was a small, flat, white quartz stone carved with a triple spiral symbol at its center.

"As you know Drew, the triple spiral symbol, or the spiral of life as it is sometimes called, is an ancient symbol that has been used in Megalithic and Celtic art and writings going back some five thousand years," he said as he held out the stone to her.

"Yes, I recognize the symbol, Dad. It appears over and over again at Newgrange!" Drew said with excitement in her voice as pieces began to come together in her head.

"That's right, Drew," said Tom.

"After Grand's funeral, your mother and I decided to put an end to the myth, thinking that if you never saw the stone, nor knew of the Campbell Family Myth, it would never come to pass," he said, looking up at her. His eyes gave way to tears, his voice cracked.

Meg got up and gently stroked Tom's shoulders.

"At my suggestion, Drew, we buried the stone in a tin at the far end of the garden where it remained until today," Meg admitted. "But now we realize that hiding it from you couldn't stop the task laid upon you by your great-grandfather all those years ago."

Drew noticed a small, rusty, dirt encrusted candy tin on the kitchen counter. "So that's where it's been these past fifteen years," she said, "Right under my nose."

Drew looked down at the stone in her father's hand and reached for it instinctively with her left hand. When the stone came in contact with her skin, the triple spirals glowed with a brilliant aquamarine light, just like the one in her painting, and again, ancient images of Newgrange flashed in her head.

Drew closed her eyes once more and tilted her head to one side as if listening to some inaudible voice calling her name. Her inner struggle gave way as the echoing voice of Eittod awakened the long forgotten memory of the words her great-grandfather spoke into her ear that snowy night fifteen years ago.

Tom and Meg watched in horror at the familiar scene playing out in front of them. Drew seemed strange somehow – distant, trance-like even. Her head tilted again as if she were listening to a voice they were not privileged to hear. Her face was soft and luminous.

As she opened her eyes and stared at the glowing radiance in her hand, Drew somehow understood the journey that lay ahead for her. But was she ready to accept it? In her heart, she had silently wished for this all of her life and here it was, an opportunity to bring peace to mankind and to the Earth itself.

"Mum and Dad, I know you can't understand what I feel and what I now know, but it's real. It's very real. And I understand your concern and fear for me, but I know Grand was right. This is my task and my task alone. Eittod has beckoned me, and...I must go now!" she said in a firm but loving voice. "I am asking you both to trust me, and please honor what I must do. Dad, will you please drive me to Newgrange?"

Tom nodded with understanding and surrender, got up from his chair and withdrew the truck keys from his pants pocket. "Come on, Meg. She'll need us both," he said soberly.

Meg began to plead with Drew, but Tom gently touched her and put an index finger to his lips, motioning for her silence.

"My dear Meg, listen to me, we have no choices left," he said, "It's out of our hands and always has been."

CHAPTER FOUR:
Newgrange

The old family pickup made its way south along the narrow, winding tarmacadam roads to the Brú Na Bóinne Visitors Centre. Sitting between her parents, Drew's mind scrambled to put together all the pieces of this unfolding puzzle: the images, the paintings, the absolute joy and exhilaration she was feeling, the faces and voices of Outpost Gypsy Tree's people, especially Eittod and his invitation for travel. The events of her birth, the Campbell Family Myth and Grand swirled inside her head. And the beautiful and intriguing carved stone she held tightly in her left hand was her ticket to it all.

Drew popped out of her bemusement as Tom navigated the truck down the hill, across the narrow bridge following the bend of the Boyne River and through the last few sharp turns into the crowded parking area of the Visitor Centre.

Newgrange, being one of the most visited ancient sites in all of Ireland, had a steady stream of tourists, both national and international, and today was no exception. Drew silently wished that all the visitors would just disappear. Right at this moment, she wanted Newgrange all to herself.

This site was one of Drew's favorite places along with the adjacent historic sites of Knowth and Dowth – all three sites built during the Neolithic period in Ireland's history. Ever since she could remember, Drew and her family had frequented these ancient sites embraced by the River Boyne and its tributary, the Mattocks – many of those times at her insistence. She felt a sense of connection, belonging – a true kinship with these mammoth stone beings of the far distant past and the intriguing stories and secrets they held; now she was beginning to understand why.

As the Campbell family made their way into the visitor's center, an elderly docent greeted them with a big smile. "Hi, Drew! No paint supplies today?" he queried in a graveled voice.

Drew had spent many hours on these grounds over the past seven years painting and sketching the various mounds, sunrises, sunsets, whooper and mute swans and the many kerbstone carvings of these ancient ruins.

"Not painting today, Michael, just visiting," she responded, giving him a big hug as he extended his arms toward her.

Michael is Drew's God-Father and a dear friend. Much of what she knew about Newgrange she learned from him. He was as close to a grandfather as she had. All of her grandparents had died before she was born. Only her great-grandfather, Grand, had remained to glimpse this Campbell family descendent.

"Everything okay?" he questioned.

Drew nodded reassuringly.

"The last shuttle's going out in a few minutes, but as usual, you're welcome to stay as long as you'd like, Drew. I'll pick you and your folks up when I come out later for my security run," he said.

Drew smiled and nodded in agreement.

Meg and Tom exchanged greetings with Michael and then quickly walked to the reception desk where a smiling, freckle-faced girl greeted them.

"Having a good summer, Drew?" she asked.

"Yes, thanks! And you, Erin?" Drew responded.

With the niceties aside and tickets in hand, the Campbell family made their way outside. Following the other visitors, they crossed the Boyne River via the footbridge to board the shuttle bus. The grassy dome of Newgrange could be glimpsed.

Finally, Drew was standing at the entrance to Newgrange. The large cairn made of many thousands of water-rolled quartz pebbles, six to nine inches across, glistened in the late afternoon sunlight. Oh, how she loved this place.

With Tom and Meg standing on either side of her, Drew placed her hands on the triple spiral symbol on Newgrange's large entrance kerbstone. As she did, Eittod's deep echoing voice summoned her. She stood motionless for a long time, trance-like, listening – her face again radiant. She turned to her parents and reached for their hands.

"Mum, Dad, it's time for me to go," she said. "Eittod is waiting for me at Outpost Gypsy Tree – my journey begins." Her voice was strangely mature, strong, distant.

"What do you mean you must go now? How? What are you talking about, Drew?" begged Meg frantically.

"I don't understand it myself, Mum. All I know is that I will simply be leaving here and going there – wherever there is. Eittod's invitation read somewhere out of the illusion of time, remember!" said Drew, musing to herself at the absurdity of her own words but knowing them to be true.

"Tom, please stop this craziness. Stop it!" demanded Meg.

"Meg, it's not craziness, and you know that," he said gently. "We both have known that there are forces at work that we have been fighting against since Drew's birth. And they are stronger and wiser than we are. Grand tried to tell us that, but we would never listen. We never really believed – not until today."

Concerned, Drew cupped her mother's face in her hands. "Mum, in my heart I have always known that someday I would find a way to help mankind, and the way is now clear for me. Please try to understand. Somehow, Grand knew it was my task. I must honor the family myth for his sake – for the sake of us all," Drew pleaded.

"Meg, she's right," said Tom. "We can't protect her nor stand in her way any longer. I think we've always known that. Over these past fifteen years, we've spent so much time talking and worrying about this day and wishing that we had listened to Grand and had asked him questions. But here it is in spite of all our efforts to prevent it. Don't you see how foolish we were to think we could change the outcome by just burying that stone and withholding the information about the myth from Drew?" he continued.

"This is well beyond our understanding and yet our Drew does understand it; Grand understood it. As hard as it is Meg, it is time for us to step down and honor her decision and her destiny."

Meg's knees buckled. Drew and Tom grabbed hold of her and leaned her against the kerbstone.

"Mum, I'll be okay. I promise. I'll be fine. I trust these people. I feel as though I have known them all of my life. I've seen into their hearts and know I'll be safe. Don't ask me how I know – I just know, Mum," Drew said lovingly, yet firmly.

"But, why must you go so soon, Drew? You're only fifteen. Can't you wait a few more years? You just found out about the stone, the family myth and these people. Please give yourself some time to think about what's going on. Digest it for a while, and then make your decision once you're older. Remember, this Eittod fellow said the choice is yours, Drew. Let's give it some time to sink in and prepare for your journey properly, alright?" Meg begged.

"Look, here comes the shuttle, Drew, let's go home," she said motioning toward the approaching shuttle.

"Attention, the last shuttle bus back to the visitor center will be leaving in ten minutes," rang Michael's voice through the shuttle speaker.

Tourists slowly began to make their way down from the mound toward the bus. Drew waved to Michael and took a deep breath – Newgrange was finally hers.

"I can't go home just yet, Mum. Nothing in my being will let me turn back at this point. Please trust me!" Drew begged.

"Please, Mum, I need you to be strong for me. Please, will you and Dad hold me as I say my transport passwords?" Drew asked.

"Remember," she continued, "Eittod promised that I will return to this precise split second in time! So you won't even have time to miss me," she laughed nervously. "Why, I'll be back before I am even gone. You'll see."

Her heart pounded with excitement and apprehension at the same time. Her mind raced with the possibilities of what the next few moments might hold.

There in the orange radiance of the setting sun, Drew's parents embraced her and kissed her gently on her cheeks.

"We love you, Drewkins; may the angels keep you safe while you are busy saving mankind," choked Tom with a forced smile.

Meg, struggling to control her fear, just nodded, holding onto Drew tightly as if this would somehow stop her flight from them.

Drew lovingly smiled at her parents. "I promise I'll be home in time for supper."

Holding her precious stone tightly in her left hand, Drew's eyes focused on the small rectangular opening just above the entrance to the Newgrange passageway as she spoke aloud the words etched in her mind.

"A peaceful, loving world is what I seek within my heart,
And I am willing to clear the way for it to happen.
I am part of the solution.
I am the solution!
I am chosen.
Eittod, this is Drew Megan Campbell.
Hear my petition for transport to Outpost Gypsy Tree!
NOW!"

With a brilliant flash of light, Meg and Tom's arms emptied.

CHAPTER FIVE:
A Forsaken Place

Far away from Drew's beloved Ireland and eons ago, or maybe just yesterday, a thick haze hung in the still afternoon air. Heat blistered everything in its wake; nothing seemed to be alive in this desolate place. The grass had long since retreated, its roots parched. The earth was powder with no breeze to disturb it. What was once a vital river lay empty; its smooth, round rocks now dry and bleached like parched bones. Its cool, babbling flow only a vague memory of days gone by; its moisture sucked into the lungs of a greedy sun. A huge, barren, solitary tree, its branches withered, stood in the middle of it all. Forsaken!

In the distance, a forest encampment laid ravaged, stripped of its beauty, its wildlife gone. The remains of stone foundations were naked and crumbled in the scorching heat, their structures long since consumed. Half-standing archways cast their haunting shadows along what were once pathways that now led to nowhere. What ancient languages laid carved here among these decayed ruins?

Who walked this land, laid these stones in place and built upon them? Where had they gone and why? There must have been a time when the air was cool and fresh, a time when these woods knew the footprints and scent of wildlife and man, a time when laughter and love rang through this abandoned site and gave it life.

Days came and went with no one to greet the sunlight. An eerie silence stood against the lasting heat; a silence only rarely broken by a faint throbbing sound from deep inside the lone tree. Tucked deep within the heart of the barren tree a slight glimmer of life remained, but for how long? It seemed an invisible force was holding this place captive, either punishing it or protecting it. Ages passed, yet the glimmer remained as if waiting for something or someone to rescue it, enliven it.

On a moonlit night, while the rest of creation slept, a breeze stirred out of nowhere carrying with it the sound of faint whispers. The breeze slowly spilled the whispers throughout the seared forest, over the crumbled stone carcasses, across the wide meadow, over the dried riverbed and encircled the lone tree as if caressing it, calling to it. The long awaited freshness had come at last. As the whispering breeze eased through, it forced the heat to withdraw its grip.

At that same moment as if working in tandem with the breeze, the moon sent slivers of light chinking into every minute crevice of the three hundred and fifty-foot solitary tree, lacing its massive trunk and long thick branches with a silvery glow. Clouds formed around and through the high branches, dressing them in a billowy white frock. Raindrops began to kiss the earth with promise. The gentle rains washed the landscape, coaxing the dormant seeds to swell. And with it, life slowly returned. Parched roots drank their fill and shot blades of green to the meadow floor. Wildflowers lifted their heads toward the sun and burst forth in festive colors. The river filled and washed over the thirsty rocks, and new life emerged from the dust.

Yet the solitary tree stood untouched, still barren but for the pale glimmer within and the occasional throb.

In the distance, the forest reached out for life once again, and it came. Nests of new life clung to strong branches and the sweet songs of birds broke the eerie silence; the rustle of hooves and the scurrying sounds of small creatures filled the once vacant air.

Seasons passed and the faint whispers on the breezes became more audible, swirling around the barren tree with a sense of pleading. A desire to be heard and acknowledged pulled at its bare branches in an effort to awaken the mammoth sleeping giant.

The occasional throbbing became more constant as the murmuring voices on the breeze grew louder and more frequent. The tree's heart was again beating and the slight glimmer swelled, eventually filling the whole of the tree with shimmering light.

Suddenly without warning, the barren tree shook violently throwing showers of light and debris in all directions like a wet animal freeing itself from years of dust and stagnation. Then it slowed to a humming vibration as if someone or something had just plugged it in. Light streamed out of every pore of its tough, wrinkled brown skin. Flares emitted from the tips of every branch sending multi-colored sparks riding across the night sky like a fourth of July celebration. The sparks collided with the murmurings, sending a lightning bolt etched with the voices of what sounded like thousands upon thousands of children into the very core of the tree. And a booming roar was set free.

Every creature, feathered and furred, halted. Their hearts pumped hard and fast, ears perked, tiny eyes searched. The trees in the distant forest bent toward the enormous sound as if expecting something more to happen. Even the blades of grass on the meadow floor stood at attention. It was as though the life blood of this place had just been put on alert.

A commanding voice echoed into the night air. "They are calling!" bellowed Eittod. "Finally, they are calling!"

All life in this place listened. Deep joyous sobs could be heard coming from the tree. Then silence. Moments later another roar from Eittod's commanding voice filled the air.

"Finally the children are calling for peace and love on the Earth! Our work begins again!"

Again more sobs, followed again by his commanding voice.

"Wake, Mingo! Can't you hear *them;* their young hearts are searching for *TRUTH!*" Eittod's voice bellowed.

"Bezen, wake up! We are called once again! Wake!"

Yet again the enormous tree shook violently, sending tremors along the ground.

"We have slept long enough, my friends; rattle your bones and open your eyes!" boomed Eittod's voice now stronger, more in control of his emotions.

Without knowing why, the inhabitants – animal, vegetable and mineral – felt vital, excited, purposeful, chosen, as Eittod's voice thundered through the night air for the first time in millenniums.

For you see, when the Earth was still forming, the Regions Authority, the supreme overseers and protectors of all seen and unseen worlds within the great vastness of the universe, brought Eittod to this protected sanctuary to teach Earth's children of the great depths of love, creativity and connection within them. Eittod taught them of the seen and unseen worlds and of their vital role in protecting creation. He taught them of the power of their thoughts, words and actions upon all Earth's species and upon its protective crystalline web.

Eittod, a vital ember of a long gone civilization far beyond Earth's galaxy, was chosen to be their guide and consented to have his vibrant spirit united with the heart energy of the solitary tree.

As millenniums passed, Earth's vital portals of light from the crystalline web became blocked by the greed, hatred, fear and pain of humanity. Mankind's darkness slowly overshadowed the Earth. It was then that Eittod, his team, and their enchanted sanctuary were put into a deep protective sleep. Their deep sleep was to continue until such time as the children of the Earth once again called out for peace, love, brotherhood and connection with the unseen worlds.

And that time has come at last. Eittod has been awakened by the pleas of countless children wanting something greater, purer and more meaningful for humankind.

Again, Eittod roared. "Wake, Mingo! Wake, Bezen! Where are you? Awaken, dear ones!" he called. His iridescent wispy form now filled the inner chamber of the mammoth tree with light.

Finally Mingo stirred. He put a hand to his mouth and yawned in a deep breath. Then he coughed it out as though it were full of dust. He sucked it back in, but deeper this time, still trying hard to open eyes that had not seen light for eons. He rubbed his eyes with his large fists hoping to wake them from their deep sleep.

With one long, loud groan, his lengthy, slender limbs stretched out as far as they could stretch without popping off. His golden hair was matted against his elongated skull, and his tongue groped for spit within a parched mouth.

Mingo, a sixteen-year-old immortal from Early Earth, has traveled through time at Eittod's side, the two like father and son, inseparable.

Eittod coaxed him impatiently, "Come on, lad! Come on! We have much work to do. Can't you hear the children pleading? We must celebrate and make ready for them!"

Mingo let out another enormous yawn, his youthful, lanky frame slowly coming to life as if a drunken puppeteer were carelessly pulling at his strings, then releasing them again. After a long pause, words began to trickle out, "Yesh, ahh...," Mingo's throat still dry, his tongue stuck to the roof of his mouth as if glued there millenniums ago.

"Yes," his words came slowly now. "Yes, I...I hee...hee...hear you and...and...ahh...," again his tongue searched for spit, but none came. "I hear *YOU*," he cried loudly, "and...and *them*!" Each syllable came with great effort.

"Come down here, lad, where I can see you!" said Eittod, eagerly. With even greater effort, Mingo, who had been perched within the interior of a high limb of the enormous tree during the long sleep, eased himself down onto the wooden floor of the snuggery and stood before Eittod.

Mingo coughed again, but all that came forth seemed like more dust; he wished for spit to return. "I hear...ahh...Eittod, help me!" he gasped.

Mingo could feel hands placing a large mug into his.

Oh yes, relief at last! he thought as he lifted the large mug to his parched lips. *It's been ages since my thirst has been quenched.*

"Drink up, lad, drink up. Your wish has been fulfilled!" encouraged Eittod eagerly.

The mug raised, and imagining spit returning, Mingo took a long drink. Gagging, he threw the mug to the floor, spitting the awful liquid unknowingly into Eittod's wispy face. "Oh! Yuk! Yuk!" Mingo sputtered.

With no sign of disgust at having been spat upon, Eittod wiped his gleeful face and then spoke with a sense of authority now.

"Well, dear one, your desire was for *spit,* was it not?" Eittod laughed.

"Ahhhhh!" Mingo released another mouthful of spit more forcefully this time.

Eittod gave him wide berth, grinned, and then seated himself.

"Oh! Eittod! You are awake all of a few minutes and already you are catching me with my own idle wishes," spat Mingo. More spit drooled down his chin.

"Ah, on the contrary, dear lad, may I remind you that it was *you!*" said Eittod. "It was you who caught yourself. I merely assisted in fulfilling your wish, did I not? Have you forgotten that your thoughts do create your reality, my boy?" he laughed heartily.

"Sir, you mean I asked for it? I probably did! *But...*a mug of cool water would have been greatly appreciated!" snapped Mingo.

"Then water is what you should have wished for in the first place, my boy," said Eittod still amused.

"Wise one, I beg you to have patience with me and this numb body of mine," said Mingo, speaking with as much respect for his elder as he could muster at the moment. His mouth was still drooling over with excess spit that now ran down onto his musty garments, and slipped between his bare toes.

"Remember, Sir, *you* got the full impact of the *whole* lightning bolt, I got but the *sparks,*" scolded Mingo, staggering to his full height of eight feet. His olive-skinned hands were firmly set on his wobbling hips and his right foot tapped to the beat of his frustrated words. His eyes squinted, still fighting the sting of the light.

Eittod, elated to be awake, laughed even harder, unable to take neither Mingo's words nor condition seriously. In fact, he laughed so hard that the large buttons on his dry-rotted vest popped off with such force that they noisily ricocheted off the walls of what was their prison only moments ago. Eittod whirled his colorful wispy presence to escape being pelted by the large, square-shaped buttons.

Mingo, unable to hold his fume with the comedic scene playing out in front of him, burst into uncontrollable laughter. He fell full-weight against Eittod, tumbling them both onto the floor into a pool of discarded spit, and their laughter rose to such a crescendo that the earth around them quaked with joy.

CHAPTER SIX:
Gypsy Tree Awakens

Eittod and Mingo's jubilation was so great it forced bright, shiny green foliage to sprout from every available limb of the solitary tree. Wispy vines of colorful gemstone beads caressed each bough. Bangles of gold, silver and crystal erupted from every crevice, shimmering in the moonlight. Rare glass bobbles of intricate designs hung like jewels on the necks of queens with no two alike. The joyful breeze played merrily through the leaves and ornamentations creating enchanting melodies.

The Gypsy Tree had awakened at last, its sights and sounds simply breathtaking; its fragrance – spicy, intoxicating and oh, so inviting.

The meadow and its creatures were stunned and awed by both the magnificent lights of the Gypsy Tree and the spectacular show before them. Lights of many colors danced in each tiny, gazing eye. Rainbows illuminated river ripples and shimmered across the shiny-backed creatures resting on the bank. The Gypsy Tree's light even reached the forest beyond and danced in the moisture droplets deposited on the leaves by the fragrant night air.

With thunderous sounds, the crumbled stones of the encampment began to move back into place on their ancient foundations as if invisible master-builders were secretly at work once again. Each stone as it moved took on its original shape, millenniums of aging now gone from them. With the cadre in place, exterior stone walls of unusual shapes and slopes rose high into the air creating a surreal structure.

As the half-standing archways rebuilt themselves stone by stone, etched writings in ancient and future languages began to reappear on the façades. As the final keystones locked into place, fluorescent green light illuminated the ancient verbiage and symbols and a radiant starburst ignited within each archway.

The innocence of Eittod's loving spirit and his deep gratitude gave life to the Gypsy Tree. His compassionate heart gave the tree its throb. His joy and laughter gave it its glimmer. But it was the innocent pleas and whispers of the children of the Earth that had freed Eittod and his team once again.

As anyone could see, with its rare beauty and enticing sounds and smell, the Gypsy Tree was like no other. This magnificent being, found by the Regions Authority in the far realms of the Great Andromeda Galaxy, consented to be transferred to this enchanted outpost within the Earth's realm for the sake of the children. In gratitude, the Regions named this enchanted sanctuary, Outpost Gypsy Tree.

Throughout the night Eittod and Mingo laughed, played and shared memories of ancient days. Their hearts were filled with joy at the sight of each other. Oh, how they loved and had missed one another. They'd been apart before, but this time was indeed the longest. The long-awaited mirth reached its crescendo; peace and contentment filled the meadow, flowed into the river and onto the distant forest. All life in this enchanted place slept easier that night.

As the sun peeked over the horizon and streamed in through Gypsy's leaves, Eittod and Mingo's laughter and joy could still be heard. Glints of sunlight danced off Gypsy's adornments and swam across the meadow. Outpost Gypsy Tree was alive once again.

"Oh, how I have missed the light of day!" cooed Eittod. "What a spectacular sight and the warmth. Ahhhh!"

Abruptly a female voice rang out in the snuggery.

"Haven't you two celebrated enough? My ears are sore from listening to the two of you all night! Surely your tongues must be blistered by now," scolded a voice.

Turning toward the voice, Eittod called out, "Bezen, where are you? Why didn't you join us last night if you were awake?"

"Oh, you know me, Eittod; I like to return at a much slower pace than you. Besides, I really enjoyed listening to you and Mingo catching up," she said with a great yawn.

"Me too, but do you think he'd let me?" cried Mingo. "Come out, come out wherever you are," he said in a sing-song voice, his eyes searching the snuggery for her wonderful face, but not finding it.

"Hey! That spit fiasco was downright brilliant and hilarious," said Bezen, letting out a whoop. "I can still see you two rolling around in that slippery mess, throwing it on each other and then rolling again, just like children! What a sight!" she roared gleefully.

"I didn't see you, Mother," said Mingo, his sparkling dark eyes still searching the snuggery for her.

"How could you, my son? You were laughing so hard I doubt you could see the nose on your handsome face through all those joyous tears," Bezen mused as she eased her soft, matronly body from between tree rings eight-thousand-six-hundred and thirty-two and eight-thousand-six-hundred and thirty-three.

"That was a great year! Great year indeed!" she murmured absentmindedly as she stepped forward to embrace her son.

Bezen, an immortal from Early Earth, and her son, Mingo, have traveled through time with Eittod to assist with the journeys and instruction of Earth's children.

"My dear Mingo, it has been so very long, my son. Let me look at you!" said Bezen as she checked him from head to toe with her motherly eyes and gently stroked his golden matted hair with her hand. "You're as handsome as ever, but a bit thin, don't you think, Eittod?"

"Well, my dear Bee, it has been a while since his last meal!" said Eittod with a mirthful laugh.

"And you!" said Bezen, now inspecting Eittod, "seems you're still not quite with us physically; and those clothes – millenniums out of style!"

Eittod, being an iridescent wisp of energy, usually takes on human form for the sake of the children. As he says, "It gives them something concrete to gaze at during those long days of instruction."

Because he's not a being of the Milky Way Galaxy, it takes Eittod much longer than the others to change form, and his skin never quite takes on the color of human flesh, but remains a collage of splendid iridescent colors.

"I suppose not, my dear Bee!" said Eittod, "But I see you have already taken on your new form for this journey, have you not? And been shopping, too?"

Bezen's tall, thin frame was now puffed out into a five-foot, five-inch middle-aged matronly shape. Her usual golden hair was now mousey brown streaked with silver tones, but her olive complexion, infectious smile and rosy cheeks gave her away.

"Indeed I have," she boasted as she twirled around for them to see. "How do I look?" she asked.

"Well fed, my dear Bee! Well fed, indeed!" said Eittod with a grin. "And what's that around your legs?"

"Janes…" a long pause, then "eh…no, jeans!" boasted Bezen. "Seems the whole world is wearing jeans, but I don't find them very comfortable, quite constricting, and the color is so drab. I still prefer the wonderful loose, colorful wraps of Egypt. And these are called sneakers," lifting up her left foot for better viewing.

"So that's what you have been up to all night, Mother!" said Mingo.

"You have been out amongst the Earth women bartering for stylish frocks! Haven't you? That's why we haven't seen you. Right?" he continued.

Being an adult immortal gives her the privilege of selecting her own physical structure and attire quite readily. Bezen has the ability to assume any likeness she so chooses, and for a woman, that's enviable in any culture or millennium.

"Yes! Yes! And I've had a grand time, which I am sure you and Eittod will never understand nor appreciate. I AM A WOMAN," she flaunted with a blush, "and style is certainly still on my list of enjoyable things, even at my age." A big smile crossed her currently plump pink face.

"I suggest you two get out of those old tattered antiques and into something more fashionable. Huh! Lose a few buttons there Eittod?" she said with a joyful grin.

"Breakfast will be thought up shortly," she said as the large wooden door of the snuggery eased opened. "We have so much readying to do for the children. How exciting! Oh, how exciting! And I am sure the Regions will be appearing to us soon. I am off to check the grounds and encampment."

The massive door of the Gypsy Tree rotated back into place behind her with a thud.

Mingo and Eittod looked at each other and burst into laughter.

"Well she's her delightful old self. How wonderful it is to be back together again!" cooed Eittod.

Yet both had noticed tears in Bezen's eyes as Mingo talked of her being out amongst the Earth women. What is Bezen aware of that they are not?

"Come lad, we best check Gypsy, and then get ourselves up-to-date on things of the Earth," Eittod urged.

Checking the status of Outpost Gypsy Tree is a major undertaking for Mingo and Bezen. Because Eittod is united heart-to-heart with Gypsy, he can only move outside the tree using a hologram. This restricts his ability to physically interact with the grounds and facilities. And although the Regions had surrounded this enchanted sanctuary and its inhabitants with protective energies before placing them into a deep sleep millenniums ago, there was still the matter of everything being operational.

CHAPTER SEVEN:
A Dim View

With the inspection of Gypsy complete, Mingo and Eittod gathered in the large sunken area of the snuggery, known as the "pit," to catch up on mankind. Mingo made his youthful body comfortable on a soft camelhair rug, and leaned a large colorful pillow against a marble pillar carved in hieroglyphics. Meanwhile, Eittod cozied down into his favorite high-backed, red and gold tufted chair and propped his colorful feet on the matching ottoman. It was business as usual at Outpost Gypsy Tree.

On Eittod's command, a large revolving crystal descended from the rafters into the middle of the pit. He and Mingo watched as present day humanity moved about their hectic daily lives. They observed the current trades and trends – what Earth's people wore. what they ate, how they traveled and what they cherished. The scene jumped from location to location all over the world. Maps of Earth changes, including old and new weather patterns, were presented along with a new and extinct species report. One moment the streets and businesses of Europe filled the snuggery; the next instant Eittod and Mingo found themselves inside of something called an airplane, an A 380 to be exact, landing on a runway in a place called Hong Kong. The images raced from Tibet and Nepal to Iraq and Afghanistan, then onto Europe and the Americas, from current day news to scenes of the genocide of the twenty-first century and back.

Faces, voices and happenings continued to fill the room. Voices of compassion were followed by voices of hate, voices of hope followed by voices of greed and condemnation. Terrorist actions were followed by a leader's plea, "I believe that freedom is the deepest need of every human soul," said America's President George W. Bush. Space exploration was a reality, "One small step for man, one giant leap for mankind," declared Neal Armstrong. Racial strife – "We must learn to live together as brothers or perish as fools," warned Dr. Martin Luther King Jr. In contrast to voices of compassion and hope, man's inhumanity to man flashed painfully around them. "You must be the change you want to see in the world," urged Gandhi. "Love and compassion are necessities, not luxuries. Without them humanity cannot survive," pleaded the Dalai Lama.

Then the images began to move more rapidly back through the centuries and millenniums to the Middle East, the New World, the Old World, South America, the Orient, Roman Empire, Greece and Egypt.

As Eittod absorbed the information, moist silvery threads streamed down his soft etched face, dripping onto his heaving chest below. His crystal blue reflective eyes grew red and puffy. Mingo seemed frozen in place, stung by the painful messages of mankind as the crystal revealed the ugly darkness into which man had thrown himself.

As the images fluxed, Eittod moved toward Mingo, placed his hands on Mingo's shoulders and then embraced him. "We are here because the children are now ready to free themselves from this ugliness, Mingo," he said in a soft, fatherly tone. "We have much work ahead of us, lad. We must prepare for the children if they are to clear the portals for humanity and open them to the light, love and peace of the ONE, the ABSOLUTE." He raised his hand and dissolved the ugly images still hovering about them.

Bezen's vibrant voice exploded, breaking the painful heaviness in which they found themselves.

"Well, now that we *all* know the challenges, let's feed our very empty, hungry bellies; we will need all the strength we can muster for the work ahead," she said.

"What shall we have for breakfast?" she whispered with enticement in her voice and rubbing her hands together. "Let me think."

Focusing and then making a quick nod of her head, a feast fit for a king and his kingdom spread out before them.

"Bee, you have simply outdone yourself. What a magnificent display!" declared Eittod as he and Mingo withdrew their chairs from the stone table and prepared to indulge.

"Mother, you're still the best cook in the universe!" boasted Mingo.

In front of them, a large stone table offered foods of all colors, shapes, aromas and flavors. Varieties of fruits from all over the world filled brightly colored, woven baskets. Juicy apples of red, blush, white, yellow and green flowed from one basket. Plump peaches, plums, mangoes, and melons flowed from another. And berries, citrus and grapes of all sizes and flavors filled and hung from yet another. A brightly colored magenta and yellow basket was laden with an enticing mixture of shelled nuts and dried fruits. Multicolored earthenware bowls brimmed with hard-cooked eggs of many sizes and colors; cut cheeses and pulled breads lay out before them. Glass pitchers of colorful juices and delicate china cups of fine teas awaited their consumption.

"Wait just one millennium!" Bezen's voice rose, shattering the mood. "I'll not have two such grubby-looking characters sitting across from me at this feast. I suggest you tidy up a bit, and do make it snappy, if you please. I am famished!" Bezen scolded, crossing her arms to her chest.

"Oh! You're right, my dear Bee!" said Eittod, relieving the massive wooden chair of his grip. "Let's put on our thinking caps, Mingo, and oblige our dear lady in...*jeans*," he said, giving Mingo a wink.

They both focused. Within seconds, Mingo and Eittod stood before Bezen bathed, combed, clothed and ready for inspection. Both were wearing...*jeans, tee shirts, sneakers*...and large silly grins.

"Does this please you, dear mother?" said Mingo as he spun around imitating her whirl.

"Let me ponder. I believe the word they use now is...COOL...or was it...PHAT?" said Mingo with an impish grin.

Eittod followed Mingo's lead and began whirling in place for inspection. By now Eittod had assumed his full human form. He was of moderate stature with a strong, pastel-colored face carved with deep wisdom lines revealing his ageless past. His crystal blue eyes reflected the youthful, playful spirit that lived within, and his silver-streaked dark hair fell softly to his shoulders.

"Now, that's more like it!" Bezen snapped, gleefully.

"Just one more thing to complete this beautiful morning feast, dear Bee," said Eittod as he focused.

Instantly the snuggery was strewn with an array of beautiful, fragrant wild flowers.

"For you, my dear!" said Eittod.

Bezen smiled and gave him a grateful embrace. "How thoughtful. Thank you!" she said. "It's been absolutely ages since anyone has given me flowers."

They all laughed, savoring the look on each other's faces; the moment felt so special, so full.

"Breakfast is indeed served. Let the feasting begin!" announced Bezen.

At last, Eittod, Bezen and Mingo were filled to bursting; they all leaned back gazing at the display they had hardly put a dent in.

"This feast was big enough to stuff the bellies of a legion, Mother!" groaned Mingo holding his stomach.

"Indeed, superb!" said Eittod, "I had almost forgotten the pleasurable sensation of juicy fruits in my mouth. Earth has so many delightful and delectable pleasures for the senses. Thank you! Now, dear Bee, may I help you clear?"

"Not to worry! I shall just put the rest back into my thoughts for another day of feasting," she said. Focusing, the remainder of the feast vanished into thin air, except for their beverages and the wildflowers which still adorned the stone table and snuggery floor.

CHAPTER EIGHT:
Business as Usual

As breakfast vanished, the Regions Authority appeared, their holographic image now present in the feasting nook area of the snuggery.

"Welcome back, Eittod!...Bezen!...Mingo! Welcome back! How good to be in your presence once again," they said in their multi-toned voice.

There before Eittod, Bezen and Mingo stood the breathtaking opalescent presence of a multitude of wise elders who spoke in unison, their deep harmonic voice similar to that of the depth and breadth of a Buddhist monk's vibrational chant.

"Earth's children have finally cried out in great numbers for peace, love and brotherhood. And we can now respond as you well know," they said with a collective nod to Eittod and his team. "Earth's light portals are in great need of clearing as you have seen, and the children are ready and eager for your guidance once again. All that is needed is your invitation to them, and we leave that pleasure to you, Eittod. We have done what we can to prepare the way, but the bulk of the work is up to you and your staff to guide, and the children to complete," they urged.

"Remember, we are here to assist you in every way possible from our side; but, of course, we do have certain boundaries that we must honor since Earth is in a free will galaxy. From our observations and upon inspection of the Earth's light portals, we have agreed that the North Portal – the portal of wisdom and love which hovers above Ireland's Hill of Tara – is the most critical to clear. Your work shall begin there," the Regions instructed. "The light, energies and information of the ONE, the ABSOLUTE, in the crystalline web that surrounds the planet, must once again reach the Earth, if mankind is to survive."

"As you request!" replied Eittod bowing his head slightly and gently placing his right fist to his heart as a reverent sign of commitment.

"Are your facilities restored to their full usage and satisfaction?" asked the Regions.

As the Regions Authority's shimmering hologram continued to fill the snuggery, Eittod looked to Bezen for her report.

Bezen rose. "My dear Regions," she began, lowering her head slightly, placing her right fist to her heart, and then straightening to full height again. "The encampment areas are fully restored and refurbished – the domicile structure containing the greeting hall, feasting nook, activity arena, instruction gazebo and the sleeping chambers. According to my calculations, the stone archways are perfectly aligned and are receiving full frequency. The grounds, with its wildlife, plant life, water and mineral elements, are reestablished and quite exquisite – especially the wildflowers," she reported, giving a side glance in Eittod's direction.

"Oh! They are very impressive indeed, as we can see," said the Regions now surveying the fragrant, colorful bouquets strewn about the stone table and snuggery floor.

As Bezen gave her report, revolving images of the forest, the stone encampment, the grounds and the archways appeared before them.

Smiling, Bezen continued. "I believe we are well prepared for our guests, and I am *so* looking forward to their arrival. Thank you!" said Bezen seating herself.

Eittod slowly turned toward Mingo and nodded; Mingo rose, bowed slightly, placed his fist to his heart and began.

"Your Regions, the upper levels of Gypsy appear to be in good order," said Mingo as various levels of Gypsy appeared and revolved before them.

"All upper branch facilities – the costuming station and the equipment center – are well restored and refurbished. The transport units and docking station in the lower branches all appear functional – we'll know better on that after a few dry runs," he said as he paused briefly to catch his breath, took a sip of his tea, and then continued.

"Our only problem seems to be located in some of the outer most limbs of Gypsy. The scumdiggalies have certainly caused some damage, but it seems to be contained in their quarters. The place is truly a shambles which, of course, given their nature to bring about havoc, is quite expected; repairs are in progress with your help as you know. Boredom does bring out the worst in some creatures, and I am sure they are eager for our guests to arrive," reported Mingo, in a low, exasperated tone.

"As for the subterranean root passageways," he continued, "all appear open on inspection from this end. Here again, we will need more time to move out along them to check the full length of each one, especially the directional passageways. I will take care of that with help from our young guests. All sub-transport vessels appear intact and functional. Of course, here again, use will verify their operational status," he finished.

Bezen smiled in her son's direction closely following him with her eyes as he took his seat, parental pride lighting up her whole face.

Eittod rose, bowed to the image of the Regions, and then spoke. "My dear Regions, business aside for a moment, I wish to express our deepest gratitude for your continued commitment to the peoples of the Earth, considering the atrocities we have witnessed today. Your patience and that of the Angelics and the ONE, the ABSOLUTE, on their behalf is always unwavering and without judgment. We are honored and humbled by your support of this enchanted space in which we so gratefully serve humanity."

"We thank you for your comments, Eittod," responded the Regions. "Humanity has much to learn about their interrelationship with all things. We trust in time, with your continued assistance and that of your staff, enlightenment and peace will come to pass for their sake and survival."

"The main trunk levels of Gypsy," Eittod continued, "all appear to be secure and in excellent condition; the time rings of Gypsy are still available to us as Bezen demonstrated for us this morning, and the main interior transport chamber is responsive. Our precious depository seems to have weathered the grip of time well. And I believe forcing the scumdiggalies into the outer limbs before Gypsy was put into her deep sleep was an excellent suggestion on Mingo's part. Thank you!" Making eye contact with Mingo, Eittod nodded his way. Mingo responded with a grateful nod and a youthful blush.

"It would appear that all is ready. Now, we leave you to your work. Again, welcome! And thank you!" The voice and image of the Regions Authority faded from the snuggery.

The snuggery, although large, was a cozy, comfortable space that reflected the delicate, airy influence of Early Earth. With the vibrant colored fabrics and solid rich woods of fertile Egypt and Persia, it held timeless treasures from around the Milky Way Galaxy.

Eittod, Bezen and Mingo enjoyed its varied textures, colors, shapes and aromas. So much time had passed since they last sat in this space together. Sunlight glistened through the crystallized amber sap crevices in Gypsy's thick bark and washed dappled golden light across their faces.

"Oh, to feel the warmth of the sun on my skin again. How easily we forget to notice the treasures of the Earth that touch us each day," said Bezen, turning her face into the light and closing her eyes.

Eittod and Mingo stretched out amongst the large pillow piles on the soft camelhair floor coverings of the pit surveying their beloved home.

The pit serves as the area of information and instruction for the light travelers and their dedicated teachers. Ancient, current and future texts, maps, carved discs, data crystals, prisms and scrolls fill the ornate bookcases. Honeycombed lattice structures laden with crystalline tubes, image vessels and air-tight vaults surround the pit. The knowledge and wisdom of all time, space and ages before and since the Big Bang, as it is referred to by Earth's scientists, are nestled here within Gypsy, courtesy of the Regions. The Gypsy Tree's time-rings hold the active existence of all civilizations past, present and to come, on and beyond the Earth and its galaxy; each ring identifies with a timeframe and location within the universe.

The main level of the snuggery houses Eittod's domicile, the pit, a feasting nook, an activity arena and the main interior transport chamber. The transport chamber allows the staff and the children access to the upper, lower and subterranean levels of Gypsy as well as transport to and from the encampment.

The fragrance of fresh wildflowers still hung in the air and mingled with the aromas of fine woods and Gypsy's spicy scent as Outpost Gypsy Tree's staff prepared for the tasks at hand. While Eittod and Mingo focused on images of the travelers to be summoned and their assignment, Bezen worked with images of the children's domicile arrangements, instruction schedules and arrival.

"The six chosen light travelers shall be summoned first, and then those who need more instruction before assignment will follow," instructed Eittod.

"Once the invitations are complete, Mingo, the youths' intuitive gifts will carry my message to them. Soon we shall celebrate their arrival."

Eittod focused, and with a gentle nod of his head, the invitations were sent.

CHAPTER NINE:
The Invitation

Light years from Outpost Gypsy Tree, in the city of Lima, Peru, Aube woke early; at least he thought he was awake. Through the partially opened window, crisp July air filled his lungs. The sun wasn't even up yet, why was he awake? he wondered. Curious images swirled in his still groggy head: a forest encampment with mysterious stone archways and pathways, a very large magnificent tree – in fact, a tree too large to even be considered real, that appeared to be decorated for the holidays. Its enchanting sounds and spicy fragrance were unforgettable. A crystal clear river and an outstretched, plush green meadow were always in this reoccurring dream. But the deep masculine voice – now *that* was definitely something new. Aube stared up at the still dark ceiling trying to decide if he was really awake or just dreaming of this strong, yet gentle, echoing voice now calling his name. His brother Gar tugged at the alpaca blanket making soft pig-like grunting sounds. Sleeping with Gar was rather like sleeping in a barnyard; he had quite a repertoire of animal snorts, snores and grunts.

I must be awake, reasoned Aube, *the dream seemed so real today – like I could walk right into that encampment and feel at home. Somehow I know those faces and recognize their voices.*

The experience was a bit unnerving, yet exhilarating at the same time. In these kinds of dreams, it was most unusual for Aube to see Gar and himself together. He was usually by himself in adventure-type dreams – separate from his twin brother. But this morning, they were together in this familiar place; and they were a vital part of something important, fun, adventurous and dangerous. Nothing in their overly protected, safe world was ever adventurous or dangerous. Their parents saw to that.

Unique and rare, Aube and Gar are handsome sixteen-year-old Peruvian conjoined twins, attached at their hips. Except for their physique, they are mirror images with their smooth, flawless chestnut-toned skin, silky black hair and the most unusual almond-shaped amber eyes. When looking at them face-on, Gar is the more muscular one to the left and Aube the leaner one to the right. Being conjoined twins renders them no privacy, not even from each other. Neither twin has ever known complete privacy and so, they really never miss it. Normal for them is togetherness, except in certain dreams.

Aube tried to piece the dream together, if that's what it was. As he focused on the echoing voice, his brow furrowed, and his eye lids squeezed tight. *The voice called me 'pure of heart' and gave me instructions on travel and key passwords,* he recalled. Aube knew in his heart that this dream was an answer to his many pleas for peace and brotherhood in his world. *This seems so crazy,* he thought, *yet so real.* Careful not to wake his brother, Aube slowly reached out his left hand and felt around on his nightstand; his fingers were around the pencil, and the pad was just beneath it. Easing the pad onto his chest, he began to write the words of the strong, masculine voice still vividly echoing in his head.

It was not unusual for Aube to write down his dreams upon waking. In fact, keeping up with his dreams and dissecting them with the help of his dream interpretation books was part of his daily morning routine. Meanwhile Gar would thumb through the morning newspaper making asides about the news and loudly broadcasting blow-by-blow information on every football game, bullfight and volleyball game played in the past twenty-four hours.

But today as Aube wrote, it was as if he were transcribing a letter being dictated by someone else, *a someone else* who was actually talking to Aube in his still groggy head. Aube's hand swept rapidly back and forth across the pad, the pencil barely coming in contact with the paper.

Dear Ones:

Your silent pleas have been heard, and today, your pure and loving hearts have answered the call of Eittod. Thank you!

You, Auben Juan Perez and your brother, Garcia Gou-Drah Perez are invited to travel to Outpost Gypsy Tree for your instructions and assignment whenever you so choose to depart. There is no need to pack, except for your massive ring; all other needs will be met on this end. Auben, it is necessary to have your brother's consent for the journey; we will know if he obliges. You both will be moving out of the illusion of time, so will not lose a moment of your linear time; hence, no need for a note to your parents. All questions will be answered upon your arrival here. Whenever you desire to return to your precise split second in time, the departure passwords will be given to you. Remember, you have free will and your choices are always honored. When and if you are ready to travel, simply repeat the following transport passwords out loud, together.

> *"A peaceful, loving world is what I seek within my heart,*
> *And I am willing to clear the way for it to happen.*
> *I am part of the solution.*
> *I am the solution!*
> *I am chosen.*
> *Eittod, this is Auben Juan Perez and*
> *Garcia Gou-Drah Perez.*
> *Hear our petition for transport to Outpost Gypsy Tree!*
> *NOW!"*

Honorably yours,
Eittod of Tulsun Minor
Ambassador to the Regions Authority
Outpost Gypsy Tree

Stunned, Aube read the message scribbled on his pad. He could scarcely believe what he had written; it didn't even look like his own handwriting, but there it was. Aube knew in his heart it was real; something very special was occurring for him, directed by some unseen force, and he was ready for it. Chills ran up and down his spine, but he was not cold. Goose flesh covered his skin and the hairs on his arms stood on end. His ears rang like church bells and tears leaked from his eyes moistening his pillow. He felt more alive at this moment than he had ever felt in his whole life.

Daybreak had slowly eked in, casting wintry grey shadows onto the ceiling, yet the glow in his room was surreal. As he looked around, everything seemed so beautiful, so alive; there were dancing circles of color around everything, even Gar and himself. The colors were intense, vivid. The smell of fresh wildflowers was pronounced, as if someone were holding a spring bouquet right under his nose. All his senses were heightened, profound. He laid in the stillness – aware of existing within two different worlds at the same time – and he loved it. The painful void he had felt deep inside for so long was gone.

Again, Gar grunted much louder than before, yawned and rubbed his eyes. Aube didn't want this moment to end; he felt so connected with a deep part of himself that was true, pure, innocent and child-like. Then remembering the message from Eittod, he excitedly poked at Gar, "You awake? Huh, Gar? You awake?"

Gar stretched his limbs. "I'm getting there. Why does morning have to come so early in the day," followed by another very long yawn and a tummy scratch. "Been awake long, Aube?"

"Oh, I don't know how long, been a while though."

Aube paused, and then said with eagerness in his voice, "I have something very special to tell you. You awake enough? Huh?" poking him again.

"Yea, yea!" followed by yet another great yawn and a butt scratch this time. "What's got you so fired up this early in the morning, huh?"

"I had a strange...ah...dream...or at least, I think it was a dream," Aube replied quickly, yet cautiously.

"Holy Christmas, Aube! You and your silly dreams! Were you at that strange encampment again?" Gar hissed.

Hesitating for a long moment, Aube took a deep breath. "I...err...we've been invited to take a trip..." he said quickly, not really sure how his brother was going to take to this news.

Gar wasn't really interested in most of the things Aube was drawn to. He didn't believe there was anything or anyone out there beyond what he could hear with his *own* ears, touch with his *own* hands, smell with his *own* nose and see with his *own* two eyes.

Aube liked reading books that spoke of the great mysteries of the world and beliefs of ancient civilizations and cultures that created sites like Stonehenge, Newgrange, the pyramids, their own Machu Picchu and Nazca Lines and matters of the unseen world. Since childhood, he'd felt a soft, loving presence around him as if something or someone was watching over him. At times, he'd swear he glimpsed an angel out of the corner of his eye. Mama told him it was probably his guardian angel, which would make Gar laugh and Mama scold. According to Mama, everyone has one, but most people don't feel them, or even acknowledge that angels exist. Even his Andean culture was full of wonderful and other-worldly stories of light beings and space craft. Mysterious happenings were even rumored to have occurred in his father's family history over a century ago, with a massive ring to prove it.

Frequently, Gar and Aube's father, Senor Juan Perez, would take the boys to San Francisco Church and Monastery, a Franciscan facility in town that housed a remarkable library filled with antique texts, some dating back to the time of the Conquistadors, who were soldiers, explorers and adventurers at the service of the Spanish and Portuguese Empires. Aube loved adventure even if it was only in books. Gar usually found something to amuse himself, such as books on astronomy or physics and the latest space explorations. Aube and Senor Perez combed the priceless documents to glean a greater understanding of their country's past and that of ancient civilizations around the world. Aube and his father harbored a similar love when it came to the study of other cultures and the unseen world. On the other hand, Gar preferred blood and guts action stuff which was much too abrasive for Aube's and Senor Perez' tastes or stomachs. Mama always calls Aube her "gentle dreamer of great dreams," and maybe he was, but this morning's experience was much more than a great dream, and he was not about to dismiss it as one.

"A trip? Where?" Gar asked eagerly. "Hey, now wait a minute! How could Mama and Papa tell you without me overhearing? Huh? After all, I am only an ear's shot away you know!" he chuckled in his condescending tone.

"No, no! Not a trip with Mama and Papa. This trip is just for you and me, Gar!" Aube said quickly, "just you and me…" his voice trailed off.

Right about now, Aube was beginning to feel quite foolish. How could he explain something so bizarre – so way out there, without expecting to be laughed at and ridiculed. Gar's dismissive attitude toward things that mattered to Aube was hurtful, yet he had to come clean on this one and take the licks. After all, he needed Gar's okay, and it was worth whatever price he'd have to pay. Whatever and wherever Outpost Gypsy Tree was, Aube desperately wanted to be a part of it.

"In my…my dream, Gar!" exclaimed Aube. "I heard about the trip in my dream! Or…ah…whatever it was!" he said quickly.

Before Gar could recant, Aube pushed the scribbled pad into Gar's hand. "Here! Read this!"

Gar began to read the message from Eittod, then paused for a moment and lifted his eyes toward Aube who was staring intently at the pad in Gar's hand. Gar continued with the message.

Aube held his breath. *What have I done?* he thought. *Gar will surely razz me about this for the rest of our life.*

Enraged, Gar shook the pad in Aube's face. "What's this rubbish? Your idea of a joke?" as he pulled them both up into a sitting position. Gar was always the stronger of the two.

"I think you've been reading too much of that weird stuff again," he shouted. "I thought you were really serious about a trip. Not funny, Auben! Just not funny!" he spat. He threw the pad to the bottom of the bed, and punched Aube hard in the arm.

"Ouch! That hurt, you big bully," Aube shouted, rubbing his right upper arm.

"Gar, I am not playing some kind of joke on you! This is *REAL!* It happened and *it's REAL!*" Aube shouted back, demanding to be taken seriously. "I know that place, and I know its people. And we're invited to be a vital part of it, a part of something exciting for once in our dull, cautious lives."

From the kitchen they could hear their mother's voice, "Auben Juan? Garcia Gou-Drah? Is there a problem in there, boys?" Senora Perez always called her sons by their full given names when she was concerned or upset with them.

"No, Mama, everything's fine. Just a difference of opinion, that's all!" Aube called back quickly. He surely didn't want his mother in on this. This was too weird even for her 'gentle dreamer of great dreams.'

Aube spoke in a softer tone as he leaned them both forward in an attempt to retrieve the pad from the bottom of the bed. "Look at the handwriting, Gar! It's not mine! Look! Yet *I* wrote it! Look at it!" He pushed the pad back into Gar's hand.

Aube shared his early morning experience with Gar, being careful not to omit a single detail, especially the part about really wanting to go and needing his brother's consent.

When Aube finished, Gar just stared at him, his amber eyes wide and wild. For Aube, seconds seemed like hours at this point. Cold beads of sweat crept over his entire body. His head was swimming.

Long moments passed in silence. Then Gar began to speak slowly and sternly through his partially clenched teeth, emphasizing each word as he spoke. "You're...dead...serious...aren't you? You really believe what you just told me is *real*, and you're asking *me* to jump into this craziness with you?" Gar shook his head from side to side as if trying to free himself of his fearful thoughts.

"Good Lord, Aube, if I did believe in your nutty fantasy world, which I *don't*, I'd say that the mangy old devil is playing evil tricks with your gullible little mind. And that's...the last...I want...to hear of it!" Gar barked, pulling them both up into a standing position and heading them toward the bathroom. Aube's feet ran swiftly sideways across the footboard and hit the floor with a painful thud as he groped at furniture and his brother for balance.

Cooperation and togetherness was a given with conjoined twins, but today, right at this moment, Aube felt abandoned – left to struggle on his own, and his best friend was furious with him. His gut knotted in pain. Never had Gar treated him like this. Never!

CHAPTER TEN:
A Brother's Struggle

The days that followed were difficult. Gar was distant, but courteous to Aube. In return, Aube was polite but ever on guard, his body still aching from his brother's betrayal. All conversation was surface and short. Their parents were concerned. They'd never known the twins to stay at odds with each other for this long, nor had Aube and Gar ever refused to share their problems with them before. This was something big, something the boys had to work out on their own, and their parents honored their need for privacy.

Aube was lonely for his brother. Although they were physically attached, Gar had cut him off emotionally and mentally. Aube knew in his heart that his brother had not just dismissed their disagreement, but that Gar was wrestling with the whole idea of an unseen world and an invitation to it.

Outwardly Gar was the stronger, but inwardly he feared everything that Aube believed in. They had always been fair and very considerate of each other's requests, and Aube was willing to wait it out. *It was just that important.* Aube reasoned he had sat through enough football, volleyball and bullfights to earn this trip and then some.

Aube continued to keep himself open to this new world. Each night he dreamt of the encampment and the familiar echoing voice beckoning him. In his dreams he roamed through the forest encampment, pondered the meaning of the archways and sat by the riverbank basking in the splendor and spicy fragrance of the great tree. Each day was spent reading and rereading Eittod's message over and over again – as if something new might appear on the pad with the next reading – and sending prayers to his guardian angel, asking for help with Gar. After all, his guardian angel had heard his cry for peace; surely the angel would hear his cry now for help with his brother's fear.

The pad became his constant companion. At school, he found himself running his fingers across the words, following the stroke of the pencil lines. As he did, images of the encampment and its people swirled through his head: a very tall, thin youth bearing a broad smile and an elongated head, a plump matronly woman with large warm eyes and rosy cheeks, and a being wrapped in what appeared to be colorful clouds of cotton candy. But his day dreams of this mysterious and inviting place could be costly. Senora Valverde, his language teacher, almost caught him with his precious pad during an examination, but his hand was quicker than her eye – at least this time. What would Mama and Papa say if he was accused of cheating?

At night, he'd slip the pad under his pillow and dream of the journey to this special place to which he'd been mysteriously invited. He could still hear Eittod's voice in his head each time he read the message. *Remember, you have free will and your choices are always honored. When and if you are ready to travel, simply repeat the following transport passwords out loud.*

Aube didn't want to lose his connection with this special place inside of him. He didn't want that deep, empty longing in his gut to return. He trusted in his brother's love and was willing to wait for Gar's decision. Aube knew in his heart that Gar's choice had to be honored, but his mind only wanted to honor his own. At times, he had dared to repeat the transport passwords in his head, secretly wishing he'd be swept off to the encampment that he had become so attached to and a part of. But without Gar's consent, it just wasn't going to happen. Eittod's warning haunted him, "*It is necessary to have your brother's consent for the journey; we will know if he obliges.*" Somehow they know he hasn't agreed, but how?

Gar's watch alarm screamed, he fumbled to find the snooze button, and then eased his head back onto the pillow. It took a few minutes before he realized that the other sound he was hearing was rain – not a sound one hears often in the city of Lima. Gar lay quietly enjoying the soft pitter-pattering sound of the rain against the glass and slowly breathed in its familiar smell. He could feel the dampness creeping in through the small opening in the window. Mama insisted on fresh air even in the winter months. Aube hadn't moved a muscle.

As Gar lay enjoying the rare sound of rain, his thoughts shifted to Aube and the events of a week ago. Actually, it had occupied his mind almost constantly for the past eight days.

Aube is certainly asking a lot of me. He knows this unseen stuff gives me the creeps; yet he asked, Gar thought. In fact, he had never asked for anything of Gar that seemed this important. *How can there be something or somebody that can't be seen or heard moving around out there?* he queried to himself. *I know the local stories of space crafts and beings from other worlds and our own eerie Perez family story concerning Lake Titicaca, but these are only stories – made up stuff to impress friends. Exaggerations. Aren't they?*

The words, *'There is no need to pack, except for your massive ring; all your needs will be met on this end,'* ran through his mind. *How do they know about our family treasure?* he thought. *Is that what they're after? Are they after the Perez family ring?*

According to the Perez family legend, the massive ring was supposedly gifted to Aube and Gar's great-grandmamma by a man from the stars over a century ago. But, this was poppycock in Gar's thinking – just an old woman's foolishness and a good story to pass on at family gatherings, that's all. Yet he knew in his mind that the ring was of a metal not found on the Earth, at least that's what the metallurgist had said. But that was so many years ago. It was probably just a mistake.

Gar's struggle continued. *And what do they mean by 'all our needs will be met on their end?' What is – and where is – their end?* Gar fearfully questioned. *And the bit about needing my permission! That's the part that really burns me, because now it's my fault that he can't go. I've not given my okay and they, whoever they are, know it!* Gar shouted in his head. *Huh! This is just too way out there to be real, so who could be pulling such a hoax on us and why? And if it is the ring they're after, why not just steal it rather than make up this outrageous scheme to tip us off?*

Gar's mind raced from one idea to the next trying to make some sense of the dilemma in which he found himself. His mind darted back to Aube's pad and the bit about *'no need to leave a note because you'll be moving out of the illusion of time.' Who are they kidding? Do they think we're that gullible? Aube maybe, but certainly not me! They can't play mind games with me. Nope. Not Garcia Gou-Drah Perez!*

For what seemed like hours, he struggled through the message, bantering each sentence back and forth, knocking holes in it, but it always came down to not wanting to disappoint Aube. And then there was the fear. Those icy fingers of fear that grip at his spine causing him to tremble – and he *hated* that feeling. It made him feel weak and cowardly. Yet his brother had always supported all his requests – well, most of them. Aube wasn't very supportive of his little league bull fighting idea or his sky diving requests. Come to think of it, neither was Mama nor Papa.

As warm memories and feelings toward Aube and their strong bond flooded in, Gar let his guard down, and his guilt and loneliness caught up with him. Hot tears seared down his smooth chestnut-brown cheeks. Had he been too hard on the one person that loved him the most, no matter what? After all, Aube was the other half of himself, inseparable. Yet he had let his fear drive him – those awful icy fingers of fear. The realization of the pain and hurt he had inflicted on his brother stung him. How could he have been so cruel, dragging Aube like that and then ignoring him?

The gentle tapping of the rain seemed to help him walk through all the thoughts, fears and regrets that had been stuffed in his head for eight days holding his brain captive.

Aube had not mentioned a word about his dream or Eittod's message for the past eight days, not even once since it happened. He had honored Gar's wishes.

Gar recalled his own words, *"And that's the last I want to hear of it!"* and his cruel actions of dragging his brother out of bed and across the room. *Holy Christmas! We've both physically paid for that thoughtless piece of rage,* he thought. *I've been pretty rough on Aube, I guess. But, where does he get off asking me such a thing anyway?* His fear was catching up with him again.

What if it was nothing more than a big hoax of some kind, a practical joke or Aube hallucinating! he thought. But worse and even more frightening was the thought that it just might be for *real.*

Aube was always the braver of the two; his world was one of facing realities and searching for truths; Gar's world was one of escape, and that realization was beginning to hit home for him.

The alarm screamed for a second time, startling Aube from a deep sleep, and their day began. As Aube rambled on about his science project for the upcoming fair, Gar's mind remained a captive of his thoughts. When pushed for an answer, he merely grunted and went back to his internal bantering. After their shower, Gar couldn't even remember if he had used soap or not and quickly sniffed his armpits. Aube laughed, "And just where are you this morning, dear brother?" Again, Gar just grunted, still locked in his inner struggle.

After breakfast, and surprisingly no sports report, they were off to catch the school bus. The rain had stopped. Rain showers were always fleeting at best here in Lima, and the dismal grey coastal fog was already closing in again. Gar pushed his mental struggle with Aube's request from his mind as they maneuvered up the bus steps together, greeting everyone as they entered. These conjoined brothers worked as one unit, each keenly aware of the other and the movements needed to accomplish their task. After sixteen years of combined motion, their balance, movements and gestures were automatic and smooth as silk.

"Good morning, boys," said Mr. Morgan in response as they moved into their reserved seats at the front. Samuel Morgan had been their bus driver ever since they could remember. He and his wife had come to Peru on vacation and never went home. He had once told Aube that he found himself in Peru, and didn't want to ever lose that feeling. Aube never understood that statement until now.

The twins were no longer a novelty at school. Their friends had finally gotten past that stage and into true and close friendships. A few classmates still found pleasure in riding them occasionally with snide remarks or snickers, but for the most part their school experiences were good. Both Aube and Gar enjoyed school and were excellent students. Although secondary school isn't compulsory in Peru, their continued education was provided by the government at a local private school.

As Mr. Morgan navigated the rickety bus through crowded, narrow, winding back streets, Aube's mind focused on his brother. He could tell that Gar was near a decision point. Their morning routine had been just a hair off today – not as synchronized as usual and the armpit sniff was a dead giveaway. Gar was in deep thought, and it just had to be about the trip.

At breakfast, Gar had acted as though he was reading the newspaper, but he made none of his usual sports comments, and his eyes didn't even go back and forth across the columns; they seemed to be focused on one spot the whole time. In fact, the spot he had been staring at for so long was a large ad for "false teeth while you wait." Then there was the matter of Gar picking up Senor Perez's cup of filtered black coffee instead of his warmed milk and spitting it out all over the morning paper. An answer was close to the surface, Aube was sure.

Aube's heart began to feel lighter and the tightness in his gut began to ease; he knew Gar was finally coming to terms with his travel request. The day seemed to glide by for Aube. This was the happiest he had felt in eight days. All seemed right in his world at last. Every cell in his body was singing, "We're going on a trip! We're going on a trip! We're going on a trip!" He could feel his muscles wanting to join in the celebration, but he restrained himself.

Aube waited. Yet another day passed with no hint of an answer from Gar. He was beginning to worry again. He could feel the heaviness returning, and the vise grip on his gut was chomping down.

He was so sure Gar had come to a decision. Now, here it was Saturday, the big day, the day Mama and Papa had promised to take the boys to a professional football game. Surely Gar's thoughts were on the game. Aube would have to wait yet another day or more for his answer. Football always came first in the life of Gar Perez. In fact, the football game of all football games was happening today – Peru vs. Argentina – and all of Lima would be on hand for it, including the whole Perez family thanks to Senor Perez's boss, Senor Sanchez.

CHAPTER ELEVEN:
The Big Game

The Perez family had relocated to the Pacific coast city of Lima from Puno, a moderate size port city on the western shores of Lake Titicaca, shortly after the twins were born. They moved for two reasons: first, the nation's capital offered far better medical facilities and schooling for the boys, and second, to protect the twins from the gawking eyes and craned necks of a multitude of tourists. Puno's largest industry was tourism due to the floating reed islands of the indigenous Uros people. Tourists found the Uros culture fascinating, and the residents of the floating islands eked out a living from foreigners' curiosity.

With the help of several local government officials, Juan Perez had secured a job with the national government as a guard at the Palacio de Gobierno, the government palace at Plaza de Armas, shortly after the family's arrival in Lima sixteen years ago. It was a very good job, and one for which the whole family was grateful. Life for Juan and Maria on the western shores of Lake Titicaca, high in the Andes, had been gentle and easy. Their lives had been wrapped around family, tradition and community. Juan spent his days as a guard at the local museum, the Museo Carlos Dreyer, which housed Nazca, Tiahuanaco, Paracas, Chimú and Inca artifacts. His thirst for knowledge of ancient cultures could never be satisfied. Maria worked alongside family members at the local market selling her native totoria reed handicrafts as souvenirs to tourists in search of a piece of the Uros culture. The twins knew nothing of that peaceful life; the bustling life of Peru's capital city with all its congestion and noise was all they knew or cared to know.

Senor Sanchez had been Juan Perez's boss from the time they arrived in Lima, and like Gar, he was a captive to all sporting events. If Gar missed a score in the morning paper, Senor Sanchez was sure to have it on the tip of his tongue by the time Juan punched his time card. It was so surprising to have been gifted the Peru vs. Argentina football game tickets to be held at Peru's Monumental Stadium.

"Hey! Juan," said Senor Sanchez, one chilly morning in early June, "Your boys like football, don't they?"

"You bet they do!" responded Senor Perez. "As you know, my son Gar checks the papers daily for the latest sports news, likes all the teams, really. Not sure if he has a favorite. Of course, he's never seen a pro game, just local stuff mostly."

"Well here, surprise the family!" said Senor Sanchez as he stuffed four tickets into Juan's hand. "I can't use them. Wasn't really thinking ahead when I bought them months ago – turns out to be my mother's birthday. Never have been good with keeping those kinds of dates in my head," he said. "We're celebrating her special day that same weekend. I didn't really put it together until yesterday. She'll be seventy-five and is looking forward to all the attention and festivities. You know how big families are; there will be bus loads of people, you can bet on that. Well, you and your family have a great time. Oh!

And here, buy the boys some souvenirs," this time shoving gift certificates for team shirts into Juan's hand.

Senor Perez stared at the tickets and the gift certificates bearing *yesterday's* date and realized they hadn't been purchased months ago as Senor Sanchez said. He'd been given free tickets before, but never to an event this big. "Thank you," he shouted as his boss rounded the gate house and was out of sight. People seemed to enjoy treating the boys to outings and giving them special gifts for no apparent reason. I guess you could say the twins were local celebrities of a sort, and they certainly never objected.

The day of the big game had finally arrived, and the excitement in the Perez household was mounting.

"Come on boys, we don't want to be late! Not today of all days. We're on our way to Monumental Stadium!" Senor Perez shouted, waving their prized tickets in his hand.

Cheerfully humming as she worked, Senora Perez could be heard scurrying in their small kitchen, putting together a lunch basket of goodies to keep her cheering squad happy.

"Sixteen-year-old boys, especially Gar, are virtual eating machines," she would gleefully boast to her friends. Maria Perez adored her family, and nothing was ever too much work for her when it came to her husband and her precious sons.

"We best get a move on Gar, Papa's about to jump out of his skin. You know, I think he's more excited about this game than you are, and that's going some," said Aube.

Preoccupied by his thoughts, Gar seemed to be in another world. His eyes appeared glassy and his skin revealed a cold sweat in progress.

"Hey, what's up with you this morning? This is the biggest game of the season," said Aube. "Aren't you feeling well?"

Gar stared into the mirror at his brother, "I am so sorry Aube. This has been an awful time for both of us. I know how much this adventure means to you. I see you reading and rereading that message, and yet you have said nothing. Do you still have our ring?"

Aube was dumbstruck. He reached into his left pocket, and withdrew the massive ring which bore a star-clustered crest on a field of black. He held it up to Gar without saying a word. He felt suspended in the moment. Time was surely standing still as Gar reached for the ring. "Do you remember the transport passwords?" asked Gar.

Again as if animated, Aube reached into his left pocket, this time withdrawing his small dog-eared pad which was opened to the message written in the strange handwriting. Aube wasn't breathing – he was afraid to. He didn't want to do anything to disturb what was happening between his brother and him at that very moment.

"I guess we need to read it together…out loud…is that right, Aube?"

Aube quickly found his voice, "Yes! Yes! That's what Eittod's message read. We both have to say it together. Out loud," he hurriedly added.

Gar looked down at the pad and began to read the transport message aloud, *"A peace…"*

Aube immediately joined him as they stared into each other's eyes in the mirror. These conjoined twins both knew the passwords by heart and both were trembling – Aube with exhilaration for the long-awaited and prayed-for journey and astonishment at his brother's decisiveness, and Gar from sheer terror of the unknown and unseen world he was possibly about to enter.

As the twins recited the passwords, Aube caught a fleeting glimpse of a very tall, chestnut-brown-skinned soldier with almond-shaped amber eyes standing behind them with a look of great pride beaming from his face.

> "...*ful, loving world is what I seek within my heart, and*
> *I am willing to clear the way for it to happen.*
> *I am part of the solution.*
> *I am the solution!*
> *I am chosen.*
> *Eittod, this is Auben Juan Perez and*
> *Garcia Gou-Drah Perez.*
> *Hear our petition for transport to Outpost Gypsy Tree!*
> *NOW!*"

With a brilliant flash of light, the mirror was quite empty.

CHAPTER TWELVE:
Arrival

"...Hear my petition for transport to Outpost Gypsy Tree! Now!"

Drew's body began to vibrate as she spoke the final words of the transport message. She could still feel her parent's hands holding her tight, yet another set of hands were reaching out for her. As she reached forward to connect with the welcoming hands, warmth enveloped her, cradling her in an invisible loving force field, soothing her. She felt weightless, joyous and vibrant as her apprehensions melted away like butter on a hot roll. The feel of her parents' presence gradually dissipated. Everything seemed to be moving in slow motion.

Glistening in the splendor of the setting sun, Newgrange slowly faded from her sight, and the hazy outline of a distant archway filled with three-dimensional, neon-colored geometric symbols filled her vision. A large shimmering spiral now slowly drew her in and upward. Then another spiral appeared and yet another. Triangles, six-pointed stars, rectangles, hexagons, infinity symbols, squares, circles and smaller spirals all seemed to be moving rapidly toward her and through her body. She felt as though her every cell was being rearranged, restructured. Drew could feel the various shapes colliding within her, and as they did, radiance glowed from her into the protective mist that embraced her. She mused at the thought of being a human headlight on a foggy night, but was she still human? she wondered. Her thoughts were so keen, so rich.

Voices, some garbled, others foreign, broke the absolute silence in which she had pleasurably found herself bathed. The familiar sweet scent of wildflowers and a spicy fragrance now filled her nostrils. After what seemed like a very long time, or maybe it was no time at all, she steadied her footing as her feet touched onto something solid. Hands were once again reaching into hers, and she was gently guided from the misty archway.

A slight breeze brushed sunlight across her face.

Eittod's voice pierced through all the other voices. "Welcome, Drew Megan Campbell. Welcome to Outpost Gypsy Tree."

Standing right in front of her was an elderly gentleman with reflective, crystal-blue eyes and a colorful body beaming at her from a hologram. And just beyond him another stone archway loomed. In awe, she moved towards him and bowed gracefully before his holographic image.

"Oh, no need! No need at all!" he said. "It is I who should be doing the bowing to *you,* brave one."

"Thank you for inviting me," said Drew in a dreamy tone. She was caught in the splendor of the magnificent being addressing her.

"Thank you very much, Eittod," and then she gasped, clapping a hand to her mouth, her eyes wide. "Oh! Beg your pardon, Sir, for being so presumptuous. Is it proper for me to call you Eittod? And am I pronouncing your name correctly, Sir?" she quickly asked.

Drew's parents had been very strict in her upbringing, and honoring one's elders was at the very top of the list. Correct pronunciation of people's names was near the top as well.

"Of course, my dear. That is my name when translated into your spoken language. And my name is pronounced *eye-todd*," he replied with a big radiant smile. "You are most welcome, and I, in return, thank you for responding to my invitation. We shall have plenty of time to talk, so not to worry. All of your many questions will be answered, Drew Megan Campbell," Eittod replied as his hologram faded from her sight.

Drew was suddenly aware that someone was still holding her hand. She turned to see the matronly lady in jeans with the large warm eyes and rosy cheeks. The lady was smiling at her.

"Hello, Drew. I am Bezen. Welcome to our home and your home away from home," she said in a motherly tone. "Your domicile and sleeping chamber have been prepared for you. My son, Mingo, will show you to the encampment," she said while motioning toward the young man with the olive-toned skin and elongated head covered in golden hair. "We will meet with you soon to formally welcome you and the others," Bezen finished.

Excited beyond belief, Drew flung her arms tightly around Bezen. "I can't believe I am really here and looking into the faces I began painting just weeks ago. I feel that I have known you all my life," she said as she looked from Bezen to the spot where Eittod's hologram had stood, and then to Mingo.

"But you have, my dear, you have," replied Bezen, stroking Drew's face with her fingertips. "We have much to share with you, but in due time. Now, off to your domicile to rest. You've had a very long journey."

Bezen's last words never reached Drew's ears, for behind Bezen, Drew glimpsed the tree – the Gypsy Tree. How glorious it was. How enormously glorious it was! She felt like a small child on Christmas morning – awe-struck, unable to take her eyes from the towering boughs above her. Drew's eyes followed up Gypsy's trunk and into the sky. Its top branches were hidden by the low moving billowy clouds. It shimmered in the sunlight; its spicy fragrance delighted her senses. And the sound! Oh, the sound! It was like nothing she had ever heard in her whole life. The sound was like angel harps and crystal chimes blended with deep, rich, vibrational undertones into a melodious symphony, beckoning and breathtaking.

She took a step forward toward the tree, but Bezen touched her arm gently, halting her. Drew recalled the image she had had in her bedroom, of herself standing in front of the giant tree wanting to go inside. She quivered. *How strange to imagine going inside of a tree. Was that even possible?* she wondered. All her mental images and paintings of the past few weeks were alive and all around her. *Am I dreaming all this? Shall I wake and find that I have gone nowhere except in a dream, like Alice and the rabbit hole?* Bezen's voice startled Drew from her inner rambling.

"Drew, this is Gypsy," said Bezen. "Gypsy will be a very valuable companion to you. Gypsy, meet Drew Megan Campbell."

The tree moved as if slightly bowing to Drew. And the sound. Oh, the glorious sound! It was better than all the magnificent orchestras on Earth combined.

"There will be plenty of time for discovering," Mingo interrupted with a broad smile. "It is a wondrous place indeed, but for now, please follow me." Mingo gestured his outstretched hand toward a stone pathway. "Come this way, Drew Megan Campbell. It's not far."

Drew paused to look back at the stone archway, wondering just how far away she was from her parents. She pictured them standing at Newgrange with empty arms, frozen in time – statue-like – waiting for her return. Tears slid down her face as she turned her back on the archway and obliged Mingo's instruction.

Drew's gait quickened as she walked beside him, taking long strides to keep up with the very tall, lanky youth and occasionally glanced back to the tree with a deep longing in her heart. As they made their way through the forest, the encampment came into view – a sight so familiar. Her heart leapt; she was really here, walking along a pathway at Outpost Gypsy Tree. Absolute joy enlivened her step. The triple spiral stone was still clutched tightly in her left fist.

Mingo and Drew were soon engulfed by the encampment with its winding stone pathways and statuary, wild flowers and hanging gardens.

Surely the gardens of Babylon must have been this magnificent, Drew thought.

Colorful water fountains graced the gardens and pathways. There were dancing waters creating a symphony of their very own. Wildlife peeked out from their hiding places to glimpse the newcomer. Drew cooed as she looked into the soft brown face and big black eyes of a fawn grazing near the path. Flowers, fruit trees and greenery of all shapes, sizes and colors met her eyes. And some of the colors she had *never seen before.* Some varieties she was sure had never existed on the Earth – or maybe endangered or gone millenniums ago.

With that thought, another one crept in. *Just where am I in relation to the Earth?* Drew wondered.

She had a million and one questions flying through her head, and many more crowding to get in. And then the strangest thing began to happen. Whenever she had a questioning thought, an answer would begin to form in her head almost immediately: names of colors, flowers, fruits and foliage and their dates of extinction or current location on the Earth or elsewhere in the heavens. She had the knowing that she was in an enchanted sanctuary nestled within a thought form in Earth's vast realm, protected by the Regions Authority. Mingo was an immortal from Early Earth. She needed to go to her domicile to complete her DNA transformation. Answers were coming as rapidly as the questions.

Eittod had promised that all her questions would soon be answered, and here they were right in her own head.

Regions? Who or what is a Regions? she asked in her head, but no answer came.

"Some questions are answered only when the time is right, Drew Megan Campbell," an unfamiliar, very sweet, soft voice resonated in her head.

Who are you, and how do you know my name and my thoughts, she asked of the voice.

"We have already met. I am Gypsy, and I am here to protect you, to teach you and to answer your questions when they warrant answering. May I call you Drew?"

Oh! Yes, you may, and may I call you Gypsy? she asked politely. Drew smiled, enjoying the direct connection with the magnificent tree. *I can't believe I am really talking to a tree,* she thought.

I imagine a question concerning Early Earth is out of bounds as well? she mused to herself.

"You imagine correctly, Drew," answered Gypsy. "And yes, you may call me Gypsy."

Drew pulled her mind away from its inner tennis match with Gypsy and focused on the edifice before her. Stark white stone walls rose into the trees at unusual angles. Slopes and futuristic geometric shapes carved the surreal beauty of the exterior. Each window and door appeared to be filled with what looked like iridescent soap bubbles.

As they approached the oval entrance, it rotated open before them, and Mingo stepped through. Drew hesitated, confused at what had just happened.

"Oh!" said Mingo, noticing her hesitation and the questioning look on her face. "You just think it and it happens for you. My thought or intention was that the energy space would open and it did. You'll get used to it. Actually, it's quite a lot of fun. Would you like to try?" he asked.

Cautiously Drew nodded in agreement. Mingo stepped out again and the door or energy space closed behind him.

"It's energy! It's alive just as you and I are, but in a different form, that's all," he reassured her. "You are living energy, everything is. Your civilization's scientists and physicists have finally rediscovered that fact, and that's just the whisker on the whale."

Drew looked at him curiously, "Do you mean like, 'just the tip of the iceberg?'"

Now, the curious look switched to Mingo's expression. Drew laughed.

"You have a nice sense of humor, Drew Megan Campbell. I like that. It will serve you well. Now, what was I saying?" he said, running his hands through his golden hair. "Oh, yes. You will learn many truths here, Drew Megan Campbell. Just be patient with yourself and with us. You will be making major leaps forward in your understanding of how our universe *really* works," he finished.

Tentatively, Drew reached out to touch the iridescent surface. She was surprised to experience a warm pulsating *something* pushing back at her, and quickly withdrew her hand. Again, Drew shot a questioning look at Mingo.

"As I have told you, it's energy. Now, I want you to imagine or *intend* the door opening, Drew Megan Campbell, and at the same time nod your head. That seems to help as you are learning. Picture it happening in your mind and *believe* it will. That's the important part, *believing!*" Mingo coached her.

Trusting, Drew focused on the space and imagined it opening as it had for Mingo, and at the same time *willed* it to happen and made a quick nod of her head. The space began to open. She gasped, and with that, it quickly closed again.

"Oh, bummy! What happened?" Drew asked chagrined, her face pinked.

"You didn't trust yourself. You didn't trust that you could do it. Your doubt closed it. The energy is responding to your thoughts, Drew Megan Campbell," he said with a slight chuckle in his voice. "It takes some getting used to for us Earthlings. It certainly did for me. And at times I still get caught by my own idle thoughts," Mingo said. He replayed the spit episode with Eittod in his head; his face warmed. "Your thoughts create your reality a lot faster here," he continued. "On Earth there is a delay between thought and action and that's probably a very good thing," he laughed.

"My thoughts create my reality?" questioned Drew, furrowing her brow.

"Yep!" responded Mingo, now casually leaning against the white façade, his arms folded across his long chest. "Everything that happens for you or to you – be it good or not so good – is a direct result of your thoughts and expectations. In fact, that's how you got here to Outpost Gypsy Tree – your thoughts or desires for peace and love in your world summoned Eittod. Didn't you know that, Drew Megan Campbell?"

"No, I didn't. I've never heard of such a thing. And why do you keep calling me, 'Drew Megan Campbell?'" she asked in an irritated tone.

"Well, because that is your true vibration is it not?" Mingo queried, surprised at her question.

"Well, it is my full name, if that's what you mean, but you can call me Drew as your mother did, can't you?"

"Drew it is! Now, let's have another go at that opening," encouraged Mingo, unable to stifle his grin.

Drew focused, determined to open the energy space. Incompetence was one thing Drew Megan Campbell didn't like to feel! After a few tries it opened and closed at her non-verbal commands. Tickled by her success, she turned to Mingo. "Well, how was that?" she questioned with a slightly pompous grin.

"Not bad for a first timer. Not bad at all," he said, grinning back. "I think we're going to get along just fine, Drew Meg...I mean, Drew. Now, into your domicile!"

"Lead the way!" she said motioning her head toward the opening. "Bummy! This focusing stuff is going to take some getting use to, that's for sure!" she muttered under her breath.

As they moved through the opening Drew had created, her eyes were once again dazzled. Everything glistened, sparkled and shone.

"Oh, it's so beautiful in here! I wish Mum could see this. But...I don't understand...?" She looked around for the light source, but didn't see lamps, chandeliers or candles anywhere. "Mingo, where are the lights coming from?"

"Everything is energy, Drew; hence, it has its own light source as do you," he replied, still smiling. He watched her with absolute delight as Outpost Gypsy Tree offered her one new experience after another – one new truth after another – and the *wonder* of it all.

Mingo lead Drew across the mosaic stone floor to the left of the large greeting hall. "It is important that you rest from your trip. Your body has been changed dramatially to accommodate this place," he said, "and yes, to answer your question, you are still human, Drew."

Drew was taken aback by his knowledge of her thoughts during her transport from Newgrange. She wondered what else he knew of her thoughts.

Pointing to many golden discs on the floor, Mingo continued, "The golden discs will be one means of transportation for you while you are here with us. Please step on one to go to your sleeping chamber," he requested.

Drew looked down. Golden discs the size of manhole covers lay at her feet. With excitement and wonder Drew stepped on one of the discs. She waited, but nothing happened. She shot Mingo a look. Mingo smiled. He so enjoyed her spunky nature.

"Remember, Drew, your thoughts create your reality. Set your intent to be taken to your sleeping chamber," he instructed her. "I'll see you later."

"Oh! Of course," she snapped as her face pinked. With a deep sigh she closed her eyes, focused, made a quick nod of her head and disappeared from the disc. In the next breath Drew found herself standing alone in front of an iridescent energy space, one that had her full name written upon it in her own handwriting. Knowing she could do it, Drew focused again, and the energy space withdrew to reveal an amazing and very welcomed site.

Before her was a large floor–to–ceiling mirror with many decorative hooks holding Irish dance awards, tiaras and wigs. Brass wall hooks displayed well-worn ghillies, and jig shoes of all sizes hung by their laces. At the base of the mirror, a scarred wooden platform covered half of the floor. A woven basket lay on the floor beside a large bed whose nightstand displayed boxes of Pop artists and Irish dance music.

"My room!" she gasped with delight. "My own room!" Eagerly looking around she sighed, "My very own room."

Drew moved into the room and sat upon her freshly made Irish sleigh bed; the linens smelled so sweet, like wildflowers. Suddenly tiredness overcame her curiosity. As she curled around her many soft bed pillows, she looked to the other side of the room where her old wooden easel stood splattered with a collage of colors. Paint boxes and glass jars containing brushes neatly lined the large window seat along with perfectly stacked art papers and canvas pads. Light shone from everything in the room. Never in her whole life had her room been this clean or bright. Absolutely never!

As Drew slowly drifted into sleep, the image of a small, child-like creature with pointed teeth came floating into her memory. Had she really seen it peeking at her through the foliage in the encampment gardens or was it just her imagination? Sleep came easily.

CHAPTER THIRTEEN:
Roller Coaster Ride

"NOW!" said the twins. The mirror was gone from sight as was the fleeting image Aube had seen behind them in the mirror – a tall handsome soldier with almond-shaped amber eyes wearing a maroon uniform. An expression of parental pride filled his face. A fine mist surrounded them obscuring their vision, and their bodies quivered uncontrollably. Concerned for Gar, Aube called out.

"Take some deep breaths, Gar. Can you hear me? We'll be okay; trust me. Just take some deep breaths."

Aube welcomed this experience with every fiber of his being. He was enjoying every sensory delight, and all the subtle nuances of this new world he had so willingly entered. But for Gar, it must surely be terrifying. The unseen world which Gar feared had just swallowed him up whole, and was carrying him off to only heaven knew where.

Gar's left hand squeezed Aube's right painfully, yet another hand was in Aube's left, a soft, gentle hand. With that touch, a warm peaceful calm washed over him, and he prayed that his brother could feel it too. Finally, Gar's grip on Aube slackened and muffled sounds could be heard.

"You okay, Gar? Talk to me! Gar, what's happening to you?" Aube couldn't see anything but the mist. "Gar, talk to me!" Aube pleaded.

"I'm okay, Aube! I'm okay! What a rush! Whee! What a ride!" his shouts echoed back at them through the mist.

Gar was intoxicated by the adrenalin rush and the soft hand in his. Aube was relieved and grateful for Gar's exuberance, for a second later a large spiral drew them upward into another spiral and then another. A large archway filled with neon-colored geometric shapes came hurdling toward them. Geometric symbols bombarded their bodies, sending flashes of light out in all directions. Squeezing each other's hands, Aube and Gar laughed and called out into the mist, which echoed back their laugher. They turned and tumbled their bodies in the gigantic, weightless void. Neither had ever been on an amusement park ride, but if they had, it would have probably been like this – but this was loads better by far. They were sure of it!

Suddenly, something solid met their feet, and hands were pulling them from the void out into sunlight. There was no need to shelter their eyes from the brightness; their pupils had adjusted to the change instantly.

Smiling faces met theirs: a plump, middle-aged woman, a teen with an unusually-shaped head and a hologram of an elderly, colorful being. Aube knew these faces and these voices greeting them and felt at home, and his heart leapt with excitement. But Gar was a stranger in this very strange land, trusting solely in his conjoined twin brother's judgment.

"Welcome, Auben Juan Perez! Welcome, Garcia Gou-Drah Perez! Welcome to Outpost Gypsy Tree, boys," Eittod greeted them.

"Eittod!" shouted Aube with great gusto as if he were unexpectedly meeting an old friend. His face turned to his brother, "Gar, this is

Eittod! He wrote us the invitation on my pad, remember? Remember Gar?" Aube glowed, his heart thumping like a tom-tom in his chest.

Eittod laughed. "Have you boys had a good trip?" he inquired.

Gar's mouth hung open, but nothing came out; his eyes were wide and searching. The trip was one thing, but a talking Crayola hologram? Now that was quite another!

Finally, Gar muttered in a soft, awed tone, "It's…it's real! This place…it's real!…Ah! Isn't it?" Gar was pale as a ghost, but his fear didn't seem to halt him. He looked around at Mingo and Bezen and back to Eittod, "It was quite a…a ride, Sir. Quite a ride. Thank you!" he finished. Mrs. Perez had raised her sons to be respectful and polite. Even in this situation her teaching shone through.

"Good!" replied Eittod. "I'll let you boys settle in, and then we'll have plenty of time to talk. I promise all your questions will be answered. My dear Bezen, I leave our travelers to you." Eittod's hologram retreated.

"Holy Christmas! What the…" blurted Gar as his eyes found the tree and followed it into the clouds. "Awesome! Is it…is it real?"

"That's the tree I was telling you about, Gar!" boasted Aube. "It's real alright. I used to come here in my dreams and sit in front of it imagining really being here, and now, here we are!" Thrilled and validated by his brother's excitement, Aube relished the moment.

"Auben! Garcia! I am Bezen and this is my son, Mingo. He'll see you to your domicile," said the matronly lady with the kind smile.

Puzzled, Gar glanced at Aube, "Domicile?" he questioned with a frozen stare.

"That would be your living quarters, or as you would say in current Earth language, 'your house,'" said Mingo. "Just follow me Auben Juan and Garcia Gou-Drah Perez," pointing to a stone pathway.

"Wait a minute! Just...just wait a minute!" said Gar anxiously, raising his hands in front of him as if to protect himself from this scary new reality.

"I know what a domicile is, thank you, but why do I need one?" questioned Gar. Icy fingers of fear were running rampant though his body again and gripping at his spine.

Coming along with Aube to satisfy his curiosity was one thing, *staying* was quite another. Gar had spent all his time struggling with the possibility of this place being real, but had never given a thought to the part about staying.

"We've come to help," Aube said, alarmed. "Gar, we've come to help Eittod. That's why we're here, Gar."

Aube reached for Gar's left hand. As he did, another hand slipped gently into Gar's right, a familiar loving hand; in fact, the same hand that he had felt in the mist just moments before. With that touch, a warm peaceful calm washed over them both. Standing beside them was Bezen – her eyes mesmerizing, her smile motherly.

"Garcia, you are safe. There is nothing to fear in this place," she said as she let go of his hand. "We have been preparing for you and Aube since before you boys were even born," she assured him. "Now, just follow Mingo. He will take you to your domicile, and I am sure you will feel very much at home there," she finished.

The twins stared at Bezen as she slowly evaporated into thin air.

"Come this way, boys. It's just a short walk," Mingo said.

"Doesn't anybody in this place just *walk* away?" asked Gar.

Mingo laughed, "Not if there's an easier way. Come along now," he said, again motioning to the pathway.

The twins followed Mingo through the forest to the encampment as Bezen had instructed. Gar seemed unusually relaxed, even enjoying himself. Aube wasn't sure what had happened between Gar and

Bezen, but he was pleased that his brother's fearful mood had changed again for the better.

With an amused look on his face, Gar nudged Aube and pointed to Mingo's head. Aube grinned.

"Where are you from, Mingo?" Gar asked.

"Actually, I live here at the Outpost, and have since I can remember. Mother and I are a part of Eittod's team. We're like a family, I guess you could say. How about you? Where are you and your brother from, Garcia Gou-Drah Perez?"

"Why don't you just call us Aube and Gar? It would be a lot simpler," Gar requested.

"If you like," Mingo replied.

"I mean, where are you from *originally*?" Gar asked again.

"Oh! Mom and I are from Early Earth. And where are you from? You didn't say."

Not even flinching at Mingo's response, Gar replied, "We're from Lima…Peru…which is in…ah…South America…" Gar paused, "Ah!…on…planet Earth." Gar felt a bit stupid saying 'planet Earth,' but it seemed to fit the conversation.

Aube giggled, amused at his brother's coping skills in this very strange situation.

"And just what was that giggle about, Aube?" asked Gar with some indignation.

"I am just enjoying myself, that's all," answered Aube, finishing with a big grin.

"So, Mingo, what's with this Early Earth stuff?" Gar asked. "You mean Neanderthal time?"

"No, no," laughed Mingo. "There is so much for you to learn and remember here. Those of your planet Earth, as you call it, have very limited knowledge of the lands you inhabit and of those who have inhabited it before and after you. Ancient Wisdom or Eternal Wisdom is always available, and the peoples of your current Earth, or time ring, are just beginning to tap into a minute piece of that wisdom. Using an expression I learned earlier today which seems to fit here, your wise ones are just at the tip of the iceberg," Mingo beamed, proud of his new verbiage. "Continuing, all knowledge of the past, present and to come has been available since the beginning of time, time being relative, according to your Einstein. Actually, time is in a circle. Many ancient and future cultures have found the route into that wisdom, only to have the greed of man and the ravages of time erase the path," Mingo finished as if this was just a casual conversation like, "How's the weather?"

Gar and Aube came to a halt, motionless, caught in the depth and implications of Mingo's words. Gar's blood went cold, his mind disconnected. On the other hand, Aube's mind and blood were racing with excitement, mentally scampering to connect the dots and fill in the gaps – and reveling in what he now knew and had somehow suspected.

Mingo glanced over his shoulder, realizing that the twins were reacting to his words. He apologized, "I have probably said too much."

"No, please go on, please," urged Aube. "I want to know more. I want to know what *you* know. I have read and searched for so long and what you just said makes so much sense to me. It fits. It all fits!" Aube shouted with glee. "Gar, Papa would love this place. Wow! Wait 'til he hears this!"

Gar was still struggling with what Mingo had just said. If this was true, then everything he had ever heard or studied up until now was pure nonsense.

"Please go on, Mingo," Aube begged.

"I must leave the instruction to Eittod. My job right now is to get you to your domicile. You must rest – that's very important. Your journey has been very hard on your physical structure. I am sure you will find your domicile very accommodating and pleasing," said Mingo.

An expression of disappointment crossed Aube's face.

"Believe me, Aube, there is plenty of time to get all your questions answered," Mingo assured him, patting him firmly on his shoulder.

As for Gar, he had already heard enough.

"Drop the subject, Aube! Drop it! *Please!*" Gar urged.

Honoring his brother's request, Aube lightened his pursuit, but was unable to curb his elation at actually being within his own dream world and interacting with it.

In an attempt to change the subject, Mingo asked, "I've never seen a two-in-one before, how did you do that?"

"Oh!" laughed Aube, "We're conjoined twins. We were born attached, and we quite like it. Medical folks back home call us pygopagus twins," Aube finished.

Gee, 'back home,' thought Aube, his own statement startling him. He'd never been out of Lima, let alone out of South America. His thoughts ran rampant. *I could even be off the Earth itself! If so, does this make Gar and me astronauts?* he wondered. *But, who would believe us? Who would ever believe we were here – wherever here is – and talking with someone from Early Earth?*

A gentle female voice eased into Aube's thoughts, "You are much more than astronauts, Aube. You boys are 'Light Travelers' – 'Protectors.'"

Now, even more questions rushed into Aube's head.

Again the gentle voice spoke, "All in good time, Aube, all in good time."

Aube mused to himself, delighted to be hearing the gentle female voice in his head.

"Who are you, and do you hear all my thoughts?" he asked in his head.

"This is Gypsy Tree. And no, Aube, just the thoughts that need answering," said Gypsy.

Still in a conversation with Mingo, Gar continued, "Yes! It's great having your best friend with you all the time – no secrets here! Right, Aube?" Gar chuckled.

If he only knew, thought Aube, *if he only knew.* Aube smiled.

As they made a turn on the path, the encampment spread out before them. They gasped – Gar in amazement at its appearance, Aube in delight at finally being here.

CHAPTER FOURTEEN:
The Gathering

Drew's eyes fluttered. She rolled over onto her back and gazed up at her favorite photos hanging on varied lengths of brightly-colored satin ribbons. She felt strangely different, but couldn't put words to it. As she glanced around the room at all her new and wonderful paintings, memories of her parents and Newgrange began to ease in. The realization of where she was hit her. She bolted from her bed and ran to the window. Stunned, Drew was sure her eyes were betraying her. There below was her father's garden, and beyond, the plush green of her beloved Ireland and the bend of the Boyne River. "What's happening?" she called out.

"All is well, Drew Megan Campbell," said Gypsy in her head. "Your sleeping chamber and your surroundings are here to comfort you. When you are ready to join the others, Mingo will meet you in the greeting hall. Just step onto the disc outside your chamber and transport."

Drew went to her mirror and checked herself from front to back and head to toe. "I look the same," she said out loud to herself, "but I feel so different – changed somehow."

In the mirror, she glimpsed a broken ceramic frame and shattered glass on the floor. She recalled Grand's photo falling when she had backed into her nightstand avoiding her parents embrace. That seemed so long ago.

Images of her parents waiting for her at Newgrange filled her thoughts again. Absent-mindedly, Drew began to gather up Grand's photo and the broken ceramic frame. He was young and handsome, with a look of absolute joy in his bright green eyes and a contagious grin on his youthful face. Mum had always remarked at how much Drew favored Grand in her looks – the bright green eyes, fair skin and red hair.

"Oh, how I would love to have known him," she mused aloud, lovingly placing the photo and frame fragments on her bed. Then she bent to gather the glass fragments. As she did a shard of glass pierced the palm of her hand.

"Ouch, that hurt. Oh, bummy!" she blurted out, "I am bleeding!" Drops of blood fell rapidly onto her clothes and the wooden floor below. Hastily, she snatched the shard from her palm and reached for the tissue box on her nightstand. In amazement she watched as the bleeding stopped as quickly as it had started. The deep cut slowly sealed itself and the crimson splatters faded from her hands, clothes and the floor below. It was as if it had never happened – all signs of the deep cut were gone. Drew opened and closed her hand, there was no pain. She stared at her hand in disbelief, her brain numbed by the experience. Slowly she raised her head to look at herself in the mirror. Thoughts began to form. Unbelievable thoughts, outrageous thoughts and downright frightening thoughts impacted her.

"It couldn't be! It just…just couldn't…be!" she stammered. Never breaking eye contact with herself in the mirror, Drew slowly dropped ragdoll-like to the floor with the realization of just how different she was.

Mingo's words and her own internal answers to her questioning thoughts exploded in her mind.

"Your body has been changed dramatically to accommodate this place, and yes, you are still human," Mingo had said.

Mingo was an immortal from Early Earth; she needed to go to her domicile to complete her DNA transformation.

Without warning, Eittod's hologram formed in front of her. "Dear child, this was not the way you were to learn of this. I am so sorry for your distress," he whispered gently.

Now Bezen was beside her, reaching out for Drew's hand.

"Yes, Drew Megan Campbell, your thoughts are correct – you are an immortal now. It just has to be that way for your human body to survive here in this place," confirmed Eittod. "Your DNA transformation seems to be complete. Know, dear one, that all is well." Eittod's colorful image dissolved.

Bezen helped her to her feet. "This has been quite a day hasn't it, Drew?" she said, smiling that calm loving smile. "Now, let's get you to the greeting hall to meet the others."

Drew took one more glance into the mirror. "I am still human?" she asked Bezen.

"Yes, Drew, you are still human, just as I am and my son. And yes, dear Drew, *you can go home again*…whenever you wish, but for now we all have work to do. Are you ready?" Bezen asked.

Drew took in a long, deep breath and pushed it out hard. "Yes! Yes, I am!" whispered Drew, her voice weak. Right at this moment, Drew craved her parent's arms around her; she needed their comfort, and they were there.

"It's okay, Drewkins, we're here and always will be," said Tom.

"Now, get on with saving mankind," said Meg, stroking Drew's cheek with her fingertips.

Then they were gone. Surprised at her experience, Drew turned to Bezen for an explanation.

"Dear Drew, you are never far from your family. Remember that!"

Bezen reached for Drew's left hand and opened it. "Your great-grandfather knew you were the 'rightful master of this stone,' as does Eittod and the Regions. Your destiny lies before you, Drew," said Bezen firmly. And again she asked, "Drew Megan Campbell, are you ready to fulfill your destiny?"

Drew pushed her shoulders back and stretched herself up to her full height. "Yes, Bezen, I am ready," said Drew in a more confident voice.

Drew stepped through the energy space feeling stronger, more vibrant. With confidence, she stepped on the golden disc, focused and a second later she was in the greeting hall looking right into Mingo's dark eyes.

"Well?' asked Mingo.

"I am ready!" she said.

"Yes, I know you are," he smiled. "Come, Drew. There are others you must meet." He led her across the greeting hall to where a small group of teens were gathered.

Drew had had enough surprises for one day, but she was about to encounter the biggest one of all.

As Mingo and Drew approached the group, they all turned to greet her with big smiles and a round of handshakes. Instinctively they knew Drew Megan Campbell of Ireland was their leader, and so did she. They all knew they would be family.

First to take her hand was a set of handsome, male conjoined twins with smooth, chestnut-toned skin and almond-shaped amber eyes. They introduced themselves as Aube and Gar Perez from Lima, Peru. Next, a young Native American girl with a long, silky black braid and large piercing eyes introduced herself as Chelli "Little Bear" Freeman from Fairbanks, Alaska.

"That's a nice name," said Drew. "How is it pronounced again?" she asked.

"It's a simple enough name, but folks do have trouble with it. It's pronounced like the *ch* in the word *chilly*, then L – E. Chelli," she said with a big smile.

Then a very slender ebony-skinned boy with twinkling dark eyes and very bushy hair stepped forward. "G'day, Penzil Kangaroo is the name, lass, and I am from down under – the Outback, Australia, you know." Penzil finished with a deep bow in front of her.

They all laughed.

"Penzil, it's a pleasure to meet you, Sir!" she responded with a deep curtsy and a big smile.

And last, a red haired, freckled-faced youth reached for her hand and began to introduce himself. "A fellow Irishman, Drew, from just outside…"

As she turned to take his hand, Drew froze and her expression sobered. "You…" she abruptly interrupted. "You look like someone…someone I know…" she said pensively. "Do…do I know you?" she asked, staring deeply into his eyes, her brow furrowed. A feeling of deep connection washed over her, and she chilled to the bone with a shiver.

Freaked out by her expression, the young man retreated. "I'd remember a pretty lass like you, Drew, but I don't think we've ever met. I am very pleased to meet you," he said extending his hand. "As I started to say, I am from just outside of Dublin and my name is Patrick Ca…"

Again Drew interrupted, "Are you *sure* we've never met before?" she asked continuing to stare more deeply now as if looking into his very soul.

"What's going on with you, Drew?" he asked as he backed away again from her advancement. "Why are you looking at me like that? You act as though you've just seen a ghost and that ghost is me!"

"I am so sorry, but...but you look so much like...like..." Drew moved close to him again as her mind flashed back to the photo of Grand that she had just laid on her bed. In a low, trembling voice, she said, "You look just like...like my great-grandfather, Grand."

Everyone had formed a circle around Drew and Patrick, all caught in the drama playing out in front of them.

Again, stumbling backwards, he retreated from her. "I...I haven't looked in a mirror since I got here, but I hope I haven't aged that much, lass," he laughed nervously.

Mingo stepped between them and laughed, "Okay, you two Irishmen, let's get moving," he said. "Irishmen! Always looking for a fight!" mumbled Mingo shaking his head. "Eittod will soon be ready to meet with you. Follow me, everyone."

Mingo put his arm around Patrick's shoulders and guided him forward. "Girls sure can be pushy," said Mingo as he led them all out through the iridescent energy space, back through the encampment gardens, past the colorful fountains and statuary, toward the double stone archways.

The young Irishman quickly moved ahead to walk with the twins. And Chelli took Drew by the arm, walking slowly behind the group.

"Strange place, isn't it? But I love it. How about you?" she asked Drew.

Drew's mind was still reeling with the images of her great-grandfather and the young man she had just met.

"I will leave you here for now. Eittod will join you shortly," Mingo said as he walked past the archways toward the footbridge and the Gypsy Tree.

All the teens began talking at once. Above them loomed the archways covered in strange symbols and ancient writings illuminated in an eerie fluorescent green. Drew was unable to pull her gaze from her new Irish friend.

"Wait up, Mingo!" Patrick called. "Please wait a minute; I have a question for you."

Mingo turned back to oblige his request, "What's your question Patrick?"

"Well, Mingo, I know that's the archway through which we arrived today," pointing to the one behind him, "but, where does the other one lead?" pointing to the one in front of him.

"Home, Earthling, home!" said Mingo cheerfully.

Drew's thoughts snapped back to her parents standing in the setting sun at Newgrange. Oh, how far away from them she was, yet she was still feeling the hug she just received from them. How strange and yet how comforting.

Aube and Gar were now in conversation with Penzil. "That's an unusual name, 'Penzil Kangaroo,' is it a family name by chance?" Aube asked.

"No mate, the name 'Penzil' was given to me by one of my Anangu elders, and I guess you could say 'Kangaroo' is a family name," replied Penzil. "Help raise me, they did!"

"You're Aborigine? Is that correct?" asked Gar.

"That's too right, Gar," confirmed Penzil

"Would it be okay if I call you 'Outback?' I've never known anyone from the Outback," asked Aube.

"Good oh, mate, don't mind at all," said Penzil with a big smile.

Gar's thoughts went to the football game he'd rather be watching right about now. Actually, any place on Earth would be okay with Gar, regretting his decision to oblige Aube's wishes.

Drew walked toward Patrick, "Where in Ireland did you say you were from, Patrick?" asked Drew, still studying him closely.

Aube and Gar approached her, cutting her path to the young man who pretended to be studying the symbols carved on the archways.

"You speak Spanish very well, Drew," remarked Aube.

"Yep! Like a native," chimed in Gar, both making idle chatter with Drew.

Surprised, Drew cocked her head to the side and ran her fingers into her copper curls. "What are you talking about? I don't speak Spanish! On the contrary, you both speak very good English."

Gar and Aube glanced at each other, shrugging their shoulders.

"We don't speak English," they responded in unison.

"Only Spanish and a smidgen of Quechua," said Aube, with a look of realization on his chestnut-toned face.

Aube called out to Penzil, "Hey, Outback, what language are you speaking right now?"

"The King's English, mate! Same as you, why?" asked Penzil who had also been studying the symbols on the archways.

"Hey, everybody, do you realize," cried Aube, "that we are all speaking our own native tongue and yet, we understand each other?"

They all stared at one another in astonishment.

Instantly, Drew knew the answer to this startling phenomenon and excitedly moved to the center of the group, catching everyone's eye.

"As we came through the archway, I believe we were gifted the ability to understand *and* speak all languages, both current and dead," pointing to the letters and symbols on the archways.

"Remember," Drew continued, "as you came through the mist, the shapes and symbols collided inside of you?"

Everyone nodded.

"Well, I believe that's when we were gifted universal language," she finished.

"I've been reading the symbols carved on the archways, and thought nothing of it. *Now*, I understand why I can read them," said Penzil in astonishment. "Way to go, mate!"

"You are right, Drew Megan Campbell. Congratulations," said Eittod, with a wonderful warm grin on his holographic face.

Drew had just stepped into her role as leader, and Eittod was elated.

Everyone applauded. Drew's face pinked.

"…And not only current and dead, but languages past, present and future. Well, my dears, another amazing discovery and many more to come, I promise you. Now, please join me inside our magnificent Gypsy Tree. She has been anxiously awaiting your arrival," said Eittod, his hologram leading the way.

Gypsy bowed, and her breathtaking sounds enticed them in.

CHAPTER FIFTEEN:
The Introduction

On their approach, the large wooden door rotated open and the spicy fragrance of Gypsy and the sweet smell of wildflowers filled their nostrils. Eager for their first glimpse of the interior, the teens tightly followed Eittod's hologram through the doorway. The door rotated shut behind them with a heavy thud. Everyone jumped.

The command center of Outpost Gypsy Tree lay before them. The space was immense, yet warm and inviting. Sunlight was streaming in through the large, crystalline, amber-colored sap crevices in Gypsy's trunk, creating a kaleidoscope of color, like a mirror ball at a homecoming dance.

To their right was a feasting nook with a large stone table strewn with wildflowers. To their left was the main interior transport chamber and beyond, an activity arena. In front of them was a very large sunken sitting area and library that would put the largest of Earth libraries to shame. Beyond the pit was a flat, circular structure of what appeared to be massive tree rings. And randomly placed carved marble and wood pillars rose into Gypsy's rafters.

"Welcome! Welcome to the snuggery," said Eittod, gesturing them toward the sunken pit area. He was no longer a hologram, but was in full human form, except for his colorful skin.

"Our first gathering begins!" he announced.

In a flurry they all moved into the pit behind him, choosing seats and pillow piles as close to Eittod as they could get. Eittod grinned from ear to ear to see all their eager faces beaming up at him. Oh, how he had looked forward to this moment.

"First, let me say on behalf of the Regions Authority and the staff of Outpost Gypsy Tree – Bezen, Mingo and myself – *thank you.* Thank you for calling out for peace and brotherly love in your world. Your calls have been heard, and have returned us to our work. We have prepared the way, and you are the solution," said Eittod, opening his hands to them.

The teens glanced around at each other, and then back at Eittod. "With that said, I know you have briefly introduced yourselves to each other, but I'd like to start with another most important introduction," he said clearing his throat.

"First, let me say that here at the outpost, expect the unexpected," he paused. "Patrick," motioning toward the young Irishman, "I know you are unnerved by Drew's reaction to you, but she has due cause," nodding toward Drew. Both Drew and Patrick eased to the edge of their seats, their eyes darting between each other and Eittod.

"Drew, I believe you know who this young man is. Am I correct?" gesturing toward Patrick.

Drew slowly stood up, her whole body quivering, "Grand...is...is that you?" she said in a loving whisper. "Is it really *you?*"

"Patrick, I'd like to introduce you to your great-granddaughter, Drew Megan Campbell," said Eittod.

The other teens gasped and froze in place waiting for what would happen next.

Patrick Campbell was dumbstruck. His face drained of color. Penzil reached out to grab him as he slipped from the edge of his seat onto the soft camelhair rug below.

"How can that be? How can that possibly be? We're...we're the same age!" he stammered. Confused and overwhelmed, Patrick tried to stand, but his knees were weak and buckling. Penzil was at his side for support, and eased him to the floor again.

Now at his side on the floor, Bezen slipped her hand into his. "Breathe deeply, Patrick, breathe," she said, mimicking a deep breath. He leaned against her and inhaled deeply.

Drew clapped her right hand to her mouth. Her eyes were wide and elated. She began to move slowly toward him, but Eittod gently stepped in her path.

"Give him a few minutes, Drew. He needs to process such news," said Eittod, "as do you, my dear Drew."

Eittod reached down and placed his hand on Patrick's shoulder. "All things are possible, Patrick. And for this journey to be successful, the Earth needs you *both*. Remember, you are no longer under the restraints of linear time as on your Earth."

Eittod reached a hand to assist Patrick into a standing position.

"All things and beings move within the eternal now, Patrick. You *both* do exist as do all beings and experiences – at the exact same time, but in a different space reality. Watch!" said Eittod as he looked up.

The large oval crystal descended from Gypsy's rafters and appeared before them. Shapes began to move inside the crystal. First, snowflakes filled the oval and swirled out into the pit. Everyone reached out to grab the fresh, cold flakes before they melted. Then images of Drew's birth and being placed into her mother's arms appeared in the crystal. Doc O'Malley called back, "You'd best let Grand know she's here, Tom. He'll want to have a look at his brand new great-granddaughter. Next, Grand touched her knee and whispered in her ear, "Remember me?" Grand named her. "Drew, that's her name! Drew! It's a good Celtic name – means courageous. And that's what she'll need, *courage*, for what lies ahead for this little lass." His voice was strangely strong.

Then it was evening and Grand knocked on the bedroom door. He placed the triple spiral stone on Drew's tiny hand declaring her the "rightful master of the stone," and the task was laid upon her. Aquamarine light flashed from the oval crystal into the pit.

"Is that me?" Patrick asked in disbelief. "Is that really me sometime in my future?"

"You are watching yourself, Patrick, as it is actually happening on the Earth. We don't do instant replays here as you can do on the Earth in Drew's Earth time. As I have said, Patrick, all things are possible when you step out of the restraints of linear time," said Eittod. "When you stand next to a moving train you see only the cars as they pass you one by one. You cannot see both the engine and the caboose at the same time. But if you stand on the hill and look down at the train, you see the whole train at one time. Am I correct?"

Patrick nodded to affirm Eittod's statement.

"It is all about perspective, my boy. It's all about perspective. It's just that simple."

Eittod asked Drew to open her left fist. He reached for Patrick's hand and placed it on Drew's left hand, upon the triple spiral stone. Again, aquamarine light flashed, but this time it filled the whole snuggery, infusing each of the teens and the staff with its powerful radiance. And the bond of these light travelers was sealed.

Patrick reached out to embrace Drew. No more questions were necessary.

Drew looked into Patrick's bright green eyes, "Grand, I have loved you all my life," she said. "And 'Grand' is the only name I have known you by. May I still call you Grand?"

"It appears that you have known me, or should I say, known of me a lot longer than I have known you. Of course you may, Drew," Patrick answered. "*But* to everyone else, *I am Patrick. Okay?*"

"Good oh, mate!" said Penzil enthusiastically.

The others answered in agreement.

Tears slid down Drew and Patrick's cheeks, and everyone was around them, embracing them. They all knew they'd never be the same again. They were now a team, family, inseparable, bonded by the Regions and by their own desire for peace and love in their world.

Eittod, Bezen and Mingo stepped back – expressions of great satisfaction and joy on their faces – nodding to each other. Eittod had chosen wisely. The journey to clear the North Portal had begun.

"Okay, Drew Megan Campbell, let's see that birthmark," said Patrick grinning. The other teens were still gathered about them.

Drew slipped off her shoe, and propped her foot up onto Eittod's red and gold ottoman. There on her left knee was a watermelon seed-shaped birthmark. Patrick touched a fingertip to it.

"Remember, this is how I shall know it is *you*, Drew, " said Patrick, more tears appearing in his green eyes. From that moment, Drew and Patrick were inseparable – they were family – they shared the same blood, Campbell Family blood – and were ready to fulfill the Campbell Family Myth.

"It's time for celebration and feasting," declared Eittod. "We'll resume instruction later. There is much for you to learn!"

Instantly, the large stone table in the feasting nook was laden with international foods and drink.

"Come on great-granddaughter, the feast is on me today!" said Patrick with a loving smile on his face as he extended an arm to her.

Drew locked arms with him, "Lead the way, Grand!" she answered. "That name is going to take some getting used to," said Patrick with a delighted grin on his face.

"I've never seen so much food in all my life," shouted Penzil.

Food was always a hard find for him, but here, food was abundant, and only a thought form away. A very slender, fourteen-year-old orphan, Penzil Kangaroo spent much of his time each day pursuing food. Raised in the harsh Outback of Australia by tribesmen and wildlife, Penzil had never known his parents. But he was grateful for his survival. Whatever or whoever had taken his parents' lives had spared his. All that he truly owned was a small weathered talisman pouch containing a triangular, black fire opal which was found around his neck as a baby.

"Who does all this cooking?" asked Chelli. "It must take days to prepare."

"My mom's the best cook on the planet," Mingo boasted. "Fill your plate, Chelli, there's more where that came from."

Bezen just smiled and shook her head.

Chelli "Little Bear" Freeman is a muscular, thickset, round-faced, fourteen-year-old Native American from the Fairbanks area of Alaska. Raised in the traditions of her Athabascan tribe, she is open to all the other-worldly experiences that Outpost Gypsy Tree has to offer.

Gar and Aube were the last ones to reach the feasting nook.

"How are you doing with all this, Gar?" asked Aube, concerned.

"It's like someone telling a joke, and I am the only one who doesn't get it. How do you think I feel? This is your element," he whispered. "I know all this way out, crazy, weird stuff makes sense to you. But it doesn't compute in my world, Aube. Great-grandfathers and great-granddaughters of the same age! Now that's beyond weird, don't you think? And food, lots of food coming from out of nowhere. It's just plain spooky if you ask me. You've always been there for me, and I am trying to cope, but honestly, Aube, I am not sure how much more I can take."

"Do you want to go outside for a while to get some fresh air and clear your head?" asked Aube.

"Sounds good," said Gar gratefully.

After filling their plates to overflowing, the twins paused in front of Gypsy's rotating door. They focused, made a slight nod of their heads and mused at their new found skill as they maneuvered their way out into the sunlight. Aube and Gar made themselves comfortable on a large tree-root bench at the edge of the riverbank where turtles were sunning on the warm river rocks.

"It's a beautiful place, Aube, and the people all seem very nice and sincere, and the warm feeling of the aquamarine light helped some, but…but I feel lost here," Gar admitted. "I'd really like to fit in. But I don't. I am just a tagalong, Aube. You're the one who was invited."

"You're wrong, Gar. The invitation was written to both of us. We both recited the transport words. What would help you to feel more at home here, Gar?" asked Aube, knowing that Gar's problem wasn't feeling lost or about being a tagalong, but about feeling his fear.

"I am not sure anything can do that, Aube. I mean, I appreciate that our room is the same as at home – that's good, really good – with all our special furniture and other stuff. And when we looked out the window, there were the streets, the smells and the sounds of Lima – that was truly amazing. Eittod's been so thoughtful. But there's this emptiness in my belly that not even this food is filling," said Gar.

Aube scratched his head. "Do we need to go back home?" he reluctantly asked. "Eittod said we could go at any time – we have free will." Aube dreaded the thought of leaving. But he understood Gar's great fear of the unknown.

At that moment, something caught Gar's eye. "Look, Aube! What do you make of that?" he shouted, pointing to a shrub moving on the other side of the river bank. He pulled them both up into a standing position.

There in the brush was a fuzzy, sweet-faced creature with pointed teeth peering at them – not human, but not animal, either. Then it was gone as quickly as it had come. They could hear it scampering deeper into the thicket.

"Holy Christmas! Did you see it, Aube, did you see it?" asked Gar, still pointing.

"Just caught a glimpse, Gar, not quite sure what it was. But it wasn't an animal, I don't think. At least no animal I've ever seen. Did you see the way it looked at us?" remarked Aube.

Gar started moving them in the direction of the scampering sounds.

"Whatever it is, it runs on all fours," shouted Gar, plowing them through the vegetation along the riverbank. Aube's feet were barely touching the ground.

"Let's not go too far away, Gar. Eittod may be calling us back any minute now," said Aube.

"Well, it's probably gone by now anyway. Whatever it was, it was moving like greased lightning," lamented Gar. "Sure would have liked to have caught up with it though."

"Maybe we're better off *not* having caught up with it, Gar," cautioned Aube. "I've never seen the likes of it in all my days and hope not to see it again. I didn't like the way it was looking at us – like it could see right through us."

Now here was a true adventure for Gar! None of that crazy mind-blowing stuff – just some good old manly hunt and trap stuff – which made Gar feel a lot better and more in control of his surroundings.

"Okay, let's head back, Aube. Maybe we can pick up its tracks later," suggested Gar. "Bet my buddy, Mingo, can solve this puzzle for us," he touted, walking with a more confident gate.

Aube took a deep breath and felt grateful to the little creature, whatever it was. As they navigated back through the heavy wooden door, Eittod's voice rang out inviting them back for instruction. As the teens made their way into the pit with plates full of food and beverage mugs, Gar caught Mingo's eye and motioned him forward.

"Mingo, I have a question for you. Could you meet us after instruction?" asked Gar.

"You got it," said Mingo with a cheerful nod and a pat on the back.

Gar beamed.

CHAPTER SIXTEEN:
Scumdiggalies

With the gathering settled in, Eittod sat in his favorite chair and propped his feet up on the ottoman. "I know each of you has many questions at this point, and hopefully I can clear up a few. First of all, I am sure you would like to know where you are in relation to your home planet, Earth," he said.

Heads nodded in agreement.

Eittod continued. "Well, Outpost Gypsy Tree is an enchanted sanctuary nestled within a thought form beyond Earth's gravitational pull. So we might say you are hovering over the Earth. Like what your scientists call a satellite, but much further out." Eittod spread his hands apart indicating the distance as his crystal blue eyes scanned the eager faces before him.

"Our outpost has been under the protection of the Regions Authority since the time of Early Earth." He went on to tell them about the Regions Authority and their role in the Milky Way Galaxy and their protection of the Earth and its inhabitants.

Everyone's attention was hanging on Eittod's every word. Well, that is except for Gar who was doing his best to ignore Eittod's every word. This was *more* information than he really wanted or needed. He looked up to examine the vaulted ceiling of the snuggery, counting each stud and beam and watching the oval crystal as it slowly revolved in place above him. Feeling a bit dizzy from the crystal's circular movement, he moved his attention to the food that was still in full view in the feasting nook, counting the variety of fruits sprawled on the large stone table. Next, his attention drifted to the jeans that Eittod, Bezen and Mingo were wearing, and he wondered if there was a shopping mall at the outpost, and if so, what kind of currency they used. He thought that maybe they could pick up a few souvenirs to take home. Then he recited in his head the names and jersey numbers of all the current players on Peru's national football team.

In spite of all Gar's efforts to ignore the instruction, Eittod's voice broke through.

"It was following the collapse of the Atlantian culture, and their flight into Egypt and parts of what are known today as the southern United States, Mexico and South America, that Gypsy and her staff were put into a deep sleep. Only the Regions, the Angelics and the staff know of the Outpost's location and purpose. Well, dear ones, that will do for now, I think. Please continue to eat, drink, talk and explore the snuggery. Take time to get to know each other. You will be each other's eyes, ears and protectors during your assignments. And that's a subject for another day," Eittod finished with a very big smile.

Mingo came up behind the twins, "You wanted to talk with me, Gar?"

Gar almost jumped out of his skin. His brain was stuck in a rat wheel running from the words *Atlantians, Angelics* and *assignments.*

This was way over the top for Garcia Gou-Drah Perez. Those icy fingers of fear began to chomp deep into his spine.

"I didn't mean to startle you, Gar. Are you okay? Your face is pale as a chamber sheet. Are you ill?" Mingo questioned at warp speed.

Aube quickly turned his head to Gar. He recognized that facial expression and that look of bone chilling terror in Gar's eyes.

"Gar, tell Mingo about the creature we saw down by the riverbank," Aube began quickly in an effort to snap Gar back from his fear place. "Remember, Gar, you wanted to ask Mingo about what we saw."

Gar looked at Aube with a blank expression, his mind still a captive of his fear. He couldn't speak.

At that moment, Eittod appeared at Gar's side, his hand on Gar's shoulder. "This is a lot to take in, I am sure, Garcia. I must give you a lot of credit for your bravery and your support of your brother and his request of you," he said, making eye contact with Gar. "You're a fine young man, and your courage, intelligence and bravery will serve us well."

Eittod's words of praise and confidence in him were just what Gar needed to hear. Maybe he wasn't just a tagalong after all. Maybe his courage was needed; maybe *he* was needed. The color began to return to his face, and his voice was under his control once again. He lifted his head up and forced his shoulders back. Eittod had called him brave and courageous. No one had *ever* called him *brave* or *courageous*.

"Ah…why thank you. Thank you, Eittod. We Perez brothers stick together – literally," he said with a slight chuckle.

They all laughed.

Drew and Patrick, hearing the laughter, joined the group as Eittod stepped away.

"Now, Gar, what question do you have for me?" asked Mingo.

Gar began to describe the creature he and Aube had seen near the riverbank and how quickly *it* had scurried off – like "greased lightning."

"Oh! You have met our troublesome scumdiggalies. It didn't take them long to present themselves," said Mingo, in his low, exasperated tone.

"So that's what I saw in the gardens when I arrived, a scum…scumdig…a what, Mingo?" asked Drew.

"They are scum-dig-ga-lies, Drew," said Mingo, slowly enunciating each syllable. "And you've seen one as well?" he asked.

"Yes, earlier as we were walking though the hanging gardens toward the domicile. Didn't you see it? I thought I had imagined the creature," she said.

"No, I didn't see it. They are like chameleons; they choose who will see them and who will not. They are very clever, very clever indeed!"

"Well, what *are* scumdiggalies?" Aube asked, "Are they animal or something else entirely?"

"Well, Aube, they are not animals. The scumdiggalies are the original inhabitants of our Gypsy Tree and natives of Elliptica in the Great Andromeda Galaxy," explained Mingo. "They are creatures who can think, reason and plan as well as you do."

Gar was beginning to regret his question.

"You see," continued Mingo, "They are the last of their kind. And troublesome as they are, their species must be preserved and protected by order of the Regions Authority."

"What do you mean they're troublesome?" asked Drew. "They are so cute and seem so timid."

"Oh! *Cute* they may be! *Timid* they are *not!*" said Mingo in a strong tone, his olive-skinned hands now firmly set on his slender hips, his right foot tapping. "They are tricksters of no moral conscience with little pea-sized hearts. They are master thieves, liars and con artists out to trick you and steal your possessions. Once they have your treasure, they *hide* it, so you can *never* find it. So, DO NOT TRUST THEM!" he stressed. "They will play with your mind and work to your weaknesses. No matter how sweet and shy they may seem, they always have their own interests afoot."

By this time, Chelli and Penzil had entered the conversation.

"Where do they live, Mingo?" asked Penzil.

"Why, right here in Gypsy, but they spend most of their time out on the grounds spying on YOU!" he said loudly, startling everyone.

"I didn't like the way it looked at Gar and me. Creepy! Really creepy – like it was looking right through us or maybe better words would be – right *into* us," said Aube with a shudder.

"Scumdiggalies may be fuzzy, sweet-faced, green-haired beauties, *but* those black gimlet-eyed rascals can see right through you – like they know all your secrets, because they probably *do*. They can outsmart you, outthink you, outwit you *and* outrun you. They are shrewd little creatures. Just remember, they are tree dwellers, so they have claws on the end of each cute little finger and each cute little toe," said Mingo glancing in Drew's direction. "And yes, Gar, they run on all-fours like *greased lightning* – as you called it," Mingo stressed.

"Are you finished scaring everyone, Mingo?" asked Bezen in her motherly tone.

"Well, they need to know what they're dealing with, Mother," he replied.

"True, son, true, but take a breath," Bezen replied as she motioned for him to lean down and then ruffled his golden hair with her hand as she passed.

"Come along, everyone. Let me show you around our dear Gypsy," ushering them toward the activity arena. "Then Mingo will give you a tour of the grounds. Oh! And do watch out for those clever scumdiggalies," she laughed, then continued. "This is the interior transport chamber. It's similar to your elevators back home. Difference is it will take you to anyplace in the outpost – no gears, no pulleys and no buttons. Just tell it where you wish to go and you're there! Great for rainy days!"

With their first day at Outpost Gypsy Tree winding down, the teens gathered in the greeting hall of their domicile. It was filled with thick, soft rugs, dozens upon dozens of colorful wraps, large pillows, study tables and overstuffed chairs. All around them were treasures from the four corners of the world and beyond. Bookcases and shelves were full of past, present and future books of all kinds. Pristine copies of some of the world's oldest and greatest works graced the shelves, some no longer in print, others not even in print yet on present day Earth. Display screens were covered with primitive art, classical art and futuristic pieces. The works of some of the world's greatest writers, musicians, dreamers, scientists, physicists, magicians, astronomers and mathematicians were gathered here.

In awe, Drew studied paintings she had only read or heard about, but had never seen with her own eyes.

"It's like being in the Louvre Museum in Paris," said Drew. "Here's Da Vinci's Mona Lisa." And pointing to one of a beautiful young woman in white, "This is Ingres' Mademoiselle Caroline Riviere. How can they be here, when I know they are *there*? Are they copies?" she asked, waiting for Gypsy's answer.

"Drew, they are originals. Speak with Bezen about these matters," Gypsy whispered in Drew's head.

Aube and Gar were checking out a miniature life-like display of the Milky Way Galaxy, its planets and constellations. Penzil was combing through current and ancient world maps. Patrick was engrossed in space exploration data as images of the international space station floated before him. Chelli was engrossed in the latest geological studies being conducted in her current Earth time. Images of soil samples and their findings floated in mid-air before her.

"The outpost is enormous. With all the space exploration that's been done, and with all Earth's digital telescopes pointed into the sky, why hasn't the outpost been noticed?" questioned Gar.

"That's a good question to ask Eittod tomorrow," replied Chelli. "I was wondering the same thing. But Eittod did stress that we're nestled in a thought form – whatever that is!"

"I can hardly believe I am actually here," said Drew. "I am living what I've been painting for weeks."

"Tell us about your paintings, Drew," asked Patrick.

Everyone gathered around her, each scooping up armfuls of pillows and snuggling into them.

Drew shared her experiences of the past few weeks – the paintings, the dancing, the voices and Newgrange. She shared her parent's story, and passed her triple spiral stone around for everyone to examine.

"Grand, have you heard about the Campbell Family Myth?" asked Drew.

"Yes, but I've not really paid much attention to it. Just considered it the ramblings of the elders," mused Patrick. "Guess I need to pay more attention from now on," he laughed. "Actually, I am quite fascinated with Newgrange and the other historical mounds around our area – like, Knowth and Dowth."

"Both my father and I have read quite a bit about Ireland's historical sites," said Aube, "and the plethora of passage mounds scattered over its landscape. We are especially interested in Ireland's Newgrange and find it quite fascinating. And you live a stone's throw away from it, Drew? How incredible is that! Do you think that's where our assignment will begin?"

Gar's icy fingers of fear were back on full alert. Why hadn't he paid more attention all those times when he, Aube and Papa had visited the library at the San Francisco Monastery?

"I don't know, Aube," answered Drew. "I just know that when I held the stone in my hand and closed my eyes, I saw an image of Newgrange, but not as it appears today."

"Hang on a tick! I've never heard of Newgrange. What is it, Drew?" asked Penzil.

"Yes, I'd like to know as well," said Chelli. "Sounds interesting."

With a big smile on her face, Drew eased from her chair down onto a pillow pile and pulled a colorful wrap around her shoulders. This was absolutely one of her favorite subjects.

"Newgrange," she began, "is a megalithic passage tomb and a major astronomical site, built around 5,200 years ago by Neolithic man. It's located at the bend of the Boyne River, about thirty miles from our nation's capital of Dublin and a short distance from my home." Drew felt like a docent giving a tour, and thought of Michael, and of her parents waiting for her there.

"Mum, Dad and I have been regular visitors of Newgrange since I can remember. At my request, Dad or Mum will drop me off, and my godfather Michael drives me out onto the property. I've spent hours there sketching and painting and being among the ancients and their magnificent edifice. I feel them on the land, and they reach out to me from their stone carvings beckoning me inward," said Drew.

Her face was glowing, and there was a misty, faraway look in her brilliant green eyes. It was obvious that Drew was back in her beloved Ireland and at-one with the spirits of her Neolithic ancestors.

"Drew! Ah, Drew?" called Aube.

"Oh!…Sorry, Aube, what?" replied Drew, realizing that she had drifted home.

"I've seen photos of the grassy mound structure with its large kerbstones and its milky-white quartz cairn. So what was different, Drew?"

"When I placed my hand on the stone in my painting, I saw whooper swans, which is not unusual. But there were many hundreds of them. Cattle and goats were grazing on the land, and other animals were in wooden pens on the hillside. And there was no great circle of greywacke stones. And what thrilled me the most, Aube, was the tidal action of the Boyne – the ebb and flow of the sea tides below Newgrange, which dates it about four to five thousand years ago," said Drew.

"I remember reading that the Great Circle was the final construction project at Newgrange while it was still in use," said Aube.

"And that was around 2,000 BCE, if I am not mistaken," said Patrick.

"You're both right!" said Drew with excitement in her voice. "So, if Newgrange *is* our destination, we're possibly going back about five millenniums." she said, with a delightful sparkle in her eyes.

Mingo appeared out of nowhere startling everyone. "Just dropped by to give you your schedules for tomorrow. It will be another busy day. I suggest you get some sleep." And he was gone.

"People keep vanishing around here," said Gar shaking his head. "Why can't people just *walk* away?"

Everyone laughed.

"We best get used to it, mates. I have a feeling we haven't really seen anything yet. Lots more over the top stuff to come, I am sure," said Penzil, "and I can't wait."

Gar's eyebrows rose to meet his hairline.

"Looks like we're in for a very busy day tomorrow," said Drew as she glanced through Mingo's schedule.

Everyone headed for the golden disks for transport to their sleeping chambers.

"We're going to be working hard together while we're here. We'll be like a family," said Drew. "So let's get some rituals started, shall we?"

"Like what?" asked Chelli. "I love ritual. Not surprising since I am Native American."

"How about a huddle," said Penzil. "It's kinda like a group hug," he said blushing.

"Sounds great!" said Patrick. "Gather round light travelers – its huddle time."

The teens formed a circle with their arms around the shoulders to either side of them and looked into each other's smiling faces.

"This is a great ritual," said Drew. "Thanks! I think we all needed a good hug after the events of this day."

"Hear, hear!" shouted Gar. "Just like a good football team."

CHAPTER SEVENTEEN:
Instruction Begins

Dawn arrived with the sweet smell of wildflowers, the joyful songs of the birds, the pattering sounds of flowing water and the melodious tones of Gypsy as the fresh morning breezes danced through her branches. Drew laid still listening to the varied sounds of Outpost Gypsy Tree. Then she realized there were no street sounds, no cars nor barking dogs. She eased from her cozy sleigh bed and glanced through her window. There before her were the breathtaking hanging gardens and colorful dancing fountains of the outpost.

Where did her beloved Ireland go? And with that single thought, with that longing, her father's garden appeared below her window. In the distance were Ireland's wildflowers, and a flock of mute swans with their grunting calls flew toward the Boyne River. Surprised at the experience, Drew set her intent for the sights and sounds of the outpost. And once again the view from her open window became that of the hanging gardens and the colorful fountains.

Drew grinned, closed her eyes and breathed in the rare spicy fragrance of Gypsy. It was intoxicating. She felt vital, vibrant and so *alive*. An overwhelming feeling of joy welled up from within her, and a deep sense of connection, belonging and oneness washed over her, penetrating her very soul. She wept. All humanity deserves to feel as she felt in this moment, she thought.

The gentle loving voice of Gypsy whispered into her mind, "And this, dear Drew, is why you are here with us. This is your pure, selfless gift to humanity."

She opened her eyes to drink in the beauty below, but staring right through her from its position near the fountain, was a bright green-haired, black-eyed cutie. Then it was gone.

"Oh, bummy!" said Drew remembering Mingo's warning. She wondered what the scumdiggalie had just learned about her – about her weaknesses.

"What are my weaknesses?" she whispered aloud.

At that moment, the delicious smell of food, glorious food, wafted in through her chamber window. Her thoughts quickly turned to breakfast and a very busy schedule of instruction. Drew hurriedly bathed and dressed, eager for the day's experiences in this enchanted place to begin. She turned to survey her room, smiled, set her intent and poof – her sleeping chamber was neat as a pin, and her bed was perfectly made with fresh linens and fluffed pillows.

"I can certainly get used to this," she said. "Mum would be proud of me." She giggled, then snatched up her schedule, and with a quick stop and a nod of her head, her chamber door opened. She stepped onto a golden disk and set her intent for passage to her domicile feasting nook. A second later she was looking right into Bezen's warm eyes.

"Good morning, Drew. I trust you slept well, my dear?" said Bezen with a big smile as she motioned Drew toward the lavish breakfast display awaiting her.

"Bezen, I have a question for you. Do you have time right now?" Drew asked.

"Of course, Drew! What's on your pretty mind this early in the morning?"

"Last evening, I noticed several paintings in the greeting hall that are also in the Louvre Museum in Paris. I thought them copies, but Gypsy said they are originals. How can this be?" Drew asked.

"Ah, Drew! Once something has been created, whether it is music, art, poetry or a garden, it is forevermore in the ethers of creativity and is eternal. With intention in the *eternal now*, anything can be brought into reality in its original form. Didn't you bring your father's garden to your window this morning?" Bezen asked.

"Well...Yes!" Drew was surprised at Bezen's knowledge of her morning experience. "It was my intention or desire for it, and it came, but an original painting?" Drew queried.

"What's the difference, Drew?"

"Well...the...the Louvre owns the original painting of Di Vinci's Mona Lisa, does it not?" questioned Drew.

"Ah! Does your father not own the garden, Drew?"

"Well...Yes!" answered Drew, "but..."

"But what?" said Bezen. "Drew, the Louvre Museum in Paris, France, is the present keeper and protector of the painting in *your* Earth time, but the creative energy, essence or ethers of the masterpiece belongs to humanity. It belongs to eternal time, the *eternal now* – past, present and to come," answered Bezen. "In your present Earth time, if someone takes the painting from the museum for selfish reasons, it is considered a crime. Is it not?"

"Y-e-s!" Drew slowly replied, unsure of where Bezen was going with the conversation.

"And the laws of your present Earthly time would rightfully be enforced. Correct?" asked Bezen.

"Well, yes!" answered Drew.

"Here at Outpost Gypsy Tree we are in eternal time. All past, present and future times merge into the *eternal now*. It's just that simple," finished Bezen.

Drew stood motionless, her eyes glazed. Her mind raced at warp speed trying to understand the truth that had just been gifted her. And then it was like a light bulb went on above her head. She understood!

"Oh! How simple it is!" she said. "I get it! I get it!" Drew flung her arms around Bezen in a big hug. "I get it! Thank you!"

"You are most welcome, my little genius! Now, it's time to fill your tummy. A very busy and exciting day lies ahead for you," said Bezen as she gently stroked Drew's cheek with her fingertips, then turned to greet the other arrivals.

One by one the teens arrived, greeted each other and filled their plates. Soon excitement and joyful chatter filled the domicile feasting nook.

"May I have your attention for a moment?" called Bezen. "Once you have finished breakfast, you will be meeting with Mingo in the domicile activity arena, followed by instruction with Eittod in the snuggery. I will see you there."

And she was gone.

Gar just shook his head and continued eating his tamales.

"These tamales taste exactly like Mama's tamales. Try one, Aube!" said Gar. "They're absolutely delicious!"

"No way could they taste like Mama's. No one knows Mama's secret Uros tamale recipe, Gar," replied Aube scooping a few onto his plate.

Gar anxiously awaited Aube's reaction.

"WOW! They *do* taste just like Mama's. How is that possible, Gar?" questioned Aube.

"I think I am beginning to understand what's going on here," said Drew. She reached for some pork rashers, and sure enough, they tasted just like her Mum's rashers. The seasoning was exact.

Drew shared with the others her conversation with Bezen concerning the Mona Lisa masterpiece, her morning experience with her father's garden and the eternal now.

"So that's how you and I can be here at the same time, Drew," said Patrick. "It's simply one's perspective, according to Eittod. It makes sense now! Yesterday Eittod said, '*All things and beings move within the eternal now.*' That you and I do exist, as do all beings and experiences, *at the exact same time*, but in a different space reality," said Patrick.

"And that's how Bezen manifests our lavish meals and even those special foods from home?" asked Gar.

"Correct!" said Drew.

"I love it! I love it! I love it!" sang Chelli, dancing around the feasting nook and waving her hands in the air. "This place is so exciting! I can't wait to find out what's coming next."

"Let's not rush things, Chelli, okay?" said Gar.

"You're an old party pooper, Gar!" said Penzil. "Where's your adventurous spirit, mate? Lighten up! And pass me some of those tamales, please. I've never eaten tamales, so I might as well start with the best ones on the planet."

Mingo was waiting for them in the domicile activity arena. "Good morning, everybody," he said with a big smile. "I trust you slept well because your real work starts today. And I am one of your trusted teachers," said Mingo with a deep bow.

Everyone clapped for him. And Gar let out a sportsman-like whoop.

"Thank you! Now, first we will practice breathing and then move on to focusing and grounding," said Mingo.

"Mate, breathing is something we do all the time!" said Penzil with a deep chuckle.

"*Well*, today you will learn how to do it *right*, Penzil," said Mingo in a commanding voice.

Mingo took his job very seriously. He knew that what he was entrusted to teach them was vital to their survival beyond the outpost.

"Each morning at sunrise you will meet me here *before* breakfast. First we will do a series of exercises or jog around the grounds, then a light breakfast, followed by breathing exercises. Then we will slowly move on to the more strenuous stuff," said Mingo. *"Got it?"*

Everyone nodded in agreement. They realized that what Mingo had said was truth. This training was no game – it was important life-saving stuff – self-survival stuff, to be exact.

"Look, I don't mean to be gruff, but we have a lot to cover in a very short amount of time. We need to get you ready for what lies ahead. And it's my job to make sure you're fit before you leave the outpost on your first assignment," stressed Mingo.

There was that word again, and Gar was concerned.

"Hey, Mingo, what do you mean by *leave on our assignment?*" asked Gar. "And what's this *first assignment* stuff?"

"Eittod will be the one to discuss that with you. I am just following orders, Gar," said Mingo.

"Okay, now let's talk about the correct way to control the breath and use it to your advantage."

"I never knew there were so many different ways to breathe," said Penzil as they walked through the forest toward the archways and the footbridge.

"It's a science in itself," said Mingo as he ducked under some of the low hanging branches along the pathway. "As I said, there is great power in the breath. Well, I'll leave you here. Just head on over the bridge to Gypsy. I am off to check on a mess the scumdiggalies made over in the meadow last night. They were celebrating something big!" said Mingo in an exasperated tone as he picked up his gait. "See you all later!" he called back.

"I wonder what that's all about," said Aube. "Did anyone hear anything last night?"

"I was fast asleep as soon as my head hit the pillow. Can't imagine what they could be celebrating," responded Gar quickly, his eyes shifting nervously.

"Well, with all the grunting and snorting you were doing, Gar, the roof could have fallen in on us, and you wouldn't have heard it," laughed Aube.

"Mingo really has it in for those scumdiggalies. Can't blame the bloke for getting upset with them. It's a no-hoper trying to keep them in line. Seems as though he's the one whose always cleaning up behind those little rascals," said Penzil.

Lagging behind the others, Drew, Patrick and Chelli were deep in conversation.

"The invitation said we were chosen. But, there are only six of us – what chance do we have against all the darkness in our world?" questioned Chelli. "It's not that I am afraid, just concerned. Eittod and the Regions are counting on *us*."

"Surely Eittod and the Regions know what they're doing, and what we are capable of with their instruction and guidance. We just have to trust and take our training very seriously, Chelli," replied Drew.

"Hopefully Eittod will share more information with us this morning concerning our assignment. I would be very excited if we were being assigned to Newgrange," said Patrick walking backwards in front of the girls. "With two of us from the Newgrange area of Ireland involved, and the Campbell Family Myth, and with the triple spiral stone brought to light, it seems to be pointing in that direction, don't you think?"

"Grand, I think you're right. I hope so, at least. I'd love to experience Newgrange in its original form," said Drew with a dreamy twinkle in her green eyes.

CHAPTER EIGHTEEN:
Truth of Their Mission

Eittod was waiting for them in the snuggery. "Good morning! Isn't it a beautiful day?" he said with a very big smile on his colorful face. "Help yourselves to something refreshing to drink and a nibble if you'd like, and please join me in the pit. Bezen has reminded me that you teens are in your larva stage and are virtual eating machines."

Everyone laughed in agreement.

"Well, there is always plenty to eat here at the outpost thanks to our dear Bezen," said Eittod.

Bezen blushed and smiled.

"Well, we have so much to do today. So, let's get started," said Eittod.

"Should we take notes, Eittod?" asked Chelli.

"No, no, no, my dear Chelli. Here at the outpost you are immortal as we discussed last evening. Hence, you have perfect recall," he replied.

Chelli sighed in relief, and snuggled into a multi-colored pillow pile for her instruction, knowing that her immortal mind was in charge of taking the notes.

"Sure would like to take that perfect recall gift back home," said Aube as he and Gar made themselves comfortable in the pit.

Everyone chimed in in agreement.

"Immortality does have its perks," said Eittod grinning as he began instruction.

"Now, I am aware that you are curious about your assignment, as you rightly should be. Each of you was chosen very carefully. Your pure hearts, genuine compassion and unwavering love for mankind drew us to you. And with our instruction and guidance, you will serve well," said Eittod glancing in Chelli's direction.

"The reason you have been called to this enchanted sanctuary is urgent to mankind. It hurts my heart to have to share with you the severity of the situation Earth and its people find themselves in, but it is vital that you realize the depth of your service. You see, the Regions need our help to clear the Earth's portals, so the light of the crystalline web that encircles your planet can once again reach the Earth and its people," said Eittod.

The oval crystal descended and before them floated images of the Earth and its protective web. Eittod got up from his favorite chair and began to pace as he talked. His hands were clasped behind him and his expression was grave as he moved among the images.

"Right now in your Earth phase, the light of the ONE, the ABSOLUTE, can no longer penetrate Earth. Earth's light portals are blocked by millenniums of hatred, greed, treachery, jealousy, judgment, pain and fear. Without clear portals, the light, energy and information from Earth's protective web can no longer reach your planet's surface. The web serves to connect each with the other and with life beyond the Earth itself. Without this light, this information, this energy from the ONE, the ABSOLUTE, Earth and its inhabitants will surely perish," said Eittod, his eyes moist.

Pin-dropping silence gripped the snuggery. Expressions of shocked disbelief and deep concern covered their faces – they were speechless, motionless.

"This painful darkness overshadows the consciousness of your world and holds it captive," he continued, still pacing.

All eyes were following his every move. They could feel his pain.

"Earth's people have turned to conflict and war, fighting over what should rightfully belong to them *all*," he continued, now sitting on the arm of his stuffed chair, his arms wrapped tight against his chest. "Once the adults pushed the mystical world – the world of all possibilities – aside and began to believe only in what they could physically touch, see, hear and own, their offspring stopped believing as well. They are taught that the time for believing in mystical things has passed; hence, the creative minds and loving hearts of children have gone into confusion. They now search outside of themselves; they no longer go within to connect with their light." He was on his feet again, shaking his head and pacing.

"They no longer trust the mystical world – the world of imagination and promise – they no longer believe that *they can make a difference* for humanity with their creative minds and their loving hearts. You who are gathered here," extending his hands out to them, "are rare, unique, precious, vital, needed." He locked his fingers and put them to his chin – as if in prayer. The love and gratitude he felt for his light travelers radiated from his face – from his whole being. They could feel it.

Gar was beginning to understand. Eittod had just described *him*, and he painfully recognized himself in this very compassionate, gentle man's words. The mystical world is what Mama has tried to share with him. Aube listened. Aube is Mama's *gentle dreamer of great dreams*. Gar fought back his fear, his tears, his guilt. Those icy fingers had crippled him for too long, and he'd had enough. Gar reached for Aube's hand. Aube understood Gar's internal struggle and pain. He gently squeezed back and said a prayer of gratitude.

Putting the oval crystal into motion again, Eittod brought forward images of the Earth's protective web forming. As the pristine images floated before them, all eyes were mesmerized by the stunning beauty, the abundance of light and its breathtaking intensity. The waters of the Earth were so clear and sparkling, and the vegetation was so green and fragrant, wholesome. They could feel the powerful love of the ONE, the ABSOLUTE, penetrating their own bodies, igniting their creative spirits, their unlimited imaginations and touching their very core. They felt as if they were one with *all* of creation.

Ever so slowly Eittod moved the image forward through time to their current Earth with its blocked portals. They gasped at the distortion and ugliness caused by humanity. They could feel the painful absence of the love, the absence of light and the lack of beauty that they had basked in just moments before.

"All living things and the Earth herself deserve to feel what you just felt moments ago, don't you agree?" asked Eittod.

Watching and reading every face carefully as they nodded in stunned agreement, Eittod continued his pacing and instruction.

"We are saddened to say Earth's children have entered into a very dark and fearful illusion – shutting out the realm of the mystical, the realm of light, the realm of the ONE, the ABSOLUTE; thus, shutting down their own powerful, creative forces within. We *must* reach *all* the children and free them from this bondage of materialism, rage, greed, hatred, bullying, fear, waste and disappointment, and open them to the wonders of their own creative minds, their own mystical spirits and their own loving hearts – hearts that now beat the lamenting sounds of pain, deep yearning and emptiness. The ONE, the ABSOLUTE, has heard you. The Regions have heard you. But only Earth's children of *pure heart* can open the portals to the light, the information and the unconditional love, and set humankind free. This is why you are here. This is what you have been chosen to do. You are the *pure of heart,* and you *will* clear the way for others to follow. *All* Earth's children of pure heart must help."

Eittod looked into their red, swollen eyes and felt their pain. He again set the crystal into motion – this time images of Earth's children filled the pit. He continued. "Earth's children have turned to outside things to find joy and fulfillment. They have turned to all avenues of illusion to kill their pain and their emptiness and to hatred and violence in order to feel and experience."

Images of bullying, fighting, destruction, vile graffiti in all languages, drugs, abusive acts against each other and child soldiers killing out of fear for their own lives flooded the snuggery. Continuous violence and fear stream into children's daily lives poisoning their minds, hardening their hearts, deadening their souls.

Senseless, murderous acts of child terrorism shattered the light travelers' minds. One by one, the teens covered their faces to block out the ugly and frightening images of the children's inhumanity to each other, and they knew the sins of the adult world were far worse.

"If this continues," said Eittod, "the people of the Earth will not only destroy each other, but will destroy the planet as well."

His voice quivered. "We *must* help them; they *must* connect once again with their soul light – the light of the ONE, the ABSOLUTE – if we are to save Mother Earth herself."

Eittod's words gripped their hearts and spirits, and the impact of his words echoed throughout the outpost. He waved his hand and the images dissolved, but the enormity of the situation was still grave and very real.

There was deafening silence in the snuggery – in the whole of the outpost. The truth of their mission weighed like mountains upon them. They seized up, stopped breathing – like existence itself stopped. The light travelers were trapped in a stunned state, unable to move or respond.

Eittod remained still, giving them time to absorb and process the gravity of his words. This depth of truth needed quiescence and consideration. He waited.

Bezen put her open hands out to the side gently, sending soothing waves of loving energy to embrace them. Mingo appeared in the feasting nook with deep concern on his youthful face. He, too, stood very still, his hands out to the side, mimicking his mother's actions. They all waited and watched as the teens mentally and emotionally struggled with the severity of Earth's situation and the magnitude of the Regions Authority's expectation of them.

Eventually, Drew's staring eyes began to flutter. Penzil's tightly clenched fists began to open and close. Life was returning. Eittod, Bezen and Mingo slowly moved among the teens, embracing them, speaking softly and rubbing their hands. In time, they – *the light travelers* – reached out for each other, comforting each other.

Again, Eittod and his staff waited.

Finally, Drew spoke firmly, "When and how do we begin, Eittod? Your light travelers are ready to serve."

"You are already on the path, my dear ones. And we are ready to assist you as are the Regions and the Angelics," said Eittod with deep compassion and conviction in his voice.

"And you can count on mother and me," said Mingo with vigor. Bezen nodded in affirmation of her son's words.

A deep tremor ran through Gypsy, startling the teens.

"Not to worry," said Bezen. "Gypsy is letting you know that she's ready to assist you in your mission as well."

The light travelers all gathered around Eittod.

"Eittod, I am ready to learn and to do all that is needed in order to free my world of this darkness," said Patrick.

"Me too!" said Chelli punching both fists into the air. "My off-spring *will* know this beautiful Earth; they *will* know the light and love of the ONE, the ABSOLUTE!"

"Count me in, mates. I'll have a go at it," said Penzil. "This darkness has met its match."

"We're in," said Aube and Gar in unison as they gave each other a high-five.

Drew withdrew her quartz stone from her pocket. She held it out in her left hand. All the light travelers placed their hands over hers. The stone began to vibrate and the triple spiral symbol glowed aquamarine filling them once again. The light travelers were truly ready.

"GOOD!" declared Eittod enthusiastically.

Putting the crystal back into motion, an image of the Earth showed once again in the pit.

"You are not alone in this service to humanity," he said, "although you are the brightest lights and the most committed. There are others on the Earth who are trying to turn the tide as well. Their deep longing for peace, love and brotherhood will serve to support you as you work to clear the portals. Their combined energies and commitment can be drawn upon when you most need their help. They are unaware of your work, but their hearts, minds and souls vibrate to the same frequency as yours.

As the Earth turned, points of light began to twinkle all over the globe. No country was without lights.

"So your work with Mingo each morning is of vital importance: controlling and learning to use the power of your breath, learning to focus and come to absolute centeredness, and finally, learning to ground your energy in order to connect with these lights before you for sustenance," said Eittod, pointing to Earth's image rotating before them.

"Children and teens from every corner of the globe are longing for peace. Before your eyes is a myriad of light bearers ready to serve humanity. And their desires have been heard as well," said Eittod. "Some of these light bearers will be brought to the outpost to serve you directly; others will serve willingly, but unknowingly."

There were big smiles on the teens' faces. They were not alone. They had their own army of light.

"Well, it is now lunch time," said Eittod. "So let's celebrate your commitment and feed those larva tummies. And you also need activity. Your bodies have been in shock and need movement. I believe the vibration pool is ready, is it not, Mingo?"

"It is, Eittod! And laps are in order, or you can just allow the water to nurture and vibrate through your body," said Mingo, "and then lunch is in order!"

"We're off to Gypsy's activity arena, and for dessert, ice cream sundaes," announced Bezen. "Let's go!"

Everyone was talking at once as they followed Bezen and Mingo into Gypsy's activity arena where a pool of light blue, vibrating water and the spicy fragrance of Gypsy greeted them. Standing at the pool's edge, they all focused, made a quick nod of their heads and swimming attire adorned their bodies. They looked at each other and childlike laughter erupted.

"Last one in is a rotten egg!" someone shouted, and Drew, Chelli, Penzil and Patrick made the plunge. *SPLASH!*

"Well, rotten egg, you ready for the slower route?" laughed Gar. "Yep!" said Aube as they reached for the steadying rails and made their way down the pool's incline. Aube had never felt as connected with his brother as he felt at this moment. They were truly of one heart, one commitment and one passion.

Much to the light travelers' delight, Gypsy's melodious sounds echoed throughout the activity arena, mixing with their voices of determined vigor and splashes upon splashes. This team was certainly up to the task laid upon them, and now they had help – an *army* of help to be exact.

CHAPTER NINETEEN:
Assignment Location

After a refreshing swim and lunch, which included ice cream sundaes of their choice with lots of whipped cream, everyone was ready for more information and instruction. Now that the teens knew their mission, they were eager to learn of their assignment location. And *how* to accomplish such a feat as *saving the world*.

As they entered the snuggery, Chelli was already in conversation with Eittod.

"Come in, everyone! Come in!" said Eittod motioning them into the pit. "Chelli has asked me to explain why the outpost has not been identified by your current Earth's satellites, telescopes or space explorations. That's a very good question and one that I have been expecting," said Eittod. "Do you remember moving through spirals as you made your way to the outpost?"

"Yes, I remember three spirals," said Drew.

"We saw three as well," said Aube.

"And we did loop de loops through them," added Gar. "It was like a roller coaster ride, I am sure. But probably better."

The others were nodding in agreement.

"Well," said Eittod, "you were traveling through space-time spirals, each one preparing you for life here at the outpost. Here, we are too small to be seen by the most powerful microscopes. And yes, your Hubble has come close, but we are undetectable, un-seeable."

"Excuse me! Don't you mean telescopes, Eittod?" asked Chelli.

Eittod laughed. "Oh, my dears, you are smaller than a mite, smaller than a nanosecond – you're at Planck time – absolutely invisible to your world, as is Outpost Gypsy Tree. If you'll remember, I told you that the outpost was nestled in a thought-form – can one see a thought? No. But it is energy, so exists at Planck time. Time is an illusion broken up into trillions upon trillions upon trillions of pieces. Each piece is able to be plucked out for a nanosecond and inserted into a new space and time dimension – just as you were when you traveled here.

"I've read about that," said Penzil eagerly.

"You know about Planck time?" asked Gar surprised. When it came to physics, Gar was a whiz kid.

"Sure do. I've nicked a few books in my day. Really love the scientific ones."

"Why don't you tell us what you know about it, Penzil," said Eittod with a twinkle in his eye.

The other teens were surprised that a boy from the Bush would know about such a sophisticated physics term. Although Penzil had grown up in the Outback of Australia – away from much of civilization – he is what people would call a "genius," whose IQ, if tested, was probably well over 145.

"We're talking *Quantum Physics,* mates, actually quantum time," said Penzil. "Planck time is a unit of time similar to a second, a minute, an hour. It is the smallest measurement of time that has any meaning in our physical universe. Any smaller division of time has no meaning according to our current Earth science. I don't rule anything out. All human experiences happen over billions of billions of billions of Planck times, making any events happening at Planck time almost impossible to detect. Talk about slow motion, we're probably moving at a trillion times slower than snail pace, mates! Our experiences right here at Outpost Gypsy Tree are an example. Is that correct, Eittod?"

"You are correct, Penzil. I couldn't have said it better myself. Very good explanation," said Eittod beaming.

The other teens were looking at each other in amazement and then back at Penzil with their jaws dropped.

"Hey, Outback, where did you learn all that?" queried Aube. "I thought you were from the Bush. You must have a great school there!"

"Too right! I am from the Bush, mate, but I am self-taught. This happy wanderer learns all he needs from books, wildlife, tribesmen, tourists, internet and life experiences. When I am catching some hotel work, they let me roam their internet. And at the hotels I meet lots of interesting tourists on vacation from all over the world. I spent last summer wandering the Bush with a physicist from the Max Planck Institute in Germany. I was his guide. He had taken some months off to rest and find himself, so I picked his noggin as much as he'd let me. We became good mates. He knows I am keen on the sciences, so he sent me some books by post once he got back home, which I devoured in just days. Actually, the bloke keeps me up on the latest stuff going on in the physics world, like updates from the Planck Institute and the newest research from CERN on particle physics and their large hadron collider – fascinating stuff!"

All the teens stood up and applauded him with calls of Bravo! Way to go! And slaps on the back bombarded him. Penzil blushed.

"There is a lot more to be learned and appreciated about each other," said Eittod, "but that will happen in due time. Right now, I am sure you are eager to learn of your assignment location."

Now their attention was locked on Eittod.

"I understand that Ireland's Newgrange or the Brú na Bóinne, as it's known in your Earth time, has been a topic of your conversations. Well, you have guessed correctly. That is precisely where you will begin – as we call it, the *palace of the gods*. The Regions Authority has charged us to clear the North Portal starting at that location," said Eittod, putting the crystal into motion. Everyone was excited at the news, especially Patrick, Drew and Aube.

As the oval crystal lowered, images of Drew's Newgrange illuminated the pit. Before their eyes on an elongated ridge loomed the great majestic mound with its pristine grassy slopes alive with graceful white whooper swans. The superbly restored Neolithic edifice was wrapped in a glistening cairn of white quartz rocks interspersed with dozens of cannon-ball sized granite cobbles and topped with a grassy dome.

Ninety-seven mammoth greywacke kerbstones placed horizontally end to end, some elaborately carved, formed its striking base. The Great Circle of twelve large upright greywacke stones encircled the sacred monument like guardians from the past. Hedgerows and fences surrounded Newgrange on all sides, protecting the ancient sleeping giant from the present. Grunting sounds of mute swans on the wing could be heard as they flew over the Boyne River and passed the Brú na Bóinne Visitor Centre and parking lot.

Drew cooed. She was home in her beloved Ireland, home with her Neolithic ancestors.

"This is Drew's twenty-first century view of Newgrange – preserved by the peoples of Ireland and their present-day United

Nations Organization as a World Heritage Site – preserved for all of humanity to experience and to dream of simpler days long past," said Eittod. "Did I get that right, Drew?" he asked.

"You certainly did, Eittod," said Drew, impressed at his knowledge of her present day Earth affairs.

The teens' eyes were glued to the images emerging from the crystal. A large entrance stone with its intriguing spiral and quadrangle carvings suddenly filled the pit. Everyone gasped and came to their feet in the center of the pit as the images moved around them.

"That's kerbstone number one or K1 as it is referred to," said Drew overjoyed.

Patrick gasped. "I recognize the large carved stone but not the site in front of my eyes. Is this really how it looks in your time, Drew?" he asked.

"Yes, Grand, this is *our* Newgrange. Amazing isn't it?" she replied. "And in your lifetime, Grand, you'll see it all happen."

"That's the same carving as on your stone, Drew," said Chelli excited.

"Yes, you're right, Chelli, it is the same. It's the triple spiral symbol," said Drew pulling her stone from her pocket to confirm Chelli's observation.

They all seemed to be talking at once – those asking questions and those trying to answer the questions. Eittod just sat back and reveled in their excitement.

Then clearing his throat, Eittod continued. "Now," he said, waving the images of twenty-first century Newgrange from the pit, "here is Newgrange as you will experience it – in its pristine original form over fifty-two hundred years ago in your far distant past."

Images of Ireland's palace of the gods now began to fill the pit. They were mesmerized by its size and beauty. There before them on an elongated ridge was the great dome as the original builders had created it. The twelve- to fifteen-foot high cairn towering above them glistened in the early morning sunlight. To everyone's surprise, the whole of the mound was covered with milky white quartz stones six to nine inches in size, interspersed with cannon-ball sized granite cobbles. Drew was awed by its brilliance.

"From space, I can imagine the mound presents an exact image of the moon's radiance," said Drew. "A replica of the moon right here on planet Earth. How amazing is that!"

"Yes, Drew, Neolithic man, as well as those who preceded and followed, recreated their heavenly deities right here on the Earth. For instance, the three pyramids of Giza – Khufu, Khafri and Menkaure – are in the exact same alignment as the three brightest stars of Orion's belt – Mintaka, Ainilam and Alnitak. The same holds true for the Thornborough triple henge site in your Great Britain."

In absolute awe, the teens moved in and around the images that gracefully floated in the pit. The intricately painted and polished entrance kerbstone close to the passage access, with its triple and double spiral engravings, drew them in. It was as if the light travelers were already standing there in their distant past, eager to fulfill their destiny.

There were no Great Circle stones of greywacke guarding the dazzling mound; those would be added toward the end of the active construction period, roughly a thousand years later. There were no fences, no hedgerows and no visitor's center.

Tidal action turned low, lapping waves of brackish water upon the shore of the Boyne River bank below as it made its way east to the Irish Sea. On ridges off in the distance, two smaller and older impressive earthen mounds could be glimpsed – Knowth to the north-west and Dowth to the north-east. The intriguing Bend of the Boyne and Matlock River, a tributary of the Boyne, encircled and cradled the three megalithic masterpieces as if guarding the sacred monuments.

Along the shore, Neolithic ancestors lashed their fishing boats, cleaned their catch and mended their nets. Women and children sat on large woven mats scattered along the hillside, weaving reeds and grasses into needed household items. Others tended crops while still others cared for livestock. Animals grazed on tall grasses while other livestock were content in wood-post pens.

Off to the southwest, smoke billowed up from stone fire rings inside huts of wood, mud-bricks and woven straw and grasses. Animal hides were hung out to dry on nearby wooden racks. Ceramic jars and woven baskets of various sizes and shapes sat on bare earth close to dwellings. Tools of polished bone, flint, stone and wood leaned next to them. Naked young children ran through the tall grasses, laughing and calling out to one another. Others were chasing behind a flock of grunting mute swans taking flight.

Could these simple people of eons ago have accomplished such a feat of architecture as was laid out before them?

As the teens viewed the images of the mound from all sides, they were amazed at the beauty of the colorful, megalithic art carved into the large hammered-smoothed stones that formed its base.

"How different it looks, Eittod. It's magnificent!" Drew sighed. "I never imagined it to be this beautiful. And the entrance stone, oh, how deep and rich its carvings are – and it was carved in place."

"Ah! The builders of this astronomical edifice dedicated to the passage of time were no ordinary race, but rather a very advanced, intelligent society. They were master mathematicians, architects, astronomers and physicists, as you will come to know," said Eittod with a spark of mystery in his voice. "Their monument holds many more surprises for you, dear ones."

"Let's take a closer look," said Eittod as he set his intent.

"Drew, why don't you give them the tour, my dear," invited Eittod as he eased into his red and gold tufted arm chair and propped his feet onto the ottoman. "I will light the way for you."

"Oh, thank you, Eittod," she replied, eagerly.

The light travelers stood amongst the images at the entrance which would lead them down the passage to the center chamber. Drew brought their attention to the rectangular roof box just above the entrance. She explained that the aperture of the roof box was of key significance. In fact, it is the meticulous placement and astronomical correctness of the aperture that precisely captures the rays of sunlight that stream over the peak of Red Mountain and down the passage to the back recess during the winter solstice.

"The center chamber of Newgrange, or should I say the palace of the gods," Drew continued, "is in total darkness except for the ten days of the winter solstice event. On our Earth calendar it would cover the days on either side of December 21 – the shortest day and longest night of the year. This was Neolithic man's celebration of the 'new sun' – the beginning of his new year. Solstice is a Greek word that means 'standing sun,'" said Drew.

"Have you ever been inside the chamber for the winter solstice, Drew?" asked Penzil.

"I have been in the passage and chambers many times," replied Drew "but never during the winter solstice. Each year, tens of thousands of people from all over the world place their names into a free lottery for the privilege of being chosen to witness the event. Only fifty names are drawn – five for each day of the solstice and standbys in case of cancellations. Each person whose name is drawn can bring another person with them. Hopefully, someday I will be blessed to have my name drawn."

"Isn't it considered a passage tomb by archeologists, Drew?" asked Aube.

"Yes! But there is still uncertainty regarding that usage, Aube. I am sure it had multiple uses down through the ages, but probably the main function was as an 'astronomical witness' to the passage of time, as Eittod mentioned," Drew answered. "In fact, Knowth, Dowth and Newgrange are astronomically aligned to not only the sun, but also to the moon, planets and other star events year round. The same is true of many other sites in the Boyne Valley."

"The passage is cruciform in shape with three recesses, one directly behind the center chamber and one to either side. Its shape resembles that of Cygnus, the swan constellation, which is cross-shaped," Drew explained.

As the images drew the teens down the passage, shimmering light filled the space, courtesy of Eittod. Drew was in awe at how perfectly aligned and polished the stone orthostat slabs were and how colorful were the engravings.

"These massive stones," she went on to explain pointing to the orthostats, "were set into place first – they formed the walls of the passage and the three recesses. They used the original shape of the stones, unlike those of the pyramids, which were cut to precise measurements. Then the kerb, or base stones, were mapped out, marking the location of the various key kerbstones such as the ones known as kerbstones 1 and 52, which are direct opposites in placement. Next, the greywacke roof slabs or lintels were laid horizontally to support the vertical standing orthostats, and eventually to support the weight of the earthen mound and flat-topped white quartz stones above," Drew instructed pointing upward.

"In our Earth time, some of these orthostats," now pointing to the massive stones of the passage wall, "are leaning inward blocking and redirecting the sunlight coming through the roof box toward the floor of the chamber, but amazingly they're still functional. Once the side walls and ceiling stones were in place, the humongous kerbstones were laid end to end horizontally to form the circumference of the palace. Then the earthen mound, with its glistening quartz stones, was set in place."

Eittod watched and listened, glowing with pride at Drew's knowledge and leadership. He and the Regions had chosen wisely.

Mingo had joined the teens in the middle of the pit taking in Drew's every word, and moving among the images, now and then asking questions. Bezen, like Eittod, gazed with pride at the intenseness with which each light traveler was engaged.

As they reached the center of the chamber images, Drew gasped. There before her in the very center of the chamber stood a colorful three-foot high, intricately carved obelisk with its pyramid-shaped top. She looked over at Eittod with a surprised expression.

"The stories of the obelisk are true?" Drew asked.

"Yes, Drew. The obelisk stories are true," said Eittod, moving toward her and laying his hand on her shoulder. "As I am sure you know, in his writings of 1725 AD, Thomas Molyneaux mentions an obelisk in the center of the chamber, but they're the last writings on the subject. Curious, don't you think? It was placed by its original builders and served a vital role. Don't ponder it now. In time you will understand. Please continue with your tour, Drew. You are doing very well," he said moving back to his chair.

Drew honored Eittod's statement and request to continue.

"If you will look up…" she said pointing to the central chamber ceiling.

Sounds of astonishment filled the pit as the teens' eyes met the breathtaking corbelled ceiling image above them. Layers upon layers of flat horizontal stones progressively overlapping each other lifted their eyes to the pinnacle – the capstone.

"…this corbelled ceiling is still water tight in our Earth time – an amazing feat of construction by its Neolithic architects and builders. According to archeologists, the builders had filled the openings between the rock slabs with burnt soil and sea salt to seal it and to keep the passage and chamber dry. According to Michael O'Kelly, who excavated Newgrange in the 1960's, *'there is no doubt that the people in charge of its construction, from the master builder and architect down to the team foremen, were intelligent and experienced,'*" said Drew.

"The ceiling looks like a rose opening up toward us, welcoming us! How beautiful is that!" said Chelli.

"I've never noticed that before. You're right, Chelli. It does look like an opening rose. I guess I've never seen it in this much light before. It's so beautiful," said Drew.

"What is burnt soil, Drew?" asked Patrick.

"I assume when the builders cleared the land for the construction, the trees, leaves, tall grasses and debris were burned and the ashes were used as part of the construction process. Is that correct, Eittod?" she asked.

"That is correct. Nothing was ever wasted by early man. Actually, cultures around your current world still use burnt soil for growing crops where soil is poor and, of course, there are other uses," said Eittod. "Good guess, Drew."

She grinned.

Everyone, including Mingo and Bezen, were captured by the beauty of the stone palace that they were privileged to witness. There were brightly-colored engravings throughout the passage, chamber and recesses, and Drew had one more very special carving to show them.

"I've saved the best until last, just as my Neolithic ancestors had done, so follow me," she said.

"It is noted," Drew continued, "that fifty–two hundred years ago when Neolithic man built this palace, the sun's rays peaked over the Red Mountain summit during the days of the winter solstice. The brilliant rays of the full sun disc aligned with the roof box, sending the light down the passage through the center of the chamber. Its golden glow rested upon the right side of the back recess, seventy-nine feet inside." Drew now moved them to the back recess images and pointed to the large stone carving.

"Lights, Eittod!" she said.

Again, expressions of wonder filled the passage as Eittod's shimmering lights hit the right side of the back recess wall image, illuminating the large triple spiral symbol and the eleven rows of colorful horizontal zigzags around it.

"Wow! That's awesome!" shouted Penzil. "What does the triple spiral carving symbolize, Drew?" he asked.

"There are many theories as to the meaning of the triple spiral symbol. Some experts claim it symbolizes life, death and rebirth. Others suggest it represents land, sea and sky. Still others believe it honors an earlier form of the holy trinity, father, mother and child. Most believe it symbolizes the accomplishment of the triple conjunction of the sun, moon and Venus on the winter solstice, which is a rare and special occurrence," said Drew.

After many questions and much exploration of the wondrous palace of the gods, Eittod called for their attention.

"This is truly an amazing structure which you will get to know very well. Very well, indeed! Let what you have heard, seen and experienced this afternoon be a part of your contemplation over the coming days," said Eittod.

Enough instruction for now," he declared. "You all need sunshine, fresh air and the sounds and rhythms of nature. Mingo, I release them to you."

"OK, everyone, let's grab some rays," said Mingo with a big grin on his face. "I learned that one from Penzil. Let's go, light travelers."

CHAPTER TWENTY:
Instruction

"Mingo sure does work us hard, but we need to be fit for what's coming, I suppose," said Gar, relieved that his fear was not chomping at his spine this morning. He and Aube made their way up the vibration pool incline after a refreshing swim.

"I love the ice plunge! It's so invigorating after all that exercising," said Chelli pulling a towel around her shoulders. "My extra pounds are just melting off. Sure wish I could take this healthier body back to my linear time frame, but I am sure that's not going to happen."

"I wonder, just how much of what we are learning and experiencing will remain in our memories once we return home?" queried Patrick.

"I've been wondering the same thing," said Drew. "Surely some of this will be gifted us."

"Maybe we should ask Mingo," replied Aube.

"Breakfast is served," called Bezen from the domicile feasting nook.

After a light breakfast, they all gathered back in the activity arena for their breathing, grounding and centering studies with Mingo.

"Okay! Now that we've all had a bite to eat, let's get started," said Mingo as he made his entrance from the feasting nook, a half-eaten apple in hand.

Mingo presents wisdom and maturity beyond his years when teaching. Yet the youthful, gleeful teen is always visible in his dancing dark eyes.

"Mingo, we have a question for you," said Aube.

"What's that?" asked Mingo.

"We were wondering just how much of all this stuff we'll remember when we go back to our precise split second in linear time?" questioned Penzil.

"Oh! Well, that's really up to Eittod and the Regions Authority, isn't it? Way out of my hands. Sorry!" said Mingo.

"Lots to cover this morning, so heads up," he said.

Mingo was all business this morning, and the teens knew they were in for some serious studies.

"Eittod was very clear about the importance of these morning studies. After all, *breath is life!* Not only do your muscles need oxygen and exercise to be strong, every cell of your being does if you are to draw energy, *prana,* from your army of light bearers. You have learned and practiced several different types of breathing since we started, and all are important. But the one you will learn and practice today is the most important – vibrational breathing," said Mingo.

"The entire universe is in vibration," he continued, his hands firmly placed on his narrow hips like a drill sergeant, "from the smallest particle at Planck time to the immense suns of our universe and beyond. If that smallest particle were to stop vibrating, it would wreck the entirety of creation. Kaboom!" he shouted, throwing up his hands.

Everyone jumped and laughed, mimicking him.

"The atoms of your physical structure," he continued, "are in constant vibration and change, always renewing. You are not the same person you were a month ago. Yes, you look the same, but virtually all of your cells have been replaced thanks to constant vibration and the divine intelligence of your body. Each of you has a distinct rhythm, and your given name is a part of that rhythm or vibration in this life experience. That is how the ONE, the ABSOLUTE, knows you. It is how the Regions, Angelics and Eittod know you. Remember, it was your vibration, your unique sound, your rhythm, that drew Eittod to you. *RIGHT*?" he asked.

"Right!" they all shouted back to their drill sergeant.

"All movement in the universe has its own vibration or sound, and is obedient to the same law – the law of rhythm," Mingo continued as the teens hung on his every word.

They loved the way he taught and his enthusiasm for the instructions entrusted to him. Each knew the instructions were for their health and welfare once out on assignment. They were like soldiers going into battle, but armed with love energy.

"By living in rhythm with your own body, you will be able to absorb great quantities of energy, or prana, which will be necessary to complete your assignment. Any questions or comments so far?" asked Mingo, taking a hearty bite of his apple.

"Mate, I've read that soldiers marching in rhythm can bring a bridge down. We're going to be working with that same principle, correct?" asked Penzil.

Mingo laughed, "Well, we won't be bringing down any bridges, per se – darkness hopefully – but that's true, Penzil. When a large group of soldiers are marching and chanting or counting off while crossing a bridge, their vibrations can, in fact, bring the bridge down and their regiment along with it. Called military cadence, this singing and marching in rhythm motivates, inspires and synchronizes their breathing to bring more energy into their bodies for long marches. When a regiment is crossing a bridge, the order goes out to *break step* to avoid that problem. Remember, vibrations from an earthquake can bring a whole city down," he explained, slowly pacing back and forth in front of the vibrational pool and keeping eye contact with each of them. It reminded the teens of Eittod's body language when he has important information to share with them.

"For you, " Mingo continued, "rhythmic or vibrational breathing, along with centering your intent in the heart and grounding yourself into the core of the Earth, will allow you to draw up needed energy and light from the Earth. Now everyone have a seat and assume correct posture."

The teens quickly seated themselves and were ready. Mingo instructed them on the sequence and count of vibrational breathing, the inhale, retain, exhale, hold, then repeat.

"First grounding! I feel you have mastered this part very well. So send your roots down into the ground as if you were Gypsy herself – nice long, strong, thick roots into the ocean of liquid iron which is in constant motion, and down into the iron core. That's four thousand miles straight down – a tad shorter if you're at the poles," he instructed, giving them a few minutes to connect with the core of their Mother Earth.

"Now today as you connect, be mindful of your army of light. Imagine the globe of the Earth that Eittod showed you with all those points of light. Without realizing it, your army is constantly sending their desire or intention for peace and love into the magnetic grid of the Earth from their own energy bodies, or light bodies. It is this energy that you will be drawing from – not from individuals – but from the energy they constantly deposit into the Earth itself. You are plugging into that powerful energy source with your intent – sort of like a toaster plugging into an electrical outlet in your current Earth time. Visualize it happening in your mind as you rhythmically breathe."

As Mingo counted off the rhythm of the breath, the teens focused on their intent and light source.

After a few minutes, he instructed them to power down and to be aware of how their bodies felt. "Could you feel a difference?" asked Mingo as he moved among them.

"Mingo, I got very warm and my whole body is tingling. I had felt that way with other breathing exercises, but with vibrational breathing and intending to connect with the energy and light of our army, I felt like I was radiating powerful light or energy out from my body," said Chelli.

"Good! Good! Who else felt a radiating out?" Mingo asked.

All the teens nodded excitedly.

"I had a similar experience when I was being transported to the outpost. I felt radiance glowing out from me into the protective mist that embraced me. Like I was a human headlight on a foggy night," Drew mused.

"Yes! Yes! That's what I just experienced, Drew," said Patrick.

"You all are amazing!" said Mingo. "You already have moved onto the next step in a brief amount of time. I don't want you to tire yourselves out though. So we're going to take this next step slowly," he said. "The important part here is keeping your roots locked into the core of Mother Earth and your intentions true and pure. No ego stuff! *GOT IT?*"

In a sing-song voice everyone answered in unison, *"GOT IT, Mingo!"*

The light travelers were well aware of the importance of keeping check on their egos. With every lesson, Mingo stressed the importance of gratitude and humility when working for the ONE, the ABSOLUTE.

At the end of the lesson, Mingo applauded them. "Good job! You all have been doing your homework and it shows. Today's lesson went very well. Eittod will be pleased at your progress. You're almost ready for the final phase," he said.

Stunned expressions covered their faces, and fear collectively gripped them to the bone.

Mingo quickly came to their rescue. "Not to worry! Not to worry! Eittod will make that decision when the time is right. I have spoken much too soon," he recanted, and immediately changed the subject.

"Eittod has an amazing surprise for you today. Follow me!" he said with excitement in his voice as he jogged them toward the hanging gardens.

Eittod's holographic image and Bezen were waiting for them in the large clearing beyond the encampment.

"I have a surprise for you on this beautiful morning. Close your eyes for a moment. Good!" Then after pausing for a few moments, Eittod instructed, "Now open your eyes!"

They gasped.

There before them on an elongated ridge stood the palace of the gods beckoning them in.

"Is it real?" asked Drew excitedly as tears of joy formed in her delighted green eyes.

"Of course it's real," laughed Eittod. "It's as *real* as *real* can get, my dear Drew. Remember, you are in the eternal now."

"Can we go inside, Sir?" asked Penzil in a whisper.

"The palace of the gods is all yours. You can do more than just go inside, my dear ones. You will become very familiar with every inch of it, inside and out, over the coming days. You must be able to move through the passage in complete darkness without disturbing anything. You must know each stone by its feel and vibration and stay steady to the center of the passage. You will study the carvings – remember you have been gifted language which includes the language of megalithic art. And at night and early morning, you will study its heavens. Bezen has provided you with bedrolls and water pouches. Remember to stay steady to the center of the passage. This is your charge, dear ones," said Eittod as his hologram faded.

Days seemed to be flying by as the light travelers moved through their very busy schedules: early morning astronomy work, then exercise or jogging and cool down, followed by a light breakfast in their domicile feasting nook. They then moved on to CGB, as they were now calling their centering, grounding and breathing lessons with Mingo.

Next it was off to the palace of the gods for several hours of hands-on experience with their assignment area, followed by a jog through the encampment and across the footbridge to Gypsy for a refreshing swim in the vibration pool and a plunge into the ice bath.

After lunch, they had 3107 BCE astronomy instruction with Eittod in the snuggery. Late afternoon included instruction out on the grounds with Mingo and Bezen on Neolithic hunting and gathering skills, which was one of Chelli's favorite lessens. After some nourishing snacks, they met Bezen and Mingo in the costuming station and equipment center in Gypsy's upper levels, followed by inter-communication skills with Gypsy.

Each evening they all gathered for a delicious dinner in the snuggery feasting nook with Eittod, which included a question and answer session on the day's activities and lessons. By late evening they were camped outside the mound mapping out the movement of the stars, planets and moon in the heavens of 3107 BCE.

"Good morning, my light travelers. Amazing!" exclaimed Eittod. "You have lived, breathed and slept the grounds and passage – all seventy-nine feet of it – and the heavens of the palace of the gods for almost two weeks, and you have absorbed much instruction. And you've got it! *BRAVO!* Your mapping of the astronomical bodies is impressive. Remember, the celestial bodies will be your only guide during your journey – no watches, no maps, no compass and no electronic devices," he chuckled.

Patrick gave him a strange look. "No 'electronic devices,' Sir?" he queried.

"These whiz kids of the twenty-first century will fill you in on 'electronic devices,' Patrick," said Eittod with a big smile on his face. "It astounds me what toys man creates for himself to track direction and the movement of time, when all he needs to do is look up into the heavens for the answers. Now just rest for a few days and enjoy each other. We all have worked very hard, especially you dear ones; so rest, relax and rejuvenate. AND HAVE FUN!" said Eittod with a look of appreciation and pride.

All the teens were on their feet and jumping up and down with joy.

"For all your hard work, Mingo and Bezen have a special treat for you just outside Gypsy's door. Are you ready, Bee?" called Eittod.

"Ready we are, Eittod," shouted Mingo and Bezen in unison.

The teens made their way out through Gypsy's large wooden door and *WHAM!!! SPLAT!!!* Snowballs were flying toward them from every direction. The ground was covered with many inches of fresh snow, and it was still coming down. On the river bank, Mingo and Bezen had built a snowman that looked just like Eittod. It was rainbow-colored, and looked very much like a large multi-flavored snow cone.

It didn't take the teens long to dress head to toe with hats, gloves, scarves, coats, boots and mischievous grins. Everyone had joined in on the fun, even the scumdiggalies. Eittod stood in the doorway; childish wonderment lit up his face with delight. Even he was caught off guard as snowballs flew past him and into the snuggery. He returned their fire with gleeful laughter.

This was their very first snowball battle, and Aube, Gar and Penzil relished in the experience. Snow is not something Lima, Peru, or Australia Outback residents get to enjoy. And they loved it! Every inch of it!

Gypsy wasn't about to miss out on any of the action. She shook her snow-covered branches sending snow tumbling down in an avalanche at Eittod's feet. Her colorful lights and melodious sounds filled the outpost with feelings of joyous holiday cheer.

Chelli called out, "Snow angels!" And within seconds Drew, Chelli and Patrick were lying on their backs in the snow, flapping their arms and legs wide. Soon everyone was on the ground creating angel-like impressions in the snow – even Bezen. They laughed and rolled into each other with fistfuls of snow in hand. Finally, when staff and teens were soaked and exhausted, Bezen invited them into the snuggery for piping hot chocolate with marshmallows and some of Meg Campbell's gingerbread cookies. Drew grinned with delight from ear to ear. Her Mom's cookies were a very special treat, indeed.

"What a glorious celebration!" declared Eittod as he brushed snow from his jeans. "I feel just like a kid again, and that's going some," he laughed. "And my palate is looking forward to those gingerbread cookies that Drew's always talking about."

"Let's face it, Eittod. You've always been a kid at heart. Promise me that you'll never grow up," said Bezen with a warm, loving smile. "We love you just the way you are!"

"Oh, Bee, you make me blush," said Eittod, his face pinked.

"You bet we love you," said Mingo, giving Eittod a big bear hug. Soon all the teens were around Eittod, joining the group hug.

CHAPTER TWENTY-ONE:
Betrayal

"I asked Eittod if we could go sledding on the palace grounds in the morning, and he gave us permission," announced Drew as they approached their domicile.

"I've never been sledding before," said Penzil excitedly. "I *love* snow! A bit on the cold side though."

"Neither have we," said Gar as they stepped through the energy space and made themselves comfortable in the greeting hall. "Should be great fun!"

"You can count me in," said Aube with a very big smile on his face.

"What a wonderful day," said Patrick. "And I actually enjoyed rollicking in the snow with the scumdiggalies. They're like little kids in the snow."

"You might want to count your fingers and your toes, Patrick. I just don't trust them," said Aube. "I don't like the way they look at me as if they know something I don't. It's a smug look."

"I know what you mean, Aube," said Drew. "Each morning as I look out my chamber window, a scumdiggalie is staring up at me from the garden near the fountain. And each time it does, I can feel myself doubting my worthiness to be here. Then I look at my stone and know that I *do* belong here. It's unnerving. They play tricks with your mind. Actually, one morning I was so distraught by the unworthy feeling that I almost threw my stone out the window. Then I noticed the excited look on its face and realized that's what it wanted – my quartz stone!"

"I like to sit by the river after supper and enjoy the croaking of the frogs," shared Penzil. "And I've had one come to me several times and tell me that my black fire opal was a bad omen stone given to me by my parents. The creature said it was willing to destroy it for me so it wouldn't draw harm to me during our assignment. But worst of all, it told me that my parents thought I was worthless and had abandoned me, hoping that the stone would draw evil upon me so I would perish in the wild. That saddened me greatly. I felt like a no-hoper," said Penzil as his eyes got red and moist. "But I was determined not to fall for its mean trickery. I told the dunny rat to nick off and not to come round again."

"I had one follow me while I was walking in the meadow gathering fresh herbs and flowers," shared Chelli. "It told me my great-grandfather's shaman bag, which I always carry, was full of evil magic. I know my Grand-Papá was a good and loving shaman healer who continues to watch over me from Brooks Mountain. I also told the creature to go away," she said, punching a fist in the air and clutching her treasured shaman bag to her heart.

Everyone looked at Aube and Gar.

"What?" asked Gar gruffly.

"Surely a scumdiggalie has approached you two," said Chelli.

"Well…a…like Aube said, they give us a smug look," said Gar, not making eye contact with Chelli.

"Sounds like those scumdiggalies have tricked none of us – we have solidarity against them," said Penzil angrily as he took his black fire opal from his weathered talisman pouch and placed it firmly on the camelhair carpet in front of him.

"Like Mingo said," Penzil continued, *"They are master thieves, liars and con artists out to trick us and steal our possessions.'* But they have none of our priceless treasures!"

Everyone followed suit placing their treasured possessions firmly onto the carpet in front of them. There on the floor lay Penzil's black fire opal, Chelli's moose-hide shaman bag decorated with colorful beads, Drew and Patrick's triple spiral quartz stone and....

"Gar!" said Aube, looking down at the items on the carpet and giving his brother a nudge with his elbow.

Gar didn't move.

Aube, looking at his brother's hand, said, "Our ring, Gar. Place it on the carpet with the other treasures!"

Still Gar didn't move a muscle.

Aube looked into Gar's face, "Gar, our Perez family ring…Give it to me," he said in a firm voice as he reached his right hand out for it.

Gar's face showed shame, guilt and regret as tears began to leak from his eyes and slide down his chestnut-toned cheeks. He turned his face from Aube.

"GAR! WHAT HAVE YOU DONE?" shouted Aube, stunned, pulling Gar into a standing position.

Gar wanted to run, to hide, to disappear. The weight of his guilt and shame was unbearable. He tried to pull Aube away from the group.

"NO! GAR! NO! You're not going to run away from this!" Aube screamed, holding his ground against his brother's strong pull. His face was beet red.

Never in his whole life had Aube stood up to his brother.

"That's what the scumdiggalies were celebrating in the meadow that first morning, wasn't it? AND YOU KNEW IT!" he shouted.

"That's what the smug looks have been about; *they knew that I didn't know about the ring!* **You have betrayed me...betrayed our fellow light travelers...betrayed Eittod and the Regions, and most of all, you have betrayed and shamed the Perez family name,"** screamed Aube from the depths of his soul.

Rage ran rampant through his quivering body as he began to kick at Gar's leg and slap at his brother's face with the back of his hand. All those years of Gar's verbal abuse and ridicule came flying out of Aube.

Gar did not defend himself.

"HOW DARE YOU! HOW DARE YOU!" Aube kept screaming as he kicked and slapped at Gar.

Penzil and Patrick were on their feet grabbing at Aube's flailing arms and legs. Drew and Chelli were pleading for Aube to calm down as they reached to protect Gar from the assault. Drew was knocked to the floor, her lip bleeding.

Bezen and Mingo appeared in the greeting hall. Bezen took hold of Aube's hands, and Mingo was holding Aube's feet as the other boys slowly lowered the twins to the floor. Aube's body was manic, his eyes crazed. Gar's body was limp.

"Aube, hear my voice. Calm down. Aube, calm down now!" said Bezen firmly. The others backed away and formed a wide circle around Bezen, Mingo and the twins.

"Are you okay?" asked Chelli as she immediately put pressure on Drew's lip with her scarf. A second later the bleeding had stopped and the cut on Drew's lip had healed.

"I love this immortal stuff," said Chelli. "Your lip is healed. Amazing!"

"Thank you, Chelli. Immortality does have its perks," said Drew. "That would have taken many days to heal. Aube sure does swing a mean upper cut. He's bound to have some Irish blood in him."

The next second, Eittod's hologram appeared in the greeting hall, "Auben! Garcia!" he said in a firm but loving voice.

The sound of Eittod's voice grabbed everyone's attention. Aube and Gar looked up at him from the floor with surprised looks on their faces.

"Auben! Garcia! I want your attention," said Eittod calmly.

Bezen released Aube's hands as Mingo and Patrick assisted the boys from the floor to a nearby couch. Aube's face was still bright red and sweaty from rage and the sting of betrayal. Gar's bloody nose and small cut above his eye were already in the process of healing. His face was red from embarrassment and guilt. Tears of regret streamed through his sweat. Both boys were shaking uncontrollably. Patrick offered Gar his handkerchief.

Bezen stood behind the twins and laid her hands on their shoulders to calm them.

"Auben, I understand your anger and rage, and I honor it. It is certainly warranted. Now, let's hear your brother out. Garcia, please explain your actions to your brother," requested Eittod.

Through Gar's sobs of shame and regret, he explained that a scumdiggalie had come to his bedside on their very first night at the outpost. The green-haired creature had told him telepathically that it was the power of the massive ring that would take them on the dangerous assignment. Without the ring in their possession, he was told, they would be unable to travel from the outpost.

The scumdiggalie told him they had saved many children from their deadly journeys, but that others who would not listen to them and had gone on, had never returned. The people of the outpost couldn't be trusted. They were using the teens for their own gain, and used gifts to seduce them – their own sleeping chambers, their own home sites from the window, an abundance of food and other pleasures. Eittod and his clever staff would say whatever they thought the teens needed to hear to gain their trust. The pointed-toothed creature claimed the scumdiggalies knew of Gar's intelligence and that he couldn't be fooled. That's why they approached him rather than Aube.

Aube's stare was stoic and detached as he watched Gar unravel his painful story of betrayal. Gar occasionally glimpsed Aube's hard face, then returned his eyes to his hands, twisting Patrick's handkerchief as he spoke. Now and then he glanced at Eittod who gave him a reassuring nod, and he continued.

"Aube, I tried to fight those awful icy fingers of fear that were chomping down on me, but I was weak and scared. I hated that tremulous feeling taking control of me. I kept repeating Eittod's words of just hours before, *'You're a fine young man, and your courage, intelligence and bravery will serve us well.'* I kept saying it over and over and over, again and again, but I was frightened of what I didn't understand at the time – frightened of the assignment. I *knew* I was *not* courageous, intelligent or brave. I *knew* I was nothing but a coward. And the creature kept filling my head with images of us bleeding to death in a dark, foreboding place, and us crying out for Mama and Papa to help us," Gar said, wiping fresh tears from his face and trying to catch his breath.

Continuing to twist Patrick's handkerchief, he went on. "I know that's not a good excuse, and I don't expect it to be. I hate what I've done. I hate and regret that I have betrayed you – betrayed us. I hate that I have shamed our family. Aube, I've wanted to tell you of my weakness, tell you what I had done, but I couldn't bring myself to do it. You seemed so happy here, and I was excited about all the new and amazing things I was learning and the deep friendships we were creating. Here again, I was a coward.

"I have come to understand what you believe and why. I too want to help Eittod and the Regions. I also want to save my world and its people, even if it does mean giving up our life to do so," said Gar stopping again to catch his breath.

Everyone was caught up in the drama playing out in front of them and did not dare to move a muscle. Tears streamed down many cheeks, and gut-wrenching, painful expressions captured their faces. They slowly reached out for each other's hands. They could feel the depth of Gar's shame and Aube's pain at being betrayed. Aube continued to coldly stare into his twin brother's distraught face.

Exhausted, Gar dropped his head into his hands, his shoulders slumped. Long moments passed in tense silence. Then, although completely spent, Gar continued.

"I am relieved that you now know," said Gar looking into Aube's cold eyes. "It's been a hellish nightmare knowing that you would eventually find out the truth of my actions. I pray you will find it in your heart someday to forgive me, Aube. And please forgive me for always bullying you and ridiculing you. I was jealous of your goodness and your courage."

"Aube, I am so sorry. I love you, and I respect and honor just how brave and courageous you are and always have been," Gar finished, again dropping his head into his hands, still unable to make eye contact with his fellow light travelers.

The tension in the room was palpable. Everyone was holding their breath, waiting for Aube's response. Aube lowered his head; his eyes darted back and forth, his forearms resting on his lap. He was taking long, deep breaths to calm himself as he considered his brother's confession. At times he placed his head in his hands for comfort as he weighed his response. A long silence followed. The room was motionless, soundless.

Eventually, Aube reached for his brother's hand, his eyes still darting back and forth, his head still down. Again, there was silence.

Gar didn't move. He knew he deserved whatever Aube had to say – and then some.

Finally Aube looked at his brother. "Gar…" he said.

Gar looked up into his brother's almond-shaped amber eyes and waited.

"Gar, I know you have been afraid of everything that I believe in. And I know it took a great deal of *courage* and…and *love* for you to agree to come here to the outpost, yet you did. I know how frightening that first day was for you. And I realize *now* that I should have been more understanding, supportive. From your description of the images the scumdiggalie forced upon you, I am sure your fear level was well over the top. Anybody's would have been, given the circumstances. I just wish you had awakened me. I wish you would have trusted me, or at least shared your experience with me that following morning. We could have worked this out somehow. Now here we are so close to our final preparations with no ring to carry us on our assignment, which saddens me greatly. But what grips at my heart and soul most is there is no ring to carry us home again," said Aube with tears of great loss streaming down his chestnut brown face.

Gar's eyes widened, stunned at what Aube had just said.

"*We can't go...go home?*" queried Gar with child-like terror in his voice. "Oh, Aube, what have I done to us?" pulling them both up into a standing position. "Maybe we can find the ring. We can search the whole of the outpost for it. We've got to find where they've hidden it. I *do* want us to go on our assignment to palace of the gods; and most of all, I want to go home again, Aube." he said, his voice cracking and filled with panic.

"Mates, count me in on the search. We can start right now! We'll use these days off to find your family's ring and the vile creature that conned it from you," said Penzil as he jumped to his feet, determination and fume in his expression.

All the teens were on their feet and talking at once. Everyone was in agreement and ready to support the brothers in their search.

"We'll comb the entirety of the outpost if need be," said Patrick. "We're a family, and in my book, family supports family, no matter what!"

"Let's get going," said Drew as she moved toward the energy space. "Those scumdiggalies have tricked this family for the last time."

"Hold on! Hold on!" said Eittod in a soft voice, motioning for them to halt.

"I am very pleased that you are this supportive of each other. That's what is needed to make your assignment successful. But we have someone who wishes to speak; Mingo, would you oblige our guest? Light travelers, have a seat."

Mingo stepped out through the energy space and quickly returned with a fuzzy, chameleon-skinned, sweet-faced, green-haired beauty in tow.

All the light travelers were back on their feet with malice in their eyes.

"Wait, everyone! Hear this creature out," said Eittod, motioning them back to their seats.

The two-foot tall creature walked tight against Mingo's leg and was shaking like a leaf in a good wind.

"Lancelot, I believe you have something for the twins," said Mingo, looking down at the frightened creature clinging to him. "Not to worry! I am right here for you. You're safe."

With Mingo at its side, the green-haired cutie slowly moved in Aube and Gar's direction, its clawed feet digging deep into the camelhair carpet. It paused and looked down at the other treasures on the floor. Chelli began to move forward to protect the treasures, but Eittod moved his hand and motioned her still.

After a long look, the scumdiggalie slowly walked around the treasures and stopped in front of Aube and Gar. Timidly, it raised its head and eyes up to meet theirs and then slowly raised its quivering, clenched right fist toward Gar. The creature slowly opened its clawed hand to reveal a massive ring with a star-clustered crest on a field of black.

Gar looked at Eittod who nodded for him to accept the ring. Gar slowly reached down and took the massive ring from Lancelot's outstretched hand. The creature lowered its hand and its head, and a very faint sound came forward.

"Very sorry!" it said in a soft whisper.

Everyone's posture and facial expressions softened as they watched the creature and Mingo slowly turn and move back toward the energy space and stop. The creature looked back at Aube and Gar, nodded its head, then proceeded out of the energy space. As it did, Gar and Aube called out, "Thank you! Thank you very much, Lancelot!" And it was gone.

"Eittod, what just happened?" asked Aube perplexed.

"Lancelot is a very rare scumdiggalie. Its heart is thrice the size of all the rest combined. It has feelings, which is unheard of for its kind. It was aware of the theft and the trickery of its kin, Liesalot. The morning after the theft, when Mingo went to the meadow to clean up the mess from their celebration, Lancelot was waiting for him. It showed Mingo where the ring had been cleverly hidden in a tree knot. Mingo, not wanting to involve Lancelot in the recovery of the item, left the ring hidden until today. Lancelot chose to be the one to return it and is saddened by the pain its kind had caused," shared Eittod.

Looking into Gar's eyes, Eittod continued, "You must have been in greater fear than any of us realized on that first night, Gar, for a scumdiggalie to have actually entered the domicile. That has never happened before, and I apologize for that. As I have said, Gar, you're a fine young man, and your courage, intelligence and bravery will serve us well." His hologram faded from the greeting hall.

Everyone gathered around the twins, shaking their hands, patting them on the back and hugging them. Aube and Gar thanked everyone profusely for their support and understanding. And Aube gave Drew a special hug and an apology for literally busting her lip.

"What are friends for?" she said with a smile. "You guys are worth it!"

"Okay, everyone, these brothers need some time to talk things out. Let's go!" said Bezen.

Once the brothers were alone, Gar reached into his pocket and withdrew the ring. "Aube, I can't be trusted with this family treasure. I think you need to carry it for us," said Gar, putting it into Aube's hand.

Aube looked at the ring for a long moment, studying the star-clustered crest on the field of black. Keeping his eyes on the ring, he spoke. "Gar, I believe our ring is a map," said Aube, pausing to take a deep breath as if trying to work up his courage. "I believe it is a map of a constellation in our Milky Way Galaxy. And I feel in my heart it will someday guide us to our great-grandfather from the stars. I have never shared that information with you before. I was afraid of ridicule.

"Gar, I am a coward as well. Like you, I have studied the stars for a long time, and this constellation appears in the northern hemisphere in the winter and the southern sky in the summer. Tonight you shared that you have come to understand what I believe and why and that you want to help Eittod and the Regions. And that you want to save our world and its people even if it does mean giving up our own life to do so.

"I feel we are now of one mind as well as one body – and that I am now safe to share my deepest beliefs and thoughts with you," said Aube, putting the ring back in Gar's hand and looking into his eyes. "I know the Perez family ring is safe in your hands, and I forgive you and I love you, Gar," said Aube.

Gar looked down at the star cluster on the field of black, "Which constellation, Aube?" Gar asked with eagerness in his voice.

"Perseus!" smiled Aube. "The Hero."

CHAPTER TWENTY-TWO:
R & R

Daybreak eased in. A light snow gently sifted down as the teens and Mingo made their way from the domicile feasting nook to the palace grounds. Greeting them were the honking sounds of hundreds of majestic whooper swans huddled on the hillside; their pure white feathers blended with the snow. A wintering ground for the large, white birds, the palace of the gods hosts the migrating flocks from Iceland every October through March.

In front of the colorfully carved entrance stone were Eittod's smiling hologram, Bezen bundled in woolly wraps, six shiny new sleds and a basket of snow goggles and helmets.

"Good morning! This is so exciting! I've been looking forward to this since yesterday," said Eittod, childish excitement filling his voice. "Your sleds are ready as promised."

The teens lit up with delight as they each claimed a sled, a pair of bright red goggles and a helmet, and prepared for the ride to the Boyne. Aube and Gar picked up the double sled, and waited for their instructions on the art of sledding from Chelli, as did Penzil. Being from the Fairbanks, Alaska, area, Chelli was certainly an expert when it came to anything associated with snow.

"Okay! Now, it's very simple guys! You can either lie on your tummy or sled sitting up. I find it easier and much more fun on my tummy, maneuvering the steering bar with my hands, rather than maneuvering the bar with my feet from a sitting position. You have much more control that way. So, put on your goggles and helmet, lie flat on your sled, heads up to see where you're going, hands gripping the steering bar, and away you go. Some folks like to get a running start, but that's up to you. Any questions?" she asked.

"Chelli, I have a very important one. How do I stop the sled?" questioned Penzil.

Aube and Gar were nodding to his question.

"Oh! Your feet serve as the brakes. Just slide them off the side and drag to a stop, or turn your steering bar hard to the side. If you can't get your sled to stop, just roll off into the snow. See you at the bottom!" shouted Chelli as she pushed off.

Mingo and Patrick gave the twins a push, then joined in the fun to the river's edge. Eittod and Bezen cheered them on.

As the sleds whizzed down the hill, the quick-paced paddling sounds of webbed feet and the labored beating of eight-foot angelic wing-spreads culminated in breathtaking celestial flight, followed by graceful touchdowns on the surface of the Boyne River below.

Everyone was caught in the splendor of the avian moment overhead and the thrill of the ride.

Penzil was so caught up in the flight of the swans that he accidently rolled himself off his sled onto his back in the snow.

"You're supposed to sled on your tummy, Outback, not on your back," yelled Aube laughing as he and Gar zoomed past Penzil.

Good spirited, Penzil just laughed, brushed himself off and was back on his sled without skipping a beat. His admiration for Aube was growing. It was as if he had a big brother for the first time in his life – a big brother who enjoyed teasing him, and Penzil loved the attention.

"Wow! This is great," yelled Gar.

"Yahoo!" shouted Aube as they sailed down the hill squealing at the top of their lungs and working the steering bar in unison.

Once everyone had reached the bottom, a snowball battle ensued. Then grabbing their sled ropes, they worked their way up through the snow to the top. Red-cheeked and out of breath, they boarded their sleds for another journey to the Boyne.

Hours later the teens and staff were enjoying hot apple cider around a fire pit in the snuggery. Wonderful sledding stories were waiting to be shared and enjoyed.

"I don't remember this fire pit being here. Not very observant, am I?" said Drew.

"Oh! You are observant enough, Drew. It's only been here since this morning," said Mingo, laughing, "We only bring it to us when we desire its warmth. Fires make Gypsy nervous."

Gypsy's melodious sounds could be heard in agreement.

"I will give you one more day of wintery fun, rest and relaxation, then it's back to work," said Eittod as he delightedly sipped hot cider from his large mug. "I do recommend you continue your research and studies for the journey though. You leave via Gypsy's time-rings for your dry run to the palace of the gods in two days. Your adventure to the past begins," he said with a very big smile on his beaming face.

Surprised and excited looks appeared on all their faces. The travelers knew they were ready for it. They had worked very hard.

"Holy Christmas! You hear that, Aube? We're ready!" shouted Gar, slapping his brother on the back and knocking Aube's empty cider cup into the air.

"You really mean it, Eittod? We are actually ready for our dry run?" asked Chelli, her eyes dancing with delight as she jumped up and down punching the air with her fists.

"Yes! You teens are more than ready, my dear Chelli. I am aware of how diligently you all have worked. Mingo, Bezen and Gypsy sing your praises. And your commitment to each other and to clearing the North Portal is evident. It shows in your hearts and in the depth of your eyes. The Regions and I have met, and they are of the same opinion, and are ready to assist your travel," said Eittod with great excitement in his voice.

"Lunch is served, and then it's back to sledding!" called Bezen. The large stone table in the feasting nook was covered with a smorgasbord of international foods awaiting their rumbling tummies.

A large pile of discarded boots, scarves, gloves, coats, helmets and colorful goggles laid dripping just inside Gypsy's wooden door.

"Wait one millennium! This mess will certainly have to go," said Bezen. With a nod of her head, the soggy pile disappeared and fresh garments and goggles lay neatly in stacks on the now dry floor, ready for the next round of fun and celebration.

The day of the dry run had arrived. Everyone rose to bright sunlight and the warmth of spring and budding blossoms. After morning exercises, cool down, breakfast, CGB studies and a trip to the costuming station and equipment center in Gypsy's upper limbs, Eittod was waiting for them in the pit.

Everyone was dressed in leather and fur from head to toe and armed with their survival packs, ready for the journey.

"Your big day has arrived; it is off to the palace of the gods for your dry run," said Eittod enthusiastically. "I take it that everyone slept well?" he asked.

"Eittod, I was much too excited to sleep last night. In my mind, I walked the length, breadth and circumference of the palace throughout the night. I familiarized myself again with the vibration of every stone and reviewed every symbol and carving. I am afraid I am exhausted, Sir. I am so sorry, but my excitement at the journey ahead overtook me," Drew apologized.

As Eittod looked around, all the travelers were sadly nodding in agreement.

"Not to worry! I expected nothing less of you, dear ones. So, get horizontal, if you please," instructed Eittod, pointing to the camelhair carpets.

The light travelers did as instructed, looking at each other and at Eittod curiously.

"Now, my light travelers, close your eyes and take a few deep cleansing breaths," he said, and then paused. "Good!" He focused and then gently waved his hands over the teens. Radiant orbs of light the size of tennis balls flowed from his hands into the resting bodies before him. He paused again, then slowly moved among them calling each by their full given name as he lightly tapped each brow.

"Awaken, Drew Megan Campbell! Awaken, Auben Juan Perez! Awaken, Garcia Gou-Drah Perez! Awaken, Penzil Kangaroo! Awaken, Chelli 'Little Bear' Freeman! Awaken, Patrick Charles Campbell!" His voice was soft, yet commanding.

Each teen was now wide-awake and refreshed as if they had had eight hours of deep, restful sleep.

"Oh! I feel so good," cooed Drew, stretching her arms high in the air and rolling her head around on her shoulders, first in one direction and then the other. "Thank you, Eittod! How are you feeling, Grand?"

"I haven't slept that good, ever!" replied Patrick. "I feel great and ready to meet the challenge!"

"Me, too!" said Penzil, stretching out his whole body and jumping up with a bounce. "Yes, thank you, Eittod."

Everyone was amazed at how calm and rested they felt from head to toe.

"Wow, Eittod, can I take that trick back home for test cramming nights?" asked Patrick.

All the teens agreed except for Penzil.

"So, what are test cramming nights?" asked Penzil with a sincere look on his ebony face.

At that question, all the teens started throwing pillows at Penzil Kangaroo until he was buried beneath the largest pillow pile Eittod had ever seen. Eittod's laughter filled the snuggery. He loved their vibrancy and youthful, joyous energy.

Mingo reached in and pulled Penzil from the pile.

"You really asked for that one, Mr. Genius!" said Mingo with a big grin.

"Way to go, Outback!" laughed Aube, throwing an arm around Penzil's shoulders.

"So, what was that all about, Aube? Is cramming that bad?" he asked.

Everyone just shook their heads in disbelief and rolled their eyes in exasperation.

"Come on, little brother, before you find yourself buried in pillows again," said Aube, leading Penzil toward a seat in the pit.

"Here, have a seat with us," said Gar, patting his hand on the large couch seat.

Penzil beamed. He'd just been called *little brother* and was invited to sit with the twins.

"Let's get to the business at hand," said Eittod, still caught up in the slapstick antics of his beloved light travelers. They so loved each other.

"Today you will travel to the 3107 BCE Winter Solstice at the palace of the gods, in what is 'Erin' then and known as 'Ireland' in your Earth time. Unlike your experience with the mound here at the outpost, you will be in the presence of Neolithic man on *his* turf. Remember, you will be able to observe him, but your vibrations will be much too high for him to witness you. Oh, he may get a glint of your light out of the corner of his eye, but that's all that he will experience of you.

"This is your trial run to experience the journey itself – the feeling of transport and the awe of your location in linear time. And you will only stay for three hours of Earth time. Bezen and Mingo will be traveling with you to observe, and are available to you if you need their help. You have studied and practiced well, and are ready. Remember, stay steady to the center of the passage. Bezen and Mingo, assist our light travelers on their journey," said Eittod now ushering them toward Gypsy's core.

"Come with us," said Bezen as she and Mingo walked them toward Gypsy's tree rings.

The teens were never before allowed in this area of the snuggery, and excitement was building within them as they moved onto

Gypsy's massive wooden core. Her spicy scent was delightful, and her melodious sounds soothed them.

"Gypsy's tree rings, as we have explained to you, hold the active existence of all civilizations past, present and to come, on and beyond the Earth and its galaxy; each ring identifies with a timeframe and location within the universe. Before we start the process of transport, does everyone have their treasured item in their possession?" Bezen asked. "It's your ticket to this journey," she reminded them.

Aube and Gar held up their massive ring and stared into each other's eyes with great love and commitment to one another and their Perez family honor. Patrick and Drew joined hands holding their quartz stone bearing the triple spiral symbol, honoring its journey through four centuries, treasured and protected by their dedicated Campbell ancestors. Penzil placed his hand over the talisman pouch about his neck, which contained a triangular, black fire opal, a gift from his loving parents. Chelli pressed her hand against the moose-hide shaman bag hanging from her shoulder. Loving thoughts of her Grand-Papá raced through her mind.

All were ready.

"Very good!" said Bezen. "We will relocate to the entrance kerbstone of the palace of the gods, winter solstice 3107 BCE Earth, two-hours prior to sunrise. The easiest way to do so is to project your desired destination and timeframe, by thought or intention, into the center of the tree rings as we have practiced. And do so NOW!" Bezen ordered.

The light travelers focused on their intended destination in 3107 BCE. Their brows furrowed with deep concentration. Within seconds, a glowing red aura formed over a hairline slit in Gypsy's core just to the right of them.

"Gypsy has identified your desired time era. Place your feet to either side of the opening forming a line, and place your hands on the shoulders of the one in front of you," Bezen instructed.

With Bezen in front and Mingo behind, Bezen continued her instructions, "Now set your intent to travel, and repeat with me as we have practiced.

> *"Gypsy, this is Drew Megan Campbell,*
> *Patrick Charles Campbell, Chelli 'Little Bear' Freeman,*
> *Penzil Kangaroo, Auben Juan Perez,*
> *Garcia Gou-Drah Perez, Mingo and Bezen.*
> *Hear our petition for transport to the palace of the gods,*
> *Winter Solstice, Earth 3107 BCE, two-hours prior to sunrise!*
> *NOW!"*

Their voices echoed through the snuggery. Eittod was like a nervous father, sending his first-born off to school for the very first time; concern as well as pride stretched across his ancient face.

With expressions of absolute awe and exhilaration on their faces, the light travelers disappeared from Gypsy's core. They felt a slight vibrational pull at their feet, causing them to tighten their grip on the shoulders in front of them for balance, each one feeling the tightened grip of the person behind. A great rush of cold air pressed in on them as if they were being tightly hugged by soft, giant snowmen. Florescent geometric shapes and symbols collided with their vibrating bodies; spiral after spiral drew them downward.

CHAPTER TWENTY-THREE:
Dry Run

In what seemed like only a split second later, the light travelers were safely standing in front of K1, the large entrance stone of the palace of the gods.

Grabbing deep breaths, the teens experienced cold, refreshing air mixed with the sweet fragrance of Scots pine and the aroma of wood fires burning in the distance. The air was indescribable: so pristine, fresh, clean, delicious even, like nothing they had ever breathed before. Intense darkness enveloped them. Their eyes quickly glanced around in the dark for each other's faces. The only light was that of the heavens. The brilliance of the Milky Way spread over the Boyne, mimicking the river's journey east to the Irish Sea, and what seemed like millions of stars twinkled before them. The absolute silence was deafening.

Awe-struck, they were beguiled and enlivened by the reality of their situation and location. Reaching out for each other's hands, they honored the stillness that felt so sacred in that moment. Could they really be fifty-two hundred years from home?

Facing the cairn, their hands reached out for the entrance stone with its engravings of a triple spiral, double-spirals, lozenges, quadrangles and concentric semi-circles. Like scurrying spiders, their fingers rapidly moved around the large, magnificent stone, feeling for its symbols and vibrations, allowing the megalithic art to speak to them.

Drew's hands found the triple spiral symbol, and her heart ached. An image of her parents standing on this very spot at Newgrange waiting for her return flashed through her mind. She closed her eyes and felt her parents holding her tightly and softly speaking to her. Tears slid down her cheeks. Oh, how she missed them. She longed to tell them all that she had learned and of her presence and footprints on the Earth five thousand years in the past.

Patrick, sensing her need, laid a hand on her shoulder and softly whispered, "You'll be home soon enough, Drew. Until then, we all have important work to do – especially you."

She reached out for her great-grandfather's hand – how nurturing was the feel of his hand in hers.

Gentle lapping sounds of the tidal action below reached their ears. Looking into the darkness in the direction of the Boyne, the teens could just make out the final embers of many campfires and silhouettes of primitive tents scattered along the riverbank. Neolithic man had gathered to witness and celebrate his ancestral accomplishment of capturing the triple conjunction of the moon, Venus and the sun's journey into the womb of the palace of the gods. In this womb, on the shortest day of the year, their sun god will be reborn, and the light of day will again begin to lengthen.

Observing the position and declination of the celestial bodies in relation to the horizon site, and using their astronomical studies charts, the teens calculated the time to be about seven o'clock in the morning – roughly two hours before the winter solstice sunrise peaks over Red Mountain. They had precisely relocated from Gypsy to their desired destination and timeframe. They were stunned.

Drew instructed her team to take their appointed positions around the outside circumference of the mound and to await further instructions. Penzil and Drew moved to the left of the cairn, counting kerbstones as they went.

"Found kerbstone 4, Drew, I'll wait for your signal," said Penzil as he placed his hands on the large greywacke stone, mindful of the ancient architect's megalithic engravings on the inner aspect of the stone.

Drew continued her journey around the mound toward the north-west, moving slowly and cautiously in the darkness.

At the same time, Patrick and Chelli moved to the right along the outside of the cairn counting stones as they went.

"Here's K93, I'll see you later," Chelli called to Patrick as he continued his journey toward the north-east, counting the kerbstones backwards from 97 as he went. Chelli placed her hands over the wavy energy field lines carved into the massive stone beneath her grip. She could feel the closeness of her Grand-Papá's spirit in this sacred place – he was with her as he had promised.

Aube and Gar remained at the entrance stone. Aube's hands laid over the triple spiral symbol on the left side of the stone. Gar's hands were over the double spirals on the right. Each was aware of the vague dividing line in the center of the entrance stone, which was aligned with the triple spiral inside the chamber and with the horizon location on the hill of Red Mountain behind them.

Meanwhile, Drew and Patrick, slightly out of breath, met at K52 on the exact opposite side of the glistening mound from Aube and Gar. Their breath was misty in the cold morning air. Drew placed her hands on the right side of the elaborately engraved, colorful stone. It was covered with multiple sets of triangles within upright and inverted, elongated arcs, overlaid with the triple-cup Orion constellation symbol enclosed in four ellipses. Patrick's hands were on the left of the large stone over the triple and double spiral carvings.

Both kerbstones, 1 and 52, had a center line which aligned with the roof box and the exact location of the horizon on Red Mountain to the southeast. The architects and builders of this monument had precisely aligned their creation with the movements of the heavens.

Drew took a long, deep breath, closed her eyes and connected with Gypsy. Through Gypsy, she sent messages to her light travelers gathered around the monument to begin their first phase of preparation. Drew waited.

Having received Drew's instructions through Gypsy, the light travelers began centering, grounding and vibrational breathing; their rhythmic cadence chant played in their heads.

Five minutes later, feeling the powerful combined vibrations of her team, Drew connected with Gypsy again, instructing her team to set their intent to draw stored energy and light through their feet from their army of light in their current Earth time. They all focused, and their vibrating bodies began to glow.

Feeling the upsurge of energy in her own body, Drew once again connected with Gypsy, instructing her team to vibrate, with intention, the kerbstone symbols beneath their hands to begin the decoding sequence. Soon the whole of the palace of the gods began to radiate with a soft fluorescent green hue. The carved symbols on the giant kerbstones glowed and stood inches out from the stone surfaces. Bezen and Mingo looked on with great pride.

Amazed at the sight before them, the light travelers realized this was no longer a game – this power is *real – very real!*

After several minutes, Drew sent out the message to slowly power down their bodies and to return to the entrance stone. Phase one of the dry run was completed.

As they appeared out of the darkness, they were vibrant, wide-eyed and still glowing slightly. Bezen and Mingo were there to cheer them on.

"We're only half way there," Drew reminded them, "retrieve your water."

Quickly, the teens removed their tanned leather water pouches from their survival packs and took long drinks.

"Remember, Eittod stressed how important it is for us to stay hydrated and grounded during this journey," said Chelli. "And remember to stay steady to the center of the passage."

"Drew, why all the emphasis on us staying steady to the center of the passage?" asked Penzil. "I don't understand."

"Neither do any of us, Penzil. But, those are Eittod's orders, and we will obey our elder, got it?"

"Got it, Drew!" everyone shouted.

"Let's move inside the mound to complete phase two of our dry run preparations," said Drew. "The moon and Venus will soon be rising over Red Mountain."

They carefully moved past K1 and stepped into the passage way. Eittod's reason for staying steady to the center of the passage became obviously clear. Both sides of the passage were lined with fresh boughs of evergreens – Scots pine, spruce, arbutus, yew and holly. The combined fragrance was intoxicating.

"It smells like Christmas in here!" said Aube. "Oh, how I love that smell. It fills me with such joy and peace."

"What a great surprise!" said Patrick. "Thank you, Eittod!" he called into the passage.

They all laughed as it echoed back.

The light travelers carefully moved along the earthen floor, staying steady to the center of the dark passage as they had practiced many times over the past two weeks. Their hands reached out for the familiar orthostats, counting as they moved and stopping to feel the vibrations of the carved stones on the right and left sides of the passage. As they did, amazing images moved rapidly through their heads: strange places, massive art work and new faces – beautiful faces who called them by strange names. The megalithic art had taken on a whole new dimension of information for them.

Eittod had not told his light travelers what to expect as they moved through their dry run preparations. He felt they were advanced enough to handle all the new and exciting experiences that this first journey to the past held for them.

They arrived at the center of the chamber, feeling around in the dark for their assigned places near the obelisk. Their fingertips were aware of the feel of each inch of stone. Above them was the corbelled ceiling, its opening rose-like image hidden in the darkness. Holding hands around the circle with their backs to the obelisk, Drew stood facing due north at the cardinal compass point zero/three hundred sixty degrees, Patrick faced due east at ninety degrees, Penzil due south at one hundred eighty degrees and Chelli faced due west at two hundred seventy degrees. Standing next to Drew, Aube fixed his intent on the center of the universe above, and Gar's intent was focused on the core of the Earth roughly four thousand miles below his feet.

"Send out your intent to connect us with the six directions, NOW!" Drew instructed.

When they did, the three-foot high stone obelisk in the center of the chamber began to hum as if it had just been plugged into an ancient electrical outlet. It was as if something or someone knew they were there. The teens turned around to face each other, their eyes wide, and their expressions full of wonderment. How blessed they all felt to have been chosen to serve mankind in this way. Who would ever believe what they are doing? But then, how much of what they are doing will they even remember?

"This is as far as we go today," Drew reluctantly reminded her fellow travelers. "We must wait a bit longer to complete the ancient sequence that will unlock the archaic code of the gods – that's for another day," she sighed. "Everyone did so well. All those hours of practice have served us today. But for now, we'll go to the entrance stone area to observe the rising of the crescent moon and the planet Venus over the hill of Red Mountain."

One by one, Drew's light travelers slowly made their way from the dark chamber through the fragrant evergreen-lined passage, emerging from the entrance opening beneath the roof box. Below, Neolithic man had awakened and could be seen mulling about, stoking his fires and preparing for his special day of celebration.

Inside the mound, Drew stood in a reverie, alone with her beloved Newgrange of fifty-two hundred years ago. Oh, how she wanted to complete the sequence, decipher the ancient code and unlock the secret of the gods. But today was only to be a dry run – a test run – *but why?*

Suddenly before her eyes, she witnessed the light travelers coming back through the passage toward the center chamber – their radiant bodies filling the whole of the palace with their light. Each stone in the passage and chambers was now glowing – the carvings were almost lifelike, radiating and vibrating out many inches from the stones. The palace of the gods was alive.

Drew called to them to power down and to return to the entrance. They continued toward her. Alarmed, she reached out to halt Penzil, but her hand went right through his chest as if he were a ghost. More startling, Drew came face to face with her own glowing image.

"What's happening?" she cried out. "What's going on, Gypsy?" she demanded as the light travelers walked right through her.

Confused, Drew watched as they moved into the chamber and faced their assigned directions around the obelisk - north, south, east, west, above and below. Drew's glowing and vibrating image gave the order to connect with the six directions.

"Drew, you are fine," answered Gypsy. "You are seeing your light travelers and yourself in your future when you *do* complete the sequence. Drew, Eittod requests that you leave the chamber immediately."

Drew considered Gypsy's response. "How absolutely bizarre to be seeing myself, sometime in my future on the exact same day and time, in my present experience," she whispered aloud to herself, struggling to comprehend. Then comprehension: *If I understand correctly what's happening, then I could stay and observe what happens when the sequence is completed.*

Again Gypsy spoke, this time more firmly, "Drew Megan Campbell, Eittod has instructed you to leave the chamber. NOW!"

Drew's passion for this journey pulled hard at her. She wanted to stay. She wanted to observe. After all, this is what she was born to do! Why must she leave now?

As Drew anxiously observed, the light travelers connected with the six directions. She saw beams of light streaming from Patrick, Penzil, Chelli and her own brow as they connected with their assigned directions. Light was shooting straight up from the top of Aube's head into the corbelled ceiling. Light glowed all around Gar's feet as he connected with the Earth – the obelisk hummed.

Drew was sure that if she were observing from the outside of the mound, she would see spokes of intense light shooting out from the mound reflecting in the milky white quartz cairn.

Beautiful grids of iridescent light began to form around each traveler's body from above their heads to below their feet. And small beads of crystalline rainbow light raced along each grid line as if busily delivering messages to all the cells of their multi-dimensional bodies. "I am seeing their DNA!" Drew whispered in disbelief. "How could that be?"

She could feel heat and vibrations emanating from the white quartz stone in her pocket. It was as if her triple spiral stone knew it had a job to do as well. With her powerful mind focused on the sequence and the unbelievable scene playing out before her, the excitement of what was to happen next soared within her. Suddenly, a strong tremor moved through the palace of the gods. Drew braced herself against an orthostat.

"What's happening, Gypsy?" she asked with alarm in her voice.

Then something or someone grabbed hard at her, forcefully dragging her into the passageway. Uncertain of what was happening, Drew fought back.

"No, Drew! No! You must come with me. Now!" said a commanding voice.

Torn from her reverie, Drew found herself being swiftly pulled through the dark passage, stumbling as she went, and out into the early morning air where Patrick let go of his vice grip on her. Everyone was staring at her with shocked expressions. The realization of what she had done impacted Drew.

"What have I done? I have disobeyed Eittod," Drew cried.

With her hands covering her face, Drew buried her head into Bezen's embrace. Shame and guilt ripped at her.

"Drew, we understand your passion, your drive. That's part of the reason Eittod chose you," said Bezen, "and why the Regions agreed to your serving as leader. We understand your love and dedication to this journey, to this place and to mankind. And they understand your desire to get on with it, rather than do this dry run. But Eittod has his reasons, and they must be respected and obeyed."

The other teens were around Drew and Bezen, stroking Drew's copper curls, lovingly consoling her and becoming part of the embrace.

"I didn't want to leave either, Drew," said Penzil. "I'd like to get on with it as well. I think we all would. But Eittod knows what's best for us. We all understand, mate."

Bezen whispered something into Drew's ear. Drew raised her head to see a procession of light snaking its way up from the river toward the mound. In the darkness, the honking of whooper swans and the sounds of large wings beating hard against the early morning air could be heard. Neolithic man made his way up the hill toward the palace entrance. He had come to honor his deities – his celestial gods of the heavens: the sun, the moon and Venus, and his earthly immortal gods: the Tuatha dé Danann who traverse the other world through the palace of the gods.

With small torches in hand, Stone Age man formed a semi-circle many layers deep in front of the great cairn – men and women with infants in arms and children in hand. In their arms, some cradled gifts of hand-crafted leather, bone, stone, reeds and fur, lovingly created for their gods. Others carried reed baskets filled with food and flora; still others bore tools of fine wood and polished stone. Staring at the entrance, they stood in silence as if waiting for something or someone to greet them.

To the teens' astonishment, three beautiful beings of light and perfection emerged from the passage; their garments, of what appeared to be fine silks, rippled gently in the morning breeze. They held bejeweled scepters of gold and silver in their hands, and diadems of tiny multi-colored moving lights graced their golden hair. Their feet barely touched the ground; their fair-skinned faces and crystal blue eyes glowed in the torch light.

"Bezen, who are those radiant beings?" whispered Chelli in awe.

"Those are the gods and creators of the palaces of the Bend of the Boyne," said Bezen. "Other-worldly and immortal, they are the architects, mathematicians, physicists, engineers, surveyors astronomers and master builders of these earthly estates. The efforts of ancient man were vital in the construction of these marvels."

Neolithic man knelt and bowed their heads low to honor their gods. Their rough exterior softened in the gods' presence. No words were spoken. Rays of iridescent light emanated from the eyes, mouths and hands of their gods, filling each worshipper with radiance. Golden tetrahedrons formed over the head of each man, woman and child, spun rapidly for several seconds, then disappeared as quickly as they had appeared. Thousands of translucent orbs – some the size of tennis balls – floated around, through and over the gathering. The sacredness of the moment felt palpable. Time stood still.

The older of the gods raised his scepter and a huge, steaming caldron appeared well off to the side of the entrance stone. The smell of a fine brew wafted in the crisp air – a gift from the Tuatha dé Danann for their people. Then as they returned to their palace of stone, the gods motioned for Neolithic man to enter. Slowly and reverently, a small group rose from their knees and followed, carrying their gifts into the passage. Others placed their gifts on the ground to the sides of the entrance. They then returned to the semi-circle, taking their seats on the cold ground, to witness the movement of their celestial gods over the horizon on Red Mountain to the southeast.

As the gods retreated, one caught Drew's eye. The radiant being looked right into her, and a slight smile washed across his youthful, illuminated face.

Astonished, Drew gasped. "He sees me!" she whispered to Bezen.

"Yes, I know," Bezen whispered back as she squeezed Drew's hand. "They all see you and your fellow travelers as well. They know who you are and why you are here."

CHAPTER TWENTY-FOUR:
Triple Conjunction

Eight o'clock approached. The crescent moon, followed moments later by Venus, the 'morning star,' would soon travel across the Boyne to peek through the aperture of the roof box. According to folklore and confirmed by astronomers, Venus made its appearance into the passage every eight years at the winter solstice.

The light travelers made their way back into the central chamber to join Neolithic man. The journey of the moon and Venus across the sky heralded the coming of the sun god. How infinitely precise was the alignment created by the architects and astronomers of the palace of the gods! Their desire to capture this precise moment in time was realized.

Drew quickly glanced around for images of her team completing the archaic sequence, but saw only the faint images of Stone Age man as he huddled together on the floor of the chamber to witness the glorious light show through the palace aperture. Everyone was mesmerized as they peered down the passageway and out through the roof box to witness the triple conjunction accomplishment of their gods and ancestors. The beautiful beings of light were nowhere to be seen.

In the back and side recesses off the central chamber, Neolithic man's gifts filled and overflowed large stone basins onto the earthen floor. A small, natural stream of water trickled from between two orthostats in the passageway just off the center chamber and gathered in a goat-skinned pouch, much like a small trough. Taking turns, Stone Age man's welcoming hands scooped up small amounts of the cold, pure, sacred water onto his palate – a gift of purification from his gods. Ever so slowly, the glow of the moon and Venus made their exits from the chamber.

"We have about half of an hour to wait for the sun's grand entrance into the chamber," whispered Drew in awe.

Again they moved slowly through the passage and out to witness the sun god's yearly performance, being careful not to disturb the fragrant greens lining the orthostats. They took deep breaths of the holiday fragrance as they passed the evergreens.

Those huddled on the hillside sat in great anticipation of their celestial god's appearance and rebirth in the womb of the palace of the gods on the shortest day of the year. Everyone was caught up in the majestic performance of the celestial bodies of the triple conjunction – the moon, Venus, and soon the sun god.

The teens, Mingo and Bezen pulled their leather and fur wraps tighter around them as they sat huddled together against the entrance kerbstone in the cold morning air, waiting for sunrise. As twilight eased in, many wood-framed skin boats could be seen dotting the shoreline of the Boyne.

"Bezen, please tell us more about the ancient gods of Ireland," asked Aube.

"Well, according to Irish mythology, the ancient gods, some of whom you witnessed this morning, are a semi-divine race who arrived in the mountains to the west sometime after the last ice age and around the time of a great flood. Their arrival was quite dramatic. The Tuatha dé Danann descended from the clouds, causing an eclipse which darkened the skies for three days. Their powers are of life, warmth and light. Tuatha dé Danann means 'the race of the gods of Danu.' Danu was the mother of all the gods of Erin. These immortal, supreme beings brought many mysterious and other-worldly gifts with them. One such gift is the great stone caldron that stands before us now," said Bezen. "It can feed hundreds upon hundreds – its gift of nourishment is endless."

"You said *one* of the gifts was the caldron. What were the other gifts, Bezen?" asked Penzil.

"Well, the most famous tangible gifts, and the ones most written about, included the Stone of Destiny, a sword and a spear. Other gifts, which you saw being given today, are far greater and more powerful. They are the sacred gifts of healing, wisdom and knowledge," said Bezen.

"I saw and felt the gifts of healing that came from their eyes, mouths and hands. My body was tingling all over. And I felt great warmth all around me, like I was being cocooned," said Gar. Aube quickly nodded in agreement.

"Yes, I felt that as well," said Chelli. "And I saw the gifts of knowledge and wisdom being given in the form of sacred geometry – the spinning tetrahedrons," said Chelli. "My Grand-Papá spoke of the great powers of the sacred symbols, and we light travelers journeyed to the outpost and to here through their vibrations. Is that correct, Bezen?" Chelli asked.

"That is correct, Chelli. The sacred symbols do hold great power. The ancient gods used the tetrahedrons to transfer knowledge and wisdom into Neolithic man's DNA. Remember, according to your current day anthropologists, it was a time in history when there was a quantum leap in mankind's knowledge," said Bezen. "It was a gift from their gods who needed stone age man's help to build their great temples and astronomical centers around the world. The gods came to the Earth to map out and study the Milky Way Galaxy, its planets and resources, and what they left behind is still of great mystery. Their unimaginable gifts continue to manifest in human kind today. Know that they were not the first visitors to do so, nor will they be the last. There is much left behind, on the earth, within the earth and under the seas, that mankind has yet to discover and understand. Areas that were once oceans are now dry land, and what were deserts are now oceans. What were tropical regions are now buried under the great poles. And the cycle of change and renewal continues. Our Milky Way Galaxy has been visited many times since its formation. Do you think we are the only ones in the ONE, the ABSOLUTE's, grand creation plan?" said Bezen.

The light travelers were awestruck by the information being imparted to them, and it all made sense. *"When TRUTH is spoken, it resonates in the soul as such,"* Eittod had told them.

"Please tell us more, Bezen," pleaded Drew, enthralled.

"I believe that is quite enough for you to chew on today," Bezen laughed. "Your enthusiasm for knowledge is so delightful. And believe me, there is more we have to share with you, but for another day. We have company," said Bezen pointing toward the southeast.

A fiery glow had just appeared from behind the hill of Red Mountain. The sun god had awakened. It was just shortly before nine o'clock. The horizon was a blaze of burnt orange and golden rays, fusing the heavens and the earth together. For a few brief, spectacular moments they were one, and time was cosmic, sacred, eternal.

Neolithic man now stood on the hillside in awe, with arms raised to the heavens, calling out greetings to their god of daylight and warmth. The children were jumping up and down and hugging each other, pointing at the gold and orange sky. They watched with great jubilation as their sun god journeyed slowly across the Boyne Valley, spreading its light and warmth on them. Then it made its journey into the roof box and passage entrance for rebirth in the womb of the palace of the gods. The golden and orange radiance of the edifice was spectacular. It was as if the palace itself were on fire.

With great anticipation, the light travelers once again made their way into the passage, following the sun's rays. Again the stone carvings glowed – only this time with greater intensity. The whole of the chamber vibrated as the sun god moved slowly and purposefully across each orthostat and onto the triple spiral symbol. As it did, within the chamber Stone Age man rose to his feet in celebration of the rebirth of his celestial god and the lengthening of the days to come. Stone Age man had come as witnesses, reverently following the intense beam of golden light and warmth, and chanting as the sun's rays slowly moved from the back chamber and along the right side of the orthostats. Their sun god's journey through the womb of the palace of the gods would last only seventeen brief minutes.

The light travelers felt the absolute sacredness of the sun's journey through the ancient site. The awe and reverence of Neolithic man for his gods was tangible, moving, holy.

The teens were touched to the most fragile fibers of their being – to the very depth of their souls.

Slowly, Neolithic man emerged from the passageway, ready for a day of celebration and feasting. The light travelers followed in their wake as they breathed in the intoxicating fragrances of the gifts of flora which lay at their feet. As they emerged from the passage, Mingo and Bezen were there to greet them.

"Quite an experience? Your glowing faces tell it all," said Bezen smiling.

"I never imagined I would ever have the privilege to witness the winter solstice from *inside* the chamber, let alone the triple conjunction – especially alongside Neolithic man," said Drew. "It was more beautiful and moving then I could ever have imagined. I can't wait to tell Mum and Dad." As she said the words, she wondered if she would even remember having experienced it.

"We leave for the outpost soon," said Bezen. "If you wish to retrace some of your preparation in the daylight, do so promptly."

The light travelers once again took their positions around the great cairn, studying their routes and pacing their steps into the dark fragrant chamber. Each knew the vibrations of every stone, the meaning of every carving. While in the center chamber, Drew shared with them her earlier experience and how captivating it was – how their radiant bodies lit up the whole of the passageway and chambers, how they walked right through her, the intensity of the light shooting from their bodies into the six directions, and of having witnessed their DNA in action.

"I am sorry I had to drag you out so forcefully, Drew," said Patrick. "But it was Eittod's command. You have never disobeyed him before. We were all stunned at your actions. But now that you have shared your experience, we understand your actions. I am sure none of us could have turned our back on that experience," he finished with a hug for his great-granddaughter.

All were in agreement.

"Thank you, Grand. I needed to hear that from you. I feel so guilty for my actions. At least I know you still love me and can understand what held me so fast this morning," said Drew with moist eyes.

"Drew, your hand really went right through my chest, and we walked right through you?" asked Penzil. "Now, how awesome is that!"

Everyone laughed and had a group hug with the dearest friends they had ever known – friends they completely trusted with their lives, no matter what.

Gypsy spoke to them in their heads, "Bezen is waiting to bring you home. Please return to the entrance stone for transport. Great job! See you soon."

They could hear her melodious sounds in their heads and could smell her spicy fragrance. Gypsy meant home to them in this far off land of 3107 BCE.

The light travelers slowly made their way to the entrance where Mingo and Bezen were waiting.

"Look at Neolithic man celebrating the victory of his gods," said Bezen, pointing toward the Boyne.

As they looked toward the river, they could see many blazing fires licking up at spits of roasting meats. Women were busy with feast preparations and children ran and laughed through the high, browned grasses. Men were ladling hot brew from the cauldron into stone vessels for transport to the feasting area near the river's edge. A newborn's squall could be heard in the distance. A new life had just emerged.

"Well, it's time to travel home, dear ones. Gypsy will get us there safely. As we have discussed, your travel back to the outpost will be similar to your tree ring departure, but you will be moving up and out of linear time. We will depart from the entrance stone," said Bezen.

Everyone gathered around the stone, holding hands and waiting for Bezen's instructions.

"Now, set your intent to travel, and repeat with me," said Bezen.

"Gypsy, this is Drew Megan Campbell,
Patrick Charles Campbell, Chelli 'Little Bear' Freeman,
Penzil Kangaroo, Auben Juan Perez,
Garcia Gou-Drah Perez, Mingo and Bezen.
Hear our petition for transport to Outpost Gypsy Tree!
NOW!"

They could feel a slight tingling and vibrational pull at the top of their heads, and a great rush of cold air again pressed in on them like soft snowmen. The familiar green florescent geometric shapes and symbols collided with their vibrating bodies, and spiral after spiral drew them upward. Within what seemed like only seconds they could feel their bodies compress and ease through a small slit in Gypsy's tree rings. They were home.

CHAPTER TWENTY-FIVE:
Home to the Outpost

Eittod was overjoyed to see them and greeted his light travelers with open arms. The teens rushed to him, and excited chatter ensued. Drew hung back in hesitation. Shame pinked her face. Eittod greeted them all individually with a big hug, praise and admiration for their role in the journey. When he reached Drew, she lowered her head in expectation of his disapproval.

"Oh, my dear Drew, how proud I am of you. The Regions Authority and I want to congratulate you and thank you on a job well done," said Eittod as he reached to lift her head, a loving expression on his colorful face.

"But...but...I disobeyed you, Sir. I disobeyed you *twice!* I am so sorry and ashamed of my actions. Please forgive me, Eittod," said Drew, tears now rapidly sliding down her pinked cheeks.

Eittod reached a hand out to wipe away her tears. "All is forgiven, my dear. We understand your passion for this journey. And we feel you have learned a very valuable lesson from your mistake. Have you not?" he asked.

"Oh, yes, Sir. I let myself become mesmerized by my desire to experience the completion of the sequence – the unlocking of the archaic code. I put my own desires above those of the mission itself. And for that I am truly sorry."

"As I have said, you are forgiven, Drew. In fact, neither the Regions nor I were aware of just how advanced your gift of multi-dimensional sight had become. For you to have been able to view yourself and your team from an overlay, or twin dimension, is quite extraordinary. You are a courageous leader. You instructed your team well and followed the sequence as you were instructed. Your connection with Gypsy was powerful, and your commands were relayed accurately. We could not have asked for more of you," he finished with a big smile.

Drew threw her arms around Eittod and hugged him dearly.

"Eittod, I promise I will not disappoint you again. Thank you and the Regions for trusting me and my fellow light travelers with this amazing journey to bring the light of the ONE, the ABSOLUTE, into the Earth once more," said Drew. "And I now understand the importance of the dry run, Sir."

With that statement, all the light travelers were around Drew and Eittod.

"It is time for a celebration, Bezen. I believe a feast is in order," said Eittod with a jovial lilt in his voice and a very big smile on his proud face.

"I agree!" said Bezen.

"Me, too!" chimed in Mingo. "I am starved. After all, I haven't eaten in fifty-one hundred years!"

The teens laughed in agreement.

With a nod of Bezen's head, a feast fit for a king was spread out on the large stone table in front of them. In the middle of the feast was a small caldron – a miniature of the one the god's had given Neolithic man – and its enticing aroma filled the snuggery. It was a fitting gift from the Regions in honor of their dry run journey.

After much celebration and debriefing, Eittod called them all to attention.

"Dear ones, your bodies, minds and spirits need nurturing, and not just with food. The journey to 3107 BCE and your entry into and out of linear time were very demanding on you. Plus, you need time with each other to process your experiences. Some time together in your domicile activity arena will serve you well. With much gratitude, I dismiss you," said Eittod with a reverent bow of his head.

After a stop at the costuming station and equipment center to turn in their gear, they made their way to their domicile via the transport chamber. Exhaustion began to set in.

"I am beginning to feel really tired," said Chelli.

"Me too, mate," said Penzil.

"The warm vibrational pool is going to feel good. I am still chilled to the bone from the early morning cold at the palace and from the travel to and from 3107 BCE," said Patrick.

"I agree! Being hugged by ice cold air was a really weird feeling. Remember, we're from South America. We don't do frigid air in Lima," said Gar with a chuckle in his voice.

Soon they were all in bathing attire, floating in the blue waters of the vibrational pool. Gypsy's nurturing sounds and aroma surrounded them. Everyone breathed sighs of relief as their bodies relaxed and absorbed the warmth and gentle massaging action of the vibrations.

"Welcome home, everybody. Great job!" Gypsy whispered.

"Thank you, Gypsy, for being with us for the dry run," said Drew.

"And for bringing us home safe and sound!" said Chelli.

"Yes, thank you, Gypsy! You're the best!" they all shouted with great and genuine enthusiasm. Their appreciative voices echoed throughout the activity arena.

"You are very welcome, my children of the Earth," she responded.

In those statements, they could feel Gypsy's love for them, and she could feel their true love for her. No further words were needed.

"This has been such an incredible day. Can you believe what we did today, and where we traveled to?" said Drew. "It's absolutely mind-boggling."

"I am so afraid I will wake up at my Uncle Titus' fish camp and find that I have gone nowhere!" lamented Chelli.

"What excites me is that we get to go back! I wonder how long we'll have to wait?" questioned Aube. "What an amazing feeling to have light coming out of the top of my head. And you witnessed it, Drew. How wondrous is that?"

"What's more wondrous," said Drew "is that one of the gods looked right into my eyes. I quickly whispered to Bezen, *'he sees me,'* and she squeezed my hand and whispered back, *'Yes, I know. They all see you and your fellow travelers as well. They know who you are and why you are here.'*"

All the light travelers gasped.

"They know who we are and why we were there!" cried Chelli. "What does that mean, Drew?"

"I don't really know. Other than they might be a part of our journey back," said Drew.

"Did you tell Eittod?" asked Penzil.

"No, I didn't think about it until just now. So much has happened today, and some of those experiences are just coming back to my memory," said Drew.

"I am sure Bezen has told him by now," injected Patrick.

"Which of the gods was it, mate?" asked Penzil.

"The young one," said Drew.

"Ahhh!" said Chelli with a grin on her face.

"Well he certainly has good taste and knows a beautiful Irish lass when he sees one," said Patrick. "But, he'll have to get my permission before any courting goes on."

They all laughed. And a splashing party ensued.

After a good night's sleep, the teens met in the domicile feasting nook looking quite refreshed. Bezen had outdone herself with a hardy, rib-sticking breakfast that included lots of goodies from home. There were piles of Maria Perez's tamales; Meg Campbell's bacon rashers, eggs, toast and gingerbread cookies; and Uncle Titus Freeman's smoked salmon. You name it, it was there.

"Wow!" Aube shouted. "How will we ever exercise after this huge meal?"

"Well according to Eittod, you have earned a day off, which means lots of goodies, lots of fun and no need to meet with Mingo for exercising. In fact, after breakfast Eittod and Mingo have a nice surprise for you. You can meet them in front of Gypsy. Eat up!" said Bezen, and she was gone.

Gar just shook his head, causing everyone to laugh.

"Thought we were past that stage, mate?" laughed Penzil.

"Just habit, I guess," smiled Gar. "And I figured you'd be expecting that response, little brother, and I didn't want to let you down."

Penzil beamed. He now had two big brothers.

Once larva tummies were full, the teens made their way through the encampment, past the archways and across the bridge to Gypsy. Eittod's hologram and Mingo were waiting for them with big smiles on their faces.

"You were remarkable yesterday. I am so proud of you. Bravo!" said Eittod, clapping his hands exuberantly. "So the Regions, Mingo and I have chosen a very special surprise for you. We know yesterday was a very wonderful but cold experience for you, so this should help warm you up some."

They followed Eittod and Mingo around to the opposite side of Gypsy's huge base. Eittod had a very impish grin on his joyful face. He loved to surprise them.

"Now close your eyes good and tight," he said.

The faint smell of salt caught their nostrils, and the sound of many birds caressed their ears.

"Now open them," he said.

The teens couldn't believe their eyes.

"Holy Christmas!" said Gar.

"Mates, my eyes must be deceiving me," cried Penzil. "Is that really an ocean?"

There in front of them was an ocean with waves splashing upon the shore; and a glistening white sand beach spread out as far as the eye could see. Tall sea grasses along the high sand dunes gently waved in the warm morning breezes. Just off shore, dolphins played in the crystal blue waters, and whale spouts could be seen further out. Overhead, squadrons of great white pelicans flew gracefully in formation along the shoreline. They periodically dipped down with their long beaks to scoop up prey in their large throat pouches, then continued their journey. Along the shore, small sea birds were scavenging, and large grey and white seagulls filled the sky.

"My dear ones, this ocean has been here for eons. It just hasn't been made visible to your eyes until today. Remember, you are in the eternal now, so everything is available and possible. Enjoy your day at the beach. You have earned it," said Eittod as his colorful hologram vanished.

"Can you believe this?" said Chelli.

"Let's get wet!" shouted Aube as he and Gar made quick nods of their heads and were suited up, ready to plunge.

As they all ran through the soft sand and into the depths of the water, dolphins surrounded them on all sides, ready for play.

"I've never seen a real dolphin before, mates," said Penzil, cautiously reaching his ebony hands out to touch one that was rubbing up against him. "This is amazing. Their skin is so smooth, slick and soft, and they are so big, yet so gentle, mates." Penzil's eyes got big as saucers as a mammal many times his size gently nudged at him.

"Yes, they are very loving and gentle," said Mingo. "The people of the Earth in your time are finally becoming aware of the great value of the dolphins, porpoises and whales – the family Cetacean. Your International Whaling Commission has established a global moratorium to protect them.

Your oceans, seas, rivers, lakes and tributaries are encoded with the history of the Earth and the evolution of mankind. It's in every molecule of water on your planet. The Cetaceans live in those waters and have access to that valuable information. And they can transfer it to your DNA – they are living libraries. They serve as the life force balance for your planet," he finished.

"Mingo, I have read of people who, after swimming with dolphins or whale watching, have had major transformations in their lives," said Drew. "Now I understand what was happening for them, or to them. What a gift to have received," she said with awe in her voice.

"Dear Drew, you are receiving those very gifts right at this moment. Don't you realize that? They are preparing all of you for the next level of your journey," he said.

They all gasped with wonder.

"That is why Eittod and the Regions chose for you to be in their presence today, light travelers," said Mingo. "Well, that's enough information for today. Let's have some fun!"

Hours later, Chelli and Drew were getting back from gathering shells. And Mingo and the others were stretched out on beach towels, just waking from naps.

Sitting next to a large sand castle that looked a lot like Newgrange was an enormous picnic basket, and the aroma wafting out smelt delicious.

"Ah! Mother has sent us some lunch!" said Mingo.

Chelli and Drew opened the basket and found fresh cold water, lemonade, juices, fruits, breads, hard eggs and cheeses of all kinds.

"How wonderful!" said Drew "And here's a checkered cloth for us to spread it out on. Bezen thinks of everything."

Soon Mingo and the teens had eaten their fill and were enjoying each other's company and conversation.

"Chelli, yesterday you said you were afraid you would wake up at your uncle's fish camp. Is that where you were when Eittod called you to serve?" asked Drew.

"Yes. I spend my summers with my Uncle Titus and Aunt Susan. There on the Yukon River I am called by my Athabascan name, 'Little Bear.' You tasted some of my uncle's smoked salmon this morning at breakfast. It's the best fish you'll ever put in your mouth. Speaking of fish," said Chelli, "let's get back into that glorious ocean."

"I sure could use some more of that Cetacean healing and DNA enhancement," said Penzil. "I think I am getting addicted to it," he finished with a very big happy smile.

"Look!" whispered Aube pointing toward the sand dunes. "Isn't that the scumdiggalie Lancelot watching us?"

"Sure is Aube, but he's not spying on you. He comes here quite often," whispered Mingo. "I think he can feel the love and the healing coming from the Cetaceans."

As they glanced toward the ocean, several dolphins were up on their powerful tails, moving backwards across the gentle waves and making clicking sounds as if communicating with Lancelot. And just at that moment one of the whales breached high into the air, landing on its back with a tremendous splash.

"I think they're talking to each other," whispered Patrick.

"I think you're right," said Mingo.

"I wonder if coming to the ocean is the reason Lancelot's heart has grown in size, mate," said Penzil.

"I wonder," said Mingo, with a knowing expression.

CHAPTER TWENTY-SIX:
Little Bear's Invitation

The light travelers' well-deserved day of rest and renewal of body, mind and spirit was coming to a close. For a non-working day, they were all looking forward to a good night's rest. Seems the light travelers play just as hard as they work!

After their usual good night huddle, they headed off to the golden discs for passage to their private sleeping chambers. "Good night," they called to each other as they set their intent and disappeared from the discs.

As Chelli eased into her pillows, images of her uncle's fish camp and Eittod's invitation to the outpost swirled in her drowsy head as dreamtime carried her off.

"That's it, Little Bear, keep us steady! The current is strong today, girl!" he shouted. "We don't want to lose these fish."

Uncle Titus straddled himself between the birch bark canoe and the fish wheel pontoon as the river current rotated the large net baskets on the fish wheel's axle. As the wheel turned, it scooped up salmon swimming upstream to spawn and dropped them into the slanted chute leading to the holding box. Knowing the importance of his instructions, Chelli pulled the ropes tighter to steady her canoe against the wooden pontoon while her uncle unloaded the salmon from the fish holding box. She loved the feel of the wet, cold fish slapping against her bare legs as the canoe filled with their mid-morning catch.

At only fourteen-years old, Chelli "Little Bear" Freeman is as strong as any man in camp and likes to prove it. Summers at her uncle's fish camp on the Yukon River in Alaska's Interior envelope her in the traditional customs of her beloved Athabascan heritage.

Uncle Titus and Chelli gut and clean their fresh catch at the river's edge saving the egg sacs, and then haul the cleaned salmon to the cutting tables nearby. Alongside other family members, Chelli helps to fillet and cut the fish into long strips. There is a constant parade of younger siblings and cousins hauling large buckets of river water to the cutting tables for washing the fillets, knives and hands. Next, the salmon strips are dipped into the Freeman family's secret salt brine recipe and hung on the covered drying racks for several days. Once dry, the strips are moved to the smokehouse for two to three weeks of smoking over a constantly burning cottonwood fire.

With twenty hours of Alaskan daylight, work went on around the clock at the fish camp, either fishing, cleaning, cutting, hauling water, hanging strips or tending the fires. Siblings, uncles, aunts, cousins, parents and grandparents worked side by side during the long-awaited weeks of the salmon run.

"Little Bear, you need some rest. You've been working hard for many hours," said her Uncle Titus as he made his way back toward the river. "Go sleep, girl. I'll come for you in a few hours for another run."

Chelli didn't argue. She knew she was spent. "Thank you, Uncle Titus," she called after him. As she slowly walked along the narrow path toward her stilted cabin, she heard her great-grandfather's voice calling to her. Startled, she followed the sound into the woods. The deeper she went, the stronger his voice became.

"I am coming, Grand-Papá, I am coming," she called to him as she continued her journey toward his voice.

Finally as she moved into a clearing, she saw his image sitting cross-legged in front of a small campfire. The smoke curled up into the trees with a wonderful smell.

"Sit with me, Little Bear," he said, motioning to her from across the fire. "We must talk." Radiance surrounded him. His body was translucent – angelic-like.

Befitting an Athabascan shaman, he was dressed in brightly colored ceremonial regalia from head to toe. His elaborate headdress of tanned moose hide was covered in intricate beadwork and feathers. His foot and leg wear was suede–like, covered with elegant stitching and wildflower beaded designs. To the Dena'ina people, their shaman was a meditator and healer who connected their natural world with the spirit world.

Dumbstruck, Chelli was unable to speak and did as he requested. Without taking her eyes from her Grand-Papá's image, she, too, sat cross-legged on the ground, across the fire from his radiant presence. Her heart pounded hard against her ribs; she could feel her blood racing wildly through her vessels. She was light-headed, mesmerized, exhilarated. It was surreal.

He spoke. "Our Dena'ina people have been called upon to serve mankind in a very special way. You, Little Bear, have been chosen by our Great Spirit father to represent us. Your pleas for peace and love in your world have been heard, and today answered. Remember as promised, I am always with you, Little Bear, and watch over you from Brooks Mountain."

When Chelli finally opened her mouth to speak, smoke swirled around her, blinding her.

And he was gone.

She had not had the opportunity to speak to the man she revered, truly missed and loved so dearly. She wept.

Had her experience been real? Or was she so tired that her mind was playing tricks on her? Sitting alone in the clearing where her dear Grand-Papá had been only seconds ago, she noticed a small scroll of tanned deer hide lying where his fire had been. As she unrolled the small scroll, confirming words met her moist eyes.

Dear One:

Your silent pleas for peace and love in your world have been heard, and today, your pure heart has answered the call of Eittod. Thank you!

You, Chelli "Little Bear" Freeman, are invited to travel to Outpost Gypsy Tree for your instructions and assignment whenever you so choose to depart. There is no need to pack, except for your shaman pouch; all other needs will be met on this end. You will be moving out of the illusion of time so will not lose a moment of your linear time; hence, no need for a note to your family. All questions will be answered upon your arrival here. Whenever you desire to return to your precise split second in time, the departure passwords will be given to you. Remember, you have free will and your choices are always honored. When and if you are ready to travel, simply repeat the following transport passwords out loud.

"A peaceful, loving world is what I seek within my heart,
And I am willing to clear the way for it to happen.

I am part of the solution.
I am the solution!
I am chosen.
Eittod, this is Chelli 'Little Bear' Freeman.
Hear my petition for transport to Outpost Gypsy Tree!
NOW!"

Honorably yours,
Eittod of Tulsun Minor
Ambassador to the Regions Authority
Outpost Gypsy Tree

It was real. She had *not* imagined it. Her Grand-Papá *had* spoken to her and *had* entrusted her to represent the Dena'ina people.

Excited beyond words, Chelli ran back through the woods to her cabin. Her mind was racing with the idea of travel, of moving out of linear time, of having been chosen to represent her people, of having the opportunity to bring love and peace into her world. And she, Chelli "Little Bear" Freeman, was ready – more than ready.

Reaching her stilted cabin and out of breath, she climbed the wooden ladder. Quickly, she scooped up her colorful beaded shaman pouch, slung the strap over her head and opened the scroll to recite her passwords to adventure.

"A peaceful, loving world is what I seek within my heart,
And I am willing to clear the way for it to happen.
I am part of the solution.
I am the solution!
I am chosen.
Eittod, this is Chelli 'Little Bear' Freeman.

Hear my petition for transport to Outpost Gypsy Tree!
NOW!"

As she said the final words, she heard her Uncle Titus calling her name. Had she really been in the woods that long? she wondered.

Daylight slowly eased into Outpost Gypsy Tree. The fresh early morning air was full of the usual fragrances of wildflowers, evergreens and Gypsy's spicy aroma. But a new scent met their nares this morning – salt air. The smell of the ocean was calling them. Without realizing the intentions of each other, the teens found themselves standing together at the water's edge.

"Good morning. I see everyone got my message to meet on the beach just before sunrise," said Mingo as he strolled toward them.

"G'day to you, Mingo, but what message, mate?" asked Penzil. "I woke, smelled the sea air and here I am!"

"That's right, Penzil, here you are. Here you all are!" said Mingo.

"Give it up, Outback! He's got us, little brother," said Aube.

"Well, with that settled, let's begin our morning routine," said Mingo with a victorious grin.

The teens donned their bathing attire and seated themselves in the soft, white sand at the water's edge, ready for their CGB class.

"I want you to close your eyes, center, ground and do some cleansing breaths," said Mingo.

After a few moments he said, "Now open your eyes and witness the glorious sunrise brought to you by the awesome power and love of the ONE, the ABSOLUTE. Let yourselves be nourished."

The light travelers watched as a soft glow began to light up the horizon. A golden ball slowly rose up from the depths of the water as if the sun were being birthed right out of the ocean itself. A brilliant orange and golden path of light stretched across the rippling surface of the water from the horizon to the shoreline, bobbing up and down with the action of the waves.

Their eyes were transfixed. Their minds went back to the palace of the gods, to the sun being reborn in the chamber and the awe of all those who witnessed the event.

Did ancient man, standing at the water's edge, believe the sun was birthed from the ocean each day? What about those who witnessed it going down into the sea each night? What were their beliefs about the sun god? The teens knew Mingo was teaching them, preparing them for what was to come next. They knew this was not just a feel good experience.

Once the sun was fully above the horizon, Mingo spoke. "Any questions?"

"I have a comment, Mingo," said Patrick. "It's like Eittod said, it's all about perspective. Early man had only his perception of the world around him — only the small piece he interacted with each day. He built belief systems around what he witnessed and understood as truth in that very limited space."

"True!" said Mingo.

"And," said Penzil, "he had what was handed down to him from his ancestors' belief systems, judgments and interpretations."

"True!" said Mingo.

"And early man had the heavens, which were a constant for him," said Drew. "He could rely on the sun, the moon, the planets and the constellations. That's why he recreated the heavens on the earth. They were his teachers, his ancestors, his inspiration and his gods."

"Very good, Drew!" said Mingo.

"So, what are we getting at, Mingo?" asked Chelli.

"Patience, Chelli," he said, holding up a finger inviting her to hold that thought.

"Drew, you were able to see yourself and your team in the chamber preparing to unlock the code. Your gift of multi-dimensional sight is more advanced than any of us realized. I believe Eittod told you that. Correct?" asked Mingo.

"Yes, but I don't understand what that means," said Drew.

"The Regions had created an overlay dimension or a twin dimension in which you and your team could practice – that was the dry run. From the overlay, you were able to see and interact with the actual assignment mission. When Eittod and the Regions realized you were witnessing the mission, they requested you to leave immediately. When you did not, Patrick was asked to retrieve you quickly, which he did. They could not take the chance of your breaking through the overlay," said Mingo, taking a moment to stand up.

Drew gasped, "Oh, bummy! No wonder they were so insistent about my leaving. I am so sorry. I could have jeopardized the whole mission."

"Exactly," said Mingo nodding his head. "They still don't know if any permanent damage occurred from the overlay. And we won't know until you are on assignment."

Now pacing with his hands on hips, he continued. "What I am getting at, Chelli, is that at times, one of you may experience something that the others do not. Each of you is very special. And each of you has a unique belief system and perspective on life and a related gift to offer the team, just like Ancient Man. That's one of the reasons you were chosen. And those gifts will manifest as needed."

Mingo stood at the water's edge, just watching them. They were deep in thought, absorbing what had just been revealed to them. The light travelers took every word of their instruction very seriously. They all wondered what gifts they might have and hoped that when called upon, they would be there for the team.

"Okay now, let's do some reviewing of the dry run. Everyone did an excellent job with centering, grounding and vibrational breathing during the dry run. Your combined rhythmic chant was very powerful and carried you to the vibrational level necessary to draw the energy from your current Earth's army of light bearers. I know we went over this when you returned, but your heads are clearer today. Are there any questions about that part of the journey?" asked Mingo.

The teens looked around at each other, then back at Mingo with shrugged shoulders.

"Good! Then let's go on," said Mingo.

"Wait...Mingo," said Drew with hesitation in her voice. "I do have an important question, but not about our technique. It's more personal and has nothing to do with ego, please believe me. "

"What's that, Drew?" asked Mingo.

"What would have, or could have, happened if I had witnessed the completion of the sequence, the deciphering of the ancient code and seen the unlocking of the secret of the gods?" she asked.

"Well, I guess none of us will be able to answer that question, Drew, because it didn't happen, did it?" responded Mingo. "Possibly once you have completed the sequence, you will be able to answer that question for yourself. Let's continue," said Mingo.

After CGB class, Mingo invited them to swim with the dolphins for their morning exercises, then to come for breakfast at the snuggery feasting nook. And he was gone. Everyone looked in Gar's direction.

"Oh, come on now! I am past that, and you know it!" said Gar with a look of exasperation.

Everyone apologized and headed for the water. There was no sign of Lancelot today.

After their morning swim, they made their way through the warm, soft sand to Gypsy for a well-deserved breakfast. The only one missing was Eittod.

"Bezen, is Eittod going to join us this morning?" asked Drew.

"Not for breakfast, but he will be here later with some guests for you to meet," said Bezen. "Now feed those tummies. I'll see you later."

Bezen made her way to the snuggery transport chamber and was gone.

"What's going on?" asked Drew. "It feels like something special is getting ready to happen."

"You're very perceptive, Drew, but be patient," said Patrick.

"I feel the same way, Drew," said Aube. "Been feeling that way since I woke this morning. I wonder what's going on."

CHAPTER TWENTY-SEVEN:
Journey to the Gods

Eittod's hologram appeared in the pit. "Good morning, my dear light travelers! Please join me," he said, motioning to the numerous pillow piles and comfortable couches. "We have a very busy morning ahead." His hologram slowly morphed into his colorful body dressed in jeans.

Having finished their breakfast, the teens hurriedly moved down into their classroom for instruction. Everyone had an excited look on their faces which matched Eittod's eager expression.

"Good morning, Eittod!" they all called to him as they gathered around their beloved teacher.

"First, let me thank you again for your well-executed dry run," he said. "Let's view some of it."

The oval crystal lowered. Images of the light travelers standing in front of the entrance stone on the winter solstice 3107 BCE appeared before them.

"Remember, this is in real time. We don't do replays here," he lovingly reminded them.

"I wish I understood that replay stuff," lamented Patrick.

As they watched, the light travelers took mental notes of their journey. They were amazed at the powerful energy and light that emanated from their bodies outside the palace as they powered up using their cadence chant and then drew up the love energy from their army of light. There before them, the palace of the gods gave off a soft florescent green glow. The carved symbols stood inches out from the kerbstones, glowing with the same eerie green hue, and sent out low murmuring sounds into the morning air. Snippets of the dry run played out as Eittod, Bezen, Mingo and Gypsy made suggestions and adjustments to the various phases. The teens also had ideas as to what might work better for the next trip.

Several hours later, Eittod brought the review to closure. "Well that should do it for that segment of instruction this morning. Thank you, everyone, for your suggestions. I think we've 'cleaned out the bugs' as you would say in your Earth time," said Eittod with a pleased smile.

And with a wave of his hand, the oval crystal slowly ascended into the rafters and rotated in place.

"We have very special guests for you to meet this morning. Remember, here at the outpost, anything and everything is possible, dear ones," said Eittod as he walked to his favorite red and gold armchair chair, seated himself and propped his feet upon the soft matching ottoman.

Everyone anxiously awaited the arrival of the guests. Moments later the breathtaking opalescent presence of a multitude of wise elders appeared before the light travelers. They spoke in unison; their deep harmonic voice was similar to the depth and breadth of a Buddhist monk's vibrational chant.

The teens gasped.

"Good morning, dear ones! We come as ambassadors of the ONE, the ABSOLUTE," they said in their multi-toned voice. "We are the Regions Authority, and are honored to meet you face-to-face. We have known you since before your first breath. We know who you are – we know you well. We know the depth of your love for humanity and your desire for peace and love in your world. We know the purity of your souls' light and your souls' commitment to this sojourn. We, the overseers of your galaxy, know of your sincere pledge to the Earth and its people as does the ONE, the ABSOLUTE. We join you and your teachers today to assist in your training. What lies ahead for you is challenging, demanding and at times dangerous."

The light travelers looked around wide-eyed at each other, and then at Eittod. He gave them a knowing nod.

"This journey is other-worldly," the Regions continued. "But then all of this…" motioning to the outpost and its people, "…was 'other-worldly' to you at the beginning. At all times you *must* trust us. We promise to bring each of you home safely. Remember our promise to you in your times of distress. And there will be *distress*, but help will always be nearby. You will not be abandoned. You are treasured children of the Earth. As the Regions Authority, this work is not for us to do, or it would have never been necessary. We cannot interfere in the affairs of a free-will galaxy. We do what we can from our side with the help of the Angelics, Eittod and his staff. Earth's children of pure heart must do the battle for humanity and the Earth itself," said the Regions.

The light travelers' concerned looks changed to alarm.

"Please don't be frightened, dear ones," the Regions continued. "Believe us – you are up to the task before you. Your outpost teachers have prepared you well, and your steel-like courage and commitment to each other will sustain you. Soon you will meet new teachers.

Know that they are of the same commitment as you and will serve you well. We leave you to your work.

"Thank you for your strength, courage and commitment. Always look for the light to guide you," they finished.

The multi-toned voice and opalescent image of the Regions Authority faded from the pit.

No one moved. There was absolute silence in the snuggery as the teens processed the words of the Regions. Eittod and his staff waited and watched. They knew the strength and courage of their light travelers. They just needed time to process.

Then knowing they were ready for more, Eittod began.

"As the Regions have told you, the next part of your journey will be instructed and guided by your new teachers whom you have seen but not yet met," said Eittod.

"I knew it! I knew it! I knew it!" said Chelli as she jumped from her pillow pile and punched into the air in excitement. "It's the beautiful gods who came out of the palace just before the triple conjunction, isn't it?" she asked Eittod.

"Well, my dear Chelli, you have guessed correctly. And you will have the honor of meeting them and being instructed by them. The Tuatha dé Danann have returned to serve mankind again as they had promised. They come to bring the light – their illumination – to the peoples of the Earth and will guide you in clearing the North Portal," said Eittod.

This was jaw dropping information for the light travelers. Their assignment was beginning to involve a whole lot more than they had ever imagined, but they were more than ready for it.

"When do we leave, Eittod?" asked Drew eagerly.

"Tomorrow, my dear light travelers, you leave *tomorrow!* And you will meet with all your outpost teachers today for last-minute instructions," said Eittod.

The afternoon went by quickly. First, a pep talk from Mingo and last-minute instructions on their hunting and gathering skills. Next Eittod went over some last-minute astronomy instructions. Then Bezen met with them in the costuming and equipment areas.

"Bezen, I talked with Mingo about taking my own bow and quiver from my sleeping chamber, rather than the outpost's equipment. He told me to check with you on that," said Chelli.

"I think that would be a very good idea. You are more familiar with your own equipment's weight and site, so yes," said Bezen. "You have my permission to take it with you, Chelli."

Chelli's face lit up with delight.

Afternoon classes concluded with inter-communications skills with Gypsy, then a refreshing trip to the beach for a late afternoon swim with the dolphins. By now the light travelers had named most of the dolphins. Penzil named his favorite dolphin Nudges. It seems Nudges liked to push against Penzil, and in return Penzil would lie on its back and gently stroke its underbelly. And the whales always preformed an amazing breaching display to dazzle them. The light travelers would miss their Cetacean friends, but they also knew that their individual DNA carried precious information encoded in them by their new friends.

After their routine goodnight huddle, the teens were off for a restful night's sleep, that is, if their busy minds would let them.

Morning eased in with its usual glory. The teens were already gathered for breakfast by the time Bezen arrived.

"You are up early this morning! Eager to get back to 3107 BCE are you?" she asked.

Excitement filled the domicile feasting nook. Everyone was talking at once.

"You're going to wear out your tongues," Bezen laughed.

"So what do you desire to eat this morning? Picture it in your heads," she paused. "Got it?" she asked.

Everyone nodded.

"Okay, now manifest it!" she ordered them with gusto.

There before them were their very own breakfast orders waiting to be consumed.

"See, you can do it as well. Good job. Your minds have become quite skilled at manifesting your desires. This will work for you as long as you are here at the outpost and in the immortal state. Remember that," said Bezen.

They looked at her with questioning expressions.

"What do you mean by that, Bezen? Here at the outpost we are immortal, are we not?" asked Gar, confused and concerned.

"Yes, here at the outpost you are," she responded. "Now, enjoy your breakfast as you have a very busy and exciting day ahead of you. We will meet you in the snuggery for transport." And she was gone.

The teens knew when a conversation was over. Whatever that immortal piece was about, they would just have to wait it out.

After breakfast they met their teachers in the snuggery. Everyone had big smiles on their faces, and Gypsy's melodious sounds were full of joy and excitement.

"Come in! Come in! Your big day has arrived, and you are more than ready for it," said Eittod.

"I see all are dressed for the occasion and your gear has been gathered for your journey. Good job! I wish I could go with you, but I must relinquish that pleasure to the gods of Erin. Bezen has mentioned that she left you hanging on a question of immortality this morning at breakfast. You see, my dear light travelers, there will be a time during your journey when you will have to relinquish your immortality *temporarily*, but know that help is nearby as the Regions have assured you. Do you have any questions?" asked Eittod.

"No questions, Eittod. We trust you, your staff and the Regions with our lives. We always have," said Drew, "and we trust that the gods of Erin will take good care of us in your stead."

"We're all in this together for the sake of mankind. Right, mates?" shouted Penzil.

"Right!" shouted the light travelers in unison.

"Let's have a huddle and get on with it," said Patrick.

The teens and staff formed a big huddle as they looked into each other's faces. They were family – a chosen family.

Eittod looked at them with great love and admiration. He loved their commitment to each other and to this mission.

Gypsy was not to be left out. She moved her branches to create a special bon voyage melody for her light travelers. Oh, the sound was glorious.

"Thank you, Gypsy!" they called to her.

Soon the light travelers were geared up and standing on Gypsy's core with their hands on the shoulders of the person in front of them. Drew was at the front of the line and Patrick was in the rear.

Drew called out the orders. They recited their destination and desired timeframe, and they disappeared through the red slit in Gypsy's tree rings.

Within what seemed like only seconds, the light travelers stood at the entrance stone of the palace of the gods. Grabbing deep breaths, the teens experienced the cold, refreshing air, mixed with the sweet fragrance of Scots pine and the aroma of wood fires burning in the distance. They looked into each other's faces and grinned. They were on their own in 3107 BCE, and they relished in it. The brilliance of the Milky Way spread over the Boyne River, and its millions of stars twinkled around them. Drew took a moment to connect with Gypsy.

"We arrived safely. Thank you, Gypsy!" Her message was telepathically sent.

"Let's get to work, light travelers. Initiating Phase One!" said Drew.

Aube and Gar took up their positions at the large entrance stone with their hands on the megalithic carvings.

Drew and Penzil moved to the left of the entrance stone along the outside circumference of the cairn. Patrick and Chelli went toward the outside right of the cairn counting off kerbstones in the dark. Soon Drew and Patrick were standing breathless at kerbstone 52. Drew placed her hands on the right side of the elaborately engraved, colorful stone, covered with multiple sets of triangles within upright and inverted elongated arcs. The arcs were overlaid with the triple-cup Orion constellation symbol enclosed in four ellipses. Patrick's hands caressed the left side of the large stone over the triple and double spiral carvings.

Once Drew caught her breath, she closed her eyes and connected with Gypsy. "Begin preparation of the kerbstones." Drew waited.

Having received Drew's instructions through Gypsy, her team began centering, grounding and vibrational breathing. With their rhythmic cadence chant playing in their heads, they honored the adjustments recommended by Mingo.

Moments later Drew felt the powerful difference in the combined vibrations of her team. They were much stronger, more vibrant. Drew connected with Gypsy again, instructing her team to set their intent to draw energy and light from their army of light bearers in their current Earth time. They all focused, and their vibrating bodies began to radiate.

Feeling an overwhelming upsurge of energy in her own body, Drew became concerned for her team. Through Gypsy, she instructed her team to once again set their intent for grounding and centering and to check in with her. One by one, each member of her team gave her an update. Patrick, who was standing next to her, gave her an okay nod.

"Drew, this is the most powerful energy that I have felt. I am doing okay though. Thumbs up here," said Chelli.

"We're glowing like roman candles, but we're maintaining. Thanks, Drew," said Aube.

"Hey, mate. Feel like I got too close to the barbie. But I can handle it," said Penzil.

Drew once again connected with Gypsy, instructing her team to vibrate the kerbstone symbols beneath their hands in order to begin the decoding sequence. Soon, the whole of the palace of the gods began to radiate with a brilliant fluorescent green hue. The carved symbols glowed and vibrated many inches out from the stone surfaces and emanated a murmuring sound.

After several minutes, Drew sent out the message to maintain and return to the entrance. Phase one of the mission was complete. As they made their way back to the entrance, they left colorful streams of light in their wake.

"Is everyone doing okay?" asked Drew.

Her team nodded in the affirmative. They were in awe of each other's light.

"Retrieve your water," said Chelli.

Quickly, the light travelers removed water pouches and took long drinks.

"And remember to stay steady to the center of the passage," said Chelli. "And enjoy the aroma."

They glanced toward the Boyne River. Gentle lapping sounds of the tidal action below reached their ears. Once again, the teens could make out the final embers of Neolithic Man's campfires and the silhouettes of their primitive tents scattered along the riverbank. They were gathered to witness and celebrate the rebirth of their sun god and the lengthening of the light of day.

"Let's begin Phase Two; the moon and Venus will soon be rising over Red Mountain," said Drew.

Stepping into the passage, the teens stayed steady to the center of the passage and took deep breaths, enjoying the fragrant fresh boughs of Scots pine, spruce, arbutus, yew and holly at their feet. As the light travelers moved along the earthen floor, their radiant bodies illuminated the whole of the interior. Their glow cast light onto the small white flowers on the arbutus branches and the small rich red berries of the yew and holly that lined the passage. Neolithic Man had decorated for the holiday.

"I've said it before, and I'll say it again. I love the smell of fresh greens, and today I get to enjoy their colorful bounty. It fills my heart with such Christmas joy and peace," said Aube.

"The greens serve a medicinal purpose for early man as well, Aube," said Chelli. "As they tread on the greens fragrant oils are released and serve as antibacterial and antiviral agents."

"Your knowledge of plants and herbs is amazing, Chelli," said Aube. "Thanks!"

As they slowly made their way through the seventy-nine-foot passage, their eager hands caressed the familiar carvings on the orthostats. At their touch, the etchings radiated out inches from the stones and created murmuring sounds like many voices whispering to them the secrets of the gods. The decoding sequence was in process. Each stone in the passage and the chambers glowed. The carvings were lifelike, radiant and vibrant. The palace of the gods was alive with light, sound and sacred information.

The light travelers arrived at the center chamber and looked up into the corbelled ceiling. Their own radiance created a warm, soft glow on the opening's rose-shaped stone creation twenty feet above them. The six light travelers moved to their assigned places, holding each others' hands with their backs toward the small obelisk. Drew faced due north at the cardinal compass point zero/three hundred sixty degrees. Patrick faced due east at ninety degrees; Penzil due south at one hundred eighty degrees and Chelli due west at two hundred seventy degrees. Standing next to Drew, Aube fixed his intent on the center of the galaxy above. Gar stood next to Patrick and focused his intent on the core of the Earth roughly four thousand miles below his feet.

"Send out your intent to connect us with the six directions, NOW!" Drew instructed.

The light travelers were aware of the light shooting out from their own bodies into the six directions. They heard the three-foot high carved obelisk begin to hum. Much to their surprise, their own radiant bodies began to hum in rhythm with the obelisk. They were in cadence with it. Once again Drew saw beautiful grids of iridescent light form around each traveler's body, from above their heads to below their feet. Small beads of crystalline rainbow light raced along each grid line, busily delivering messages to all the atoms and molecules of their multi-dimensional bodies. This time their DNA appeared richer and more dynamic than before, thanks to their Cetacean friends, Drew was sure.

"Power down slightly and maintain," Drew commanded. "We are connected."

As they powered back, the light radiating from their bodies into the six directions dimmed, then slowly faded. At that moment all the carved symbols throughout the passage and chambers blinked on and off in strange patterns and sequences, then dimmed to a soft continuous glow. They could hear the musical calibrations of the ancient code playing out in their heads. The archaic Neolithic code was alive with sound as well as light. The teens turned to face each other, their eyes opened wide and their expressions full of wonderment.

The light travelers realized they were surrounded by many loving beings. The Regions Authority and the gods were with them. The Tuatha dé Danann made reverent nods of their heads, and they were gone. The teens knew the gods were outside the entrance, blessing, healing and encoding the DNA of Neolithic Man. The Regions stepped back into the shadows and faded from sight.

"Look! The moon and Venus are making their entrance into the roof box," said Patrick moments later. The triple conjunction had begun.

The light travelers slowly moved back from the center of the chamber to observe the crescent moon make its entrance along the passage floor, followed by Venus, the morning star. One by one the glow of the heavenly bodies rested on the triple spiral symbol on the right side of the back chamber entrance. Then the glow slowly made its exit from the right side of the passage.

In what seemed like only minutes, the first chink of sunlight streamed through the roof box and slowly began to ease along the passage floor and orthostats on the left side of the passageway. The teens were stunned.

"Drew, what's happening?" asked Penzil in an anxious tone. "We should have had at least thirty-five minutes between their entries."

Alarmed as well, Drew connected with Gypsy.

"Time is collapsing," responded Gypsy in their heads. "Drew is closer to breaking through the twin dimensions than we ever imagined. Go quickly."

Drew's eyes widened and her jaw dropped.

"We're good, Drew. Don't worry," said Patrick, reassuringly. "Start the next phase when you're ready."

"We have no choice; zero hour has arrived. Is everyone ready to do this?" Drew asked. Her voice was strong, steady. She listened for each affirming voice. "Here we go light travelers. We will begin phase three on my signal!"

All the teens were proud of Drew. She didn't let this throw her off course. And they were ready to follow their very brave and capable leader.

The light travelers waited and watched as the sun god continued its journey. Caressing each stone and each ancient carving, it made its way toward the center of the chamber. Drew knew she had to wait until the sun illuminated the triple spiral carving near the back chamber before she could initiate phase three.

She reached into her pocket and retrieved her stone which was warm and vibrating. The sun's rays finally reached the back chamber and illuminated the triple spiral symbol. The sun god was reborn.

With her eyes fixed upon the pinnacle of the small humming obelisk before her, Drew Megan Campbell slowly rubbed the small white quartz stone between her hands. As Eittod had instructed her, she held the stone just inches above the tip of the obelisk's pinnacle. She sucked in a deep, nervous breath; her heart pounded hard against her ribs and her flushed face tensed.

This was what she was born to do; it was her task, and hers alone, her great-grandfather had said. She had to trust, even though she did not yet know the outcome of her next action. Her fellow travelers' eyes were transfixed upon her. Their fate rested in Drew's hands.

As the triangular notch on the underside of the small quartz touched onto the pinnacle, three things happened in rapid succession: brilliant aquamarine lights flashed throughout the stone chamber blinding them, the earth began to tremble and the heavy, scraping sounds of moving rocks deafened them.

It can't end like this, we've come too far, Drew thought, bracing herself as the ground below her feet shifted. Drew's life flashed before her.

CHAPTER TWENTY-EIGHT:
The Other World

Locking eyes with Patrick, they both instantly knew it just couldn't end like this! The others stared at Drew with concerned eyes as the earth below their feet rumbled. The light travelers reached for each other's hands and gripped tight. The stone chamber descended like a modern-day elevator. But there was no light board indicating the number of floors below or above, nor was there piped-in soothing music. Instead, ear-splitting scraping and groaning sounds of ancient heavy rocks vibrated through their bodies, rattling their bones and clattering their teeth. It was as if the ancient chamber was devouring them whole.

The aquamarine flashes became more intense, more tangible, surrounding them as if holding them all safely in place. An avalanche of thoughts spilled through their heads, but no one made a sound. It was all happening in slow motion, freezing them speechless. Drew could feel their fear, hear their thoughts. Telepathically through Gypsy, she reminded them of her kinship with Patrick, hence this can't be the end. Through all the scraping and groaning noises she heard sighs of relief from her team.

With a sudden thud they had arrived. But where? Darkness enveloped them. Eittod had asked for their trust. The Region's had promised safe passage.

"Is anyone hurt?" Drew called out, concerned. "Sound off!"

She listened for each name and their okay signal.

"It sounds as if everyone's been shaken, but intact," said Drew.

"Now quickly move away from the obelisk," she instructed.

As they moved back into the unknown darkness, a sudden quivering coolness enveloped them and the aquamarine light moved tight against them pinning them against the wall as if protecting them. Electrical prickles covered their bodies. The deafening sounds of moving rock began again. The central chamber slowly began to move upward. Quickly, Drew tried to reach for her stone on the pinnacle, but the aquamarine light held her fast.

"Oh, bummy!" cried Drew. "My stone!"

The stone and the chamber were gone. They heard Patrick's voice echoing in the distance above them.

"No, Drew! No! You must come with me. NOW!" he shouted.

The light travelers were stunned.

"That was close," lamented Drew. "Too close!" She and Patrick locked eyes.

"We're okay, Drew. You did a great job," he reassured her.

When the aquamarine light dissipated, Drew connected with Gypsy. "Please let Eittod know that we have arrived beneath the chamber and that we are safe at this point. But my triple spiral stone is still on the pinnacle and out of reach. What should I do?" she asked.

"Eittod is very pleased with his light travelers. Do not worry about your stone. Bezen will retrieve it. Just watch for the light as the

Regions have instructed. It will guide you," responded Gypsy. "Safe journey, dear ones!"

"Eittod has instructed us to watch for the light and follow it, and I sense that was our last contact with Gypsy," said Drew sadly. "We are on our own, but we're okay," Drew reassured them. "We have each other."

"Drew, we are in a dark tunnel with a very small bright light at the end. Are you sure we're okay?" asked Gar. "This looks like a near death experience to me!"

"Yes, Gar, we're fine. I can feel my body, can't you?" Drew said impatiently.

"No, Drew, I can't feel your body – it's too far away," said Gar, "but if you move over..."

"That's not funny, Gar," snapped Drew. "I meant that we don't take our bodies with us when we cross over."

"Oh well, now that you mention it, yep! Our body is still here," said Gar as he reached out and poked Aube. "Guess we're okay," he snickered.

Aube giggled.

"It's getting a bit warm in here, mates. Have you noticed?" asked Penzil.

Everyone laughed.

"Cut that out. This is serious stuff, team," said Drew quickly, noticing that her face felt very flushed.

"Hey, that's my great-granddaughter you're flirting with, Garcia Gou-Drah Perez. We need to have a talk!" said Patrick. "Remember, I am an old-fashioned guy from the roaring twenties – nineteen twenties that is."

Again laugher broke out, and smiles returned to strained faces.

"Well, back to the task at hand," said Chelli. "All dark tunnels lead somewhere," she nervously laughed. "Let's see where this takes us, shall we?"

As they slowly moved down the dark, narrow tunnel toward the small light, they could hear an enchanting sound, and a sweet fragrance met their nostrils.

"That smell is heavenly," said Drew.

"Told you!" called out Gar.

Everyone was laughing and slapping on backs and shoulders.

Gar's humor helped to break up the depth of anxiety that everyone was feeling but not admitting.

"What was that?" cried Chelli.

"I felt it too!" said Penzil, alarmed.

Simultaneously, they had again felt a quivering coolness and electrical pricks around their bodies. A sudden strong breeze caught their breath causing them to grab for air, and a slight shimmer glowed around their bodies.

"I think we just walked through a gateway or threshold into another dimension," said Drew. "It's similar to what we felt a few minutes ago as we came down into the tunnel. I feel enlivened, energized this time."

"Me too," said Patrick. "I think you're right, Drew. We definitely have moved into a whole new space."

"Look ahead of us team. Are they fireflies?" questioned Aube.

Just a few yards ahead of them in the tunnel, miniature moving lights were blinking off and on, leaving a greenish-yellow afterglow.

"The lights seem to be moving forward, guiding us," said Penzil.

"So, let's just follow the light as the Regions instructed," said Drew.

The further they went, the larger and brighter the light became at the end of the tunnel.

"I think we're almost there, wherever there is," said Chelli.

Eittod had not told them what to expect once Drew placed the stone on the pinnacle. He trusted his light travelers, and wanted them to enjoy all the surprises and experiences that presented for them. Eittod had told them, *"Knowing what lays ahead takes all the joy and excitement out of the adventure."*

They came to the end of the tunnel and reached out for each other's hands.

"Here we go, team," said Drew. "On three! One, two and *three!*" she shouted.

Together they jumped out into the light. It was as if they had moved through yet a third force field. Again their bodies quivered with coolness, and electrical pricks covered every inch of their bodies.

"Holy Christmas!" said Gar.

"Amazing!" cooed Drew.

There before them, a breathtaking garden awaited. Everything appeared to be alive with color, light and sound. The sun was a golden ball of fire, and rainbows danced between billowy clouds. Whooper swans and mute swans covered the landscape and filled the sky along with other colorful birds.

In the crystal blue waters of a nearby lake, large long-necked, white swan-like birds gracefully glided. Pink fuzzy plumes adorned the tops of their heads and swirled around their necks as the swans repeated what sounded like "wally wamp, wally wamp."

Spectacular multicolored crystal pillars shot from the garden soil high into the tropical foliage above. The teens were dazzled by the beauty all around them.

"Welcome, children of the Earth. Welcome to the world of the gods," said a voice.

The light travelers were speechless as they turned to see a group of magnificent Tuatha dé Danann gods addressing them.

"We trust you have had a good journey?" asked the oldest of the gods.

"Yes, an interesting journey so far, Sir," Drew said, politely.

"My name is Dagda and this is my son, Aonghus, and his mother, Bóinn," said the god.

They were all magnificent – surrounded with radiance.

The light travelers bowed and introduced themselves.

"Yes, we know who you are, dear children of the Earth," said Bóinn in a loving tone. "We have been anticipating your visit with us."

"Welcome to the Other World," said Aonghus. "Please follow us."

Drew recognized the youth as the one who had looked directly into her eyes the morning of the dry run. He was handsome, about seventeen, with shimmering long blonde hair, fair skin, and he had the biggest blue eyes that Drew had ever seen.

They walked toward an iridescent rotunda of pure light surrounded by living statues of humanity of all races. Some faces were very ancient, others futuristic – all beautiful. The light travelers were captivated by the images before them.

"This is humanity. They represent all the races of children on the Earth – past, present and future, as you call it," said Bóinn in an endearing tone.

"Come!" said Aonghus, anxiously motioning them forward.

They walked through lavish gardens with fountains of fire and water. There were tall obelisks carved with all the languages of the Earth. Surprisingly, off to the side was a brightly-colored playground with monkey bars, slides, swings and an abundance of wildlife grazing.

"You may visit the gardens later. Right now, we have instructing to do, my children," said Dagda.

They followed Dagda into the enclosure of pure light where a marble mosaic spread across the floor at their feet, and breathtaking frescos graced the iridescent walls that surrounded them.

When the light travelers looked down at the mosaic, their own beautiful faces stared back at them. They gasped.

"As I have told you, my children, we know you well," said Dagda, pointing to their faces in the mosaic.

"Here you are known as *Copper Rings*," said Dagda, pointing to Drew. She loved it.

The light travelers anxiously waited to receive their names from the gods of the Other World.

"You are the *Two-in-One*," said Bóinn, pointing to Aube and Gar. The twins slapped their hands together in the air. They remembered Mingo having called them that on their first day at the outpost.

"You are *Little Bear*," said Aonghus, pointing to Chelli.

Chelli grinned from ear to ear. That name was given to her by her Grand-Papá, whom she loved dearly. *Did he know then of my journey to this other world?* she wondered.

Penzil stepped forward for his name. "You are known as *Roo, From the Land Beneath*," said Bóinn. Penzil smiled. His dark eyes sparkled.

Patrick awaited his new name. "And you are *The Elder*," said Dagda, "and the most revered." Patrick's cheeks flushed as red as his hair.

"You are the chosen ones we have been waiting for these many eons. Your Earth and its people are now ready for the quantum leap into the heart," said Dagda.

"Remember Eittod's words and Mingo's reminders – '*no ego stuff*,'" said Bóinn.

All the light travelers grinned. Oh, how they loved and respected Mingo and wished he were with them.

"You must enter your chosen work for the ONE, the ABSOLUTE, with gratitude and humility," said Dagda.

The teens all nodded in agreement.

"Now we move on," said Bóinn.

"Excuse me, may I call you Bóinn?" asked Drew, reverently.

"Of course, my child," Bóinn replied. "And this is Dagda and Aonghus to you."

"Bóinn, who are these beings in the frescos with us?" asked Drew, pointing to the many faces looking down at them from the rotunda walls.

"In due time, my children. In due time," she said. "Let's move on."

As they followed her from the rotunda into a small cozy room, Aube couldn't help but grin. His heart pounded, and his excitement was hard to contain. In the fresco, Aube had recognized the very tall, almond-shaped amber-eyed, chestnut-brown-skinned soldier in the maroon uniform who had stood behind them in their mirror in Lima.

"Instruction begins!" said Dagda.

The light travelers were reeling as they emerged from the cozy space several hours later.

"So this is how one saves the world!" exclaimed Drew, her mind groping for some sense of sanity.

Eittod, Bezen, Mingo and Gypsy had entrusted them to the Tuatha dé Danann. Oh, how the teens longed for their beloved teachers in whom they had unwavering trust.

This was craziness. No, this was sheer madness. Did Eittod know about this? Was this sanctioned by him for his light travelers? Unbelievable thoughts bombarded their frazzled minds. Would they ever get home again? But the Regions Authority had promised to bring them all home safely. They promised help would always be at hand. Just follow the light.

But, where was the light now – now, that they were so unraveled? All they could do was hold on to each other. Who else could they trust in this other-worldly place?

The light travelers wandered out into the gardens speechless. The living statues of mankind surrounded them. The statues represented all those of the Earth who needed their help, their courage, their dedication to move the Earth of twenty first century and its people into the dimension of the heart – the fourth dimension and beyond – as the gods had instructed them.

But to achieve this feat, they would have to retrieve the blue crystals from the Hill of Tara, some fifteen miles southwest of the palace of the gods. The kicker was that in order to do so, they would have to move through the Cave of Damnation in their *mortal* state – absolutely vulnerable. Their journey through the cave would be riddled with challenges to test the purity of their hearts, their intentions and their worthiness to touch the blue crystals. They remembered the Regions warnings, *"What lies ahead for you is challenging, demanding and at times dangerous. Remember our promise to you in your times of distress. And there will be distress."*

Still without speaking, the light travelers walked together hand-in-hand toward the gardens. Although this was a team of teenagers, right now they all felt like scared little kids – abandoned and alone. As they looked toward the playground, they noticed fireflies swarming around the monkey bars.

Here were the lights as promised. The light travelers quickly climbed onto the bars. Somehow, here near the miniature lights, the teens felt safe yet still vulnerable. Here they could feel the presence of the Regions and their beloved teachers, Eittod, Mingo and Bezen.

Finally Drew spoke. "I know the instruction from the gods was a shock to each of us, but let's try to reason this out," she said. "Eittod trusts that we can do this. The Regions Authority trusts us. And together we have to trust in each other and believe that as a team we can do this. Let's take it one step at a time. I know the piece that is haunting all of us the most is the vulnerability of mortality in the Cave of Damnation. So what are our strengths as mortals?" she asked them.

Still perched on the bars, they responded.

"Well, I know the wisdom of the Athabasca. My Grand-Papá taught me from the time I could walk how to gather and use the medicines of the herbs and plants, and my shaman bag is well-stocked, thanks to the outpost meadow. I have my bow and quiver with me, and I know how to hunt and fish. And Mingo has taught us what foods are safe and what to stay away from here in this ancient land. I can read the land where animals and man have walked before me. And I am strong," said Chelli, ready to serve her fellow travelers.

"Well, Drew, Gar and I can read the heavens for direction and time, day or night. And I am a dreamer of great dreams which means I am intuitive, as you are. And I have the determination of an oxen," said Aube.

"Team, I am willing to do whatever it takes to serve you and protect you. I build great fires. I am very knowledgeable when it comes to math and the sciences. I am strong and, as Aube mentioned, determined to see this through," said Gar.

"Yep! He's a real pyro!" said Aube with a chuckle.

Their light-heartedness was beginning to return.

"Mates, in my culture I am considered a healer. With my inner vision, I can read the signs of the body. With the energy of my hands and my intention, I can halt bleeding, heal wounds and ease pain. And I can smell water, even in the rocks," said Penzil, now moving to a higher bar.

"Like Gar, I am willing to do what I can to serve. I have a level head and do a fair job at cooking vittles. I know how to clean and cook fish and wild game. And I would appreciate a few of your tasty herbs to spice things up, Chelli. Collecting wood is one of my specialties," laughed Patrick. "Our only defense against the cold and damp in Ireland is a roaring fire. And I've built plenty."

"Wow! Sounds like we have a very efficient team and all the skills needed to keep us alive, healthy and fed. As your leader, I will certainly do my part. I recently took a first aide course at our local Irish Red Cross Office. And according to Eittod, I am doing very well in multi-dimensional vision. After all, I almost wrecked our journey with it, didn't I," laughed Drew.

The team was ready for whatever the Cave of Damnation had to throw their way as mortals. They knew that together they could do whatever was asked of them.

As they climbed out of the monkey bars, Aonghus approached.

"We are ready for your next instruction. Please come!" he said, motioning toward the rotunda. They fell in line behind Aonghus. Aube and Gar moved up even with him.

"So where are you from originally, Aonghus?" asked Gar.

"A very long time ago in your Earth time, my people traveled from many far-away star groups and through many time-gates," said Aonghus. "We came to the Earth with our wisdom, knowledge and gifts for humanity, with the permission of the Regions Authority."

"Oh, we've met them. Cool dudes, that's for sure," said Gar, changing the subject. Gar knew he was getting braver, but space cadets he just wasn't ready for – at least not today.

"Cool dudes?" asked Aonghus.

"Sorry, Earth slang," Gar replied quickly.

"Earth slang?" asked Aonghus.

"Hmm!" said Gar. "I guess being gifted with universal language doesn't include slang."

"I guess not," said Aonghus with a questioning grin.

When they reached the rotunda, Aube halted Gar as the others moved ahead into the cozy room for their final instructions.

"Gar, look at the almond-eyed face in the fresco," said Aube, pointing to the soldier in the maroon uniform.

"So?" asked Gar.

"Gar, I think that's our great-grandfather from the stars – from Perseus," said Aube.

"How do you know that?" questioned Gar.

"I saw him behind us in the mirror as we recited our petition for travel to the outpost."

"You might be right, Aube. I've never seen eyes like ours before," said Gar. His amber eyes flashed with delight.

"And maybe, just maybe, our ring is a map, Aube."

CHAPTER TWENTY-NINE:
Hill of Tara, 3107 BCE

After their final instructions and a heavenly lunch fit for the gods, as Gar had humorously noted, the Tuatha dé Danann led them to a pathway surrounded on all sides by an arbor covered in a thick mass of delicate flowers.

Drew cooed. "Oh, this is where the heavenly aroma is coming from. What are these flowers, Aonghus?" she asked.

"They are named the purple flower of magic," he said as he reached to pick one.

"Put out your hand, Copper Rings," Aonghus requested.

As she did, he placed the delicate purple flower in her hand and closed her fingers around it. "From me to you – for remembrance," he said.

Drew quickly opened her hand.

"But I will smother it that way," she cried.

"No, Copper Rings, you won't," said Aonghus, gently reaching out to close her hand again. "It's immortal. Its beauty will never die."

Drew blushed.

"Let's move on then, shall we?" urged Patrick.

Dagda stepped forward. "Follow this covered pathway until you come to a clearing. Just ahead will be the cave you are seeking. Safe journey, light travelers," he said. "Remember all that you have been taught. It will serve you well. And as the Regions have told you, *trust us.*"

Bóinn reached out and lovingly hugged each of the light travelers. "You will be fine, my children, less we would never send you out on this mission," she said.

As the teens entered the fragrant covered pathway, they were soon engulfed in deafening silence and greeted by a quivering coolness and electrical pricks on every inch of their glowing bodies.

"Gateway number one!" announced Penzil. His voice echoed in the void. "Two more to go, I presume. They always seem to come in threes. I wonder why that is?"

"There's an old saying that there is power in threes," said Patrick, his voice reverberating back at him.

"I think that's an old vampire legend, Patrick," said Aube, "which is as weird as this void."

They all laughed.

"Aube's just playing with your mind, Patrick. Actually, there is truth in the power of three. Marketers use it all the time, as do motivational speakers, speech writers and teachers. In fact, the power of three is considered one of the important 'truths in advertising.' They pick three main topics or points and stick with that, or they lose their listeners," said Gar.

"One marketing class, and he's an expert," said Aube.

"Aube wasn't too fond of that class, but I insisted, and he tolerated it," said Gar. "Correct, brother?"

"It was either that or fencing," said Aube, "and I am not fond of sharp objects."

Patrick slapped them both on the back, "You guys are unbelievable! I pity your poor parents!"

After miles of playing with the echoing void and two more gateway experiences, the light travelers found themselves in the clearing that Dagda had described.

"Oh, it feels so good to be out of that soundless place. It gave me a very creepy feeling," said Chelli as she shook her body to free herself of it.

"I recognize this place," said Drew surprised. "We're not far from the Mound of Hostages on the summit of Tara, which was constructed around the same time as the monuments of the Boyne Valley. Let's move up to the summit; the view will be spectacular from there."

Once on Tara's summit, the light travelers looked out on a sprawling vista of unspoiled Irish countryside. Many small stone structures dotted both the base of the summit and the massive summit itself. A stiff breeze wrapped around the teens, forcing the afternoon wintery chill into their fur and leather garments. They huddled together to keep each other warm.

"Tell us more, Drew," asked Chelli. "Knowing about these sites helps us to appreciate them even more."

"Well, I do love to talk about Ireland. Tara was the epicenter of activity in the Neolithic Period and into the Bronze Age," shared Drew, shifting into her tour guide mode. "It was Ireland's first capital – the home of Kings. That stake wall around the summit," pointing to tall, tightly lashed vertical tree trunks, "was their way of protecting their capital and its treasures from invaders. Parts of it can still be seen today in our Earth time."

The teens observed Neolithic Man gathering for the celebration of three important settings over the Hill of Tara: the winter solstice sun, the "walker god" constellation known as Orion and the brightest star in the heavens, Sirius, which appears just below and to the left of the walker god's three-starred belt.

"I think we need to get on with our assignment," said Drew. "It's been fun just enjoying the Hill of Tara, but we do have a cave to visit, remember?"

Everyone was nodding in agreement, but the smiling faces of just moments before had turned to frowns. The teens made their way down from the summit and back toward the cave entrance just below the summit. Once there, an elderly man brushed past Aube, shoving something hard into his hand. The stooped man was gone as quickly as he had appeared. The light travelers were startled.

"How could he see us? We are not visible to Neolithic Man due to our higher vibrations!" cried Patrick.

"What did he hand you, Aube?" asked Penzil.

"I am not sure what it is," said Aube, holding up an angular piece of metal roughly a quarter of an inch thick.

They all gathered around him to get a closer look. Each took a turn studying the strange object, then passed it on to the next person. Once everyone had a chance to examine it, they began to throw out ideas.

"For someone to have seen us, they would have to be vibrating at the same high vibration and in the same dimension as we are," said Drew, "which leads me to believe it's a gift from Eittod, the Tuatha dé Danann or the Regions."

"I think you're right, Drew. The Regions did promise that help would always be nearby. But what is it?" questioned Chelli.

"It's either bronze or copper, which means it could be from the Bronze Age, which immediately follows the Neolithic Period. As far as I know, there was no metal found in any of the Neolithic mounds," said Drew. "Maybe what we're seeking isn't of the Neolithic Period, but the Bronze Age, or later. The blue crystals may have been placed in the chamber below the Hill of Tara at a much later time in history."

"The vertical bend of the metal is an acute angle, about seventy degrees," said Gar.

"I agree," said Penzil.

Aube turned the object upside down, right side up and sideways, examining the etching on the inner surface of the six inch by seven inch object.

"What do you make of the counter relief etchings on the inner surface?" asked Aube.

"If it were a language, we would be able to read it," said Patrick.

"Hey, mate, maybe it's a map of some kind," suggested Penzil. "If we press something soft against the etchings, like mud, we might get a better image."

With that suggestion, they gathered up moist soil and pressed it against the etched surfaces. When they peeled the mud overlay back, they were just as confused about the object's use as before.

"If this is a gift from our teachers, it must be to assist us with our journey through the cave. So, why didn't they give us some kind of clue as to how to use it?" asked Chelli exasperated.

"Well, whatever it is, I am sure in due time we'll figure it out. Until then, we best be getting on with our mission," said Drew.

At the opening of the cave, they reached out for each other knowing that their gift of immortality was about to be dissolved. Gar and Aube stepped forward.

"Aube and I would like to take the lead," said Gar. "We've discussed it, so no arguments, okay?"

"Okay, guys, I'll take the end position with Penzil in front of me," said Patrick. "Put the girls in the middle."

There were no objections. The light travelers were a cohesive team that thought as one.

"It's going to be pitch black in there, so keep a hand on the shoulder of the one in front of you," instructed Drew, "and please keep your eyes, ears and sensors alert. I don't think this is going to be a very friendly place if they're testing our worthiness," said Drew. "Those blue crystals must be very special stones."

"Remember, light travelers, we need to prove that our intentions are pure," said Gar in the lead, "so before we enter, let's take a few minutes to do some cleansing breaths and center, ground and connect with the earth and our army of light."

Gar kept hearing Eittod's words playing over and over in his head. *"You're a fine young man, and your courage, intelligence and bravery will serve us well."* He wondered, *Was this what Eittod had been referring to? And if, so am I really up to the challenge and the trust?*

The light travelers slowly moved into the mouth of the cave, each wide-eyed and alert to their surroundings and their bodies. They had only gone fifteen feet into the darkness when they encountered large boulders blocking their way. Without hesitation, Aube intuitively reached out, placed his hands hard against the stones and set his intent. The boulders dissolved at his touch.

"Way to go, Aube!" said Gar.

"Thanks, Gar," Aube responded with a grin. Praise from his twin brother felt very good, very good indeed right at this moment.

As they continued forward, they could hear the large boulders moving back into place behind them with a thud. The teens realized the only way out was forward. With each step the teens felt their bodies changing. The cold, damp air of the cave felt colder; and with each step their bodies seemed to be getting heavier.

"I feel like I've gained ten pounds within the last few minutes," cried Drew.

"Me too," complained Chelli. "And I am so cold. Brrrr."

"You're not the only one. My teeth are chat…chattering," said Penzil. "We're mortals again for sure, ma…mates."

"Hold up!" shouted Gar reaching his hands out. "There is something just in front of me."

Everyone halted and remained still, waiting for instructions from the twins.

Gar and Aube felt around in the darkness.

"Ouch!" said Gar. "I just got pricked by something sharp here on the right."

"Wait, Gar," said Aube "the metal object in my survival pack is vibrating."

When Aube held the metallic object up in front of him in the dark, he noticed the inside etchings were glowing. As he brought it up closer to his face, he realized he could see through the etchings into the surrounding area.

"I can see through the etchings," Aube shouted in surprise. "It's like a night vision scope, and is definitely twenty-first century AD technology in 3107 BCE."

"What do you see in front of us?" asked Penzil.

"Spikes! Very sharp, wooden spikes coming out of the right side of the cave wall at different angles and lengths. It's going to take some maneuvering to get through this obstacle," said Aube. "You okay, Gar?" he asked.

"I am fine. Just a puncture, but it's starting to sting," Gar replied.

"We'll need to pass the etching back and forth as we ease ourselves through. If Gar and I can maneuver it, the rest of you should do okay," said Aube.

Aube passed the metal piece to Gar.

"This is going to take some doing, brother," said Gar as he surveyed their predicament. "We'll need to face the spikes, so you'll need to lead us in, Aube. Be careful. Those spikes have a bite to them," he said passing the etching back to Aube.

While the other teens waited in the dark, occasional yelps and a few Holy Christmas exclamations could be heard as Aube and Gar slowly eased their bodies through the maze.

"We're finally through," called Aube. "I feel like a human pin cushion. Just take it slow, everybody; these spikes are sharp, and they do sting."

Aube slowly reached back through the spikes to hand the glowing etching off to Drew.

"Be careful, Drew. Take your time," said Gar.

Each light traveler, in turn, made their way through the maze of sharp spikes and emerged safely on the other side with multiple stinging punctures to prove their effort.

Chelli quickly used the glowing metallic etching to view the contents of her shaman bag and retrieved a small jar of yellow salve.

"This salve will help to ease the burning. Just dab a little bit on each spot," she said, passing the jar around. "If anyone needs help, just let us know."

"Oh, that feels much better, Chelli. Thanks!" said Aube.

"It takes the sting right out of it," said Gar. "You're amazing, Chelli. Thanks!"

"I think the tips of the spikes were coated with an irritant that caused the sting," said Chelli. "I just hope that's all it was," she said with trepidation in her voice.

After everyone had soothed their burning skin and had a snack and drink from their survival packs, they were ready for the next obstacle on the journey.

"Wait! What's happening?" cried Penzil. "My wounds feel wet. Let me have that etching for a minute, Aube."

"Mates, I'm oozing *blood!*" said Penzil, alarmed.

Everyone examined their sores in the glow of the etching and saw small beads of blood seeping from their multiple wounds.

"We don't have any more time to waste. We need to get through the cave, then we'll take care of whatever this is," said Drew with urgency in her voice.

"You're right, Drew, we need to get out of here first. Heaven only knows what lies ahead for us," said Gar in agreement. "Let's just tough it out, team. Okay? Chelli and Penzil will take care of us later."

"You bet, mates," said Penzil.

"Let's get on with it," said Chelli, punching the air.

"Would you like me to take the lead for a while, Gar?" asked Patrick. "You and Aube have the most wounds."

"Thanks, but Aube and I are good. Right, Aube?" asked Gar.

"Yep!" said Aube. "Onward light travelers, obstacle number two completed."

Gar had a need to prove Eittod correct, and to prove to himself that he was worthy of the trust his teacher and his team had in him. He held the etching up to his face and moved the group slowly through the cave. Everyone's senses were heightened in anticipation of the next challenge. After a two mile walk, a dripping cave ceiling, narrowing cave walls, scurrying rats and a multitude of screeching bats and ugly spiders, the passage forked.

"Bad news team, we've come to a fork in the passage. The area around the fork looks clear though, but I have no clue which way to go," said Gar. "All you intuitives, get your sensors going. That's not my department."

"Why don't we walk a short distance down each passage," said Drew. "One of the passages may be blocked."

"Good idea. Let's try that, Gar," said Aube. "Intuitively, I am not getting a yea or nay on either path."

"Same here!" said Drew.

"Is everyone okay with doing that?" Gar asked.

After getting the okay from the team, Gar chose to start with the right fork.

After a short distance Chelli spoke up, "I don't like the smell in here. It's a smoky smell. Does anyone else smell it?"

"I am beginning to smell it too!" said Patrick, alarmed.

Within seconds everyone was coughing and rubbing their eyes.

"Let's get out of here," ordered Drew.

As they turned, they realized the path back to the fork no longer existed. Their only alternative was to go through the smoke. But what was ahead in the smoke?

"Don't anyone move until we can figure out what's ahead of us. We don't want anyone getting hurt," said Patrick. "What are you seeing in the etching, Gar?" he asked.

"It's hard to tell with all this smoke. No wait! Wait! The images are beginning to clear. Oh, Holy Christmas!" said Gar in a terrified voice.

"What is it, Gar?" everyone was asking.

"There's a fire pit...just ahead of us – and...it's huge," cried Gar. "Take a look, everyone. I've never seen anything like this."

The light travelers were becoming unraveled. Being mortal in this situation was taking its toll on their bravery, and their bleeding was increasing. They passed the etching around, and in turn, each one gasped.

There, before them, was a fire-belching pit throwing lava high into the air above it. Flames licked the sides of the cave walls. With every second that passed, the pit seemed to be getting larger, crowding them back. There was no sign of a way around it, and at this point, they knew there was no way out.

"We're trapped, mates!" said Penzil, with dread in his voice.

The light travelers stood in stunned disbelief at their situation. They had been promised safe passage, but they could feel the weakening effect of their bleeding wounds. Fear was overtaking them.

"Wait a minute!" bellowed Drew, stomping her feet. Her face was as red as her copper curls, and her hands were propped on her hips.

"We've allowed ourselves to become *victims* just because we have lost our immortality," she scolded, pacing in the firelight in front of the encroaching fire pit.

"We have forgotten *who we are and what's at stake here!* We are the *light travelers,* and we have *promised* to clear the North Portal for mankind and the earth itself! We have an army of light bearers who walk beside us, whether we are mortal or immortal. This fire pit is feeding off our fears just as the darkness in the portal feeds off mankind's pain, fear, rage and greed and magnifies it. **Now, let's show this Cave of Damnation just who we are, that our intentions are pure and we are absolutely worthy!**"

The other light travelers were cheering her on and jumping up and down. Chelli was punching the air, and Penzil was ready for positive action. Absolute pride in his great-granddaughter crossed Patrick's face in the firelight.

Following Drew's commands, they formed a circle in front of the fire pit with their backs to each other. They grounded, centered and connected to the Earth and their army of light bearers and began their vibrational breathing.

"Start your cadence chant out loud, NOW!" Drew commanded as the fire pit drew dangerously close. The heat was searing their flesh.

She could feel their courage and power mounting. She waited. Then with all the power she could muster, she shouted her orders.

"Send out your intent to connect us with the six directions, NOW!" Drew commanded.

As they did, the fire pit began to recede.

Their bodies of light illuminated the whole of the cave. They were no longer in darkness. As their radiant bodies began to hum, their powerful combined energies blew the Cave of Damnation wide open.

They were standing in the fresh open air with hundreds of fireflies swarming around them. They had proven that their intentions were pure, and that they, the light travelers, were worthy.

"Power down," Drew commanded, with a very proud look on her face. "We are connected," she said softly.

The light travelers surrounded Drew, and hugs and bravos ensued.

"Great job!" she said. "We are a team – an amazing, powerful team! It took all of us to prove our worthiness. And in those fleeting seconds, I realized the only ones we needed to prove our worthiness to were ourselves. We are the only ones who truly know if our intent is pure. We know our own hearts and the hearts of each other," said Drew in a loving tone, "and I believe our immortality has just been returned to us."

They all looked down at their burns and blood-soaked wounds. They were healing. Big smiles covered their faces.

"Look at the heavens," said Patrick in awe.

There in the twilight, the re-born sun god of the winter solstice was slowly setting in the southwest. Also setting above them was Orion the walker-god, whose three-starred belt pointed to the Dog Star, Sirius – the brightest star in the heavens.

After setting up camp and feeding their larva tummies, they did their usual good night huddle. The light travelers tucked into their bedrolls on the winter grasses close to their fire and gazed with wonder into the splendor of the night sky over Tara.

Drew reached into her pack to retrieve her purple flower of magic. It was as fresh as when Aonghus had placed it in her hand. She laid it on her bedroll next to her face, took a deep breath and drifted off to sleep with its heavenly scent wafting in her head and the crystal blue eyes of a young god gazing into hers.

It had been a challenging day in which they had proven their pure intent and worthiness. Tomorrow they would enter the chamber of the blue crystals beneath the Hill of Tara as immortals.

CHAPTER THIRTY:
Mound of Hostages

As the first glow of daylight slowly reached across the Irish countryside, it found the light travelers already moving about. Close to camp, Patrick was gathering firewood and kindling. Chelli and the twins were off hunting. Drew and Penzil had hiked to a nearby well for fresh water. The teens were aware of Neolithic Man moving about near them in another dimension.

Patrick had collected armfuls of dry wood and twigs and had a good fire going by the time the others returned.

"Great fire there, mate!" said Penzil, with his usual big smile and twinkling dark eyes. Slightly out of breath, he lowered the two water bladders that hung from his shoulders onto the cold ground. "The well was a bit further north than Drew remembered, but she has a good sense of where things are around here which really helps. She'll be back soon; she's cutting some fresh evergreens."

Within minutes Drew re-entered the campsite with an armful of greens and water that she eased to the ground next to Penzil's.

"That was quite a walk, but the brisk morning air of Ireland is wonderful – no matter the millennium," she said in a dreamy tone, feeling the kinship with her homeland and ancient ancestors. "Penzil really *can* smell water. He took us right to it," said Drew, laying fragrant greens about the campsite.

"You're in trouble in the Outback, mate, if you don't have a nose for tracking water," replied Penzil. "Those who don't must resort to divining rods. The elders tell me I have the gifts of the ancestors."

Drew moved to the fireside to warm her hands. "Oh, this fire feels so good. Thank you, Grand," she said as she held her hands over the flames, then placed them on her cold red cheeks.

"Penzil, what does it mean to have the gifts of your ancestors?" asked Drew.

"I reckon it means I carry their wisdom and knowledge of the Earth in my DNA, Drew. From my research, I've learned that all our tribal ancestors had an innate connection and respect for the land. They had great foresight and a deep understanding of their relationship with the Earth – it supported their lives. It was their mother. All the indigenous tribes of the Earth have the same wisdom and knowledge. And they are finally talking with each other and sharing their stories. As a result, they are realizing that it is all the same information. It's very exciting. I sense that all us light travelers are very connected with our ancestral gifts."

"How exciting that the various aboriginal groups are beginning to share with one another," said Drew. "That kind of information and connection will benefit all of mankind."

"Too right!" agreed Penzil.

"Have you seen any sign of our fierce hunters, Patrick?" Penzil asked with a grin.

"Not yet, but I am sure they'll return soon with a good breakfast in hand. I am hungry enough to eat a bear!" growled Patrick. "Bezen has us spoiled with her *'lavish displays of culinary delights,'* as she puts it."

"She's quite the gastronomer!" said Drew.

"The what?" asked Patrick, confused.

"It means she's a connoisseur of good food," said Drew, "a gourmet."

"Can't you just say she's a good cook?" replied Patrick.

"But she doesn't cook, Patrick. She recreates food," said Drew.

"Oh, mates, I sure do miss Bezen, Eittod and Mingo. They've become family as well," lamented Penzil.

Patrick put more dry branches on the fire.

"Drew, you were amazing yesterday; I hope you realize that. Your leadership, courage and insightfulness got us through that harrowing situation in the cave," said Patrick.

"Thank you, Grand," said Drew, giving her great-grandfather a loving hug. "I truly felt Eittod by my side, guiding me through it. It was like he was standing right there, directing me and watching over us."

"Didn't mean to eavesdrop on a family moment, but I could feel him too, Drew. I don't think he's ever far from us, mates," said Penzil in a reverent tone.

"You're family as well, Penzil," said Drew.

"You bet!" said Patrick as he and Drew gave him a bear hug.

Penzil blushed.

"I've never had a family until now, mates. I feel such deep kinship with all my light travelers," said Penzil with moist eyes. "Thanks for the hug. I needed one that was *all* mine," he said with a grateful grin. "And I agree with Patrick; you were awesome yesterday, Drew."

They sat close together on their bedrolls, enjoying the warmth of the fire as they waited for their colleagues to return.

As the guys talked, Drew reviewed in her mind their instructions from the gods on how to enter the chamber under the Hill of Tara and how to safely retrieve the crystals from their resting place.

"Looks like our hunters are back," said Penzil, pointing toward the east. Chelli and the twins could be seen approaching in the distance; the soft glow of a golden sky made itself visible behind them. The hunters waved their hands in the air and shouted something about breakfast.

Patrick, Penzil and Drew made their way out to meet them.

"WOW!" yelled Patrick. "It's not a bear, but it has breakfast written all over it. What a wonderful sight!"

"This girl is a master hunter with that bow, and we have the game to prove it," Gar said as he and Aube held up three buck rabbits and a grouse.

Chelli was all smiles.

"And we found some hazel trees that had given up their bounty to the ground for the picking," bragged Aube. "You did say the nuts had to be picked from the ground and not the tree, right Drew?"

"That's right, Aube. When the hazel nut is ripe for the eating, it drops from the tree. There's a lot of folklore and superstition around the hazel tree, from its use as a divining rod to its protection from evil spirits. And it's considered bad luck to pick the nuts directly from the tree," said Drew.

"Well, with the task ahead of us, the last thing we need today is bad luck," said Gar.

"We also have fresh mushrooms that we can cook on green sticks like marshmallows," said Chelli. "And we were very careful in choosing them. Mingo's instructions were very specific as to the species that were safe. Ireland has lots of varieties. It seems the prettier they are, the more poisonous they are."

"Just like women, they lure us with their beauty," said Gar with a hint of sarcasm in his voice.

"Don't get yourself off on the wrong foot today, brother," warned Aube. "Remember who bagged your breakfast."

Everyone was excited and looking forward to a hardy meal provided by the Irish countryside and their expert archer.

Soon the guys had the rabbits skinned and cleaned, and the girls had plucked, cleaned and prepped the grouse using some of Chelli's herbs.

Patrick and Penzil lifted the meat-laden spit onto the green forked boughs and took turns rotating it. Chelli and Drew cracked and shelled the hazel nuts on a nearby rock. Meanwhile, Aube and Gar warmed their butts near the fire.

"We should have enough nuts for breakfast and an afternoon snack as well," said Chelli. "The hazel trees are so mesmerizing with their curlycue branches going hither and yon."

"They can lure you into a dream or meditative state if you focus on the twisting branches long enough. Its fruit is considered a brain food," shared Drew. "I've done several watercolors of hazel trees and have had the same mesmerizing experience."

The wonderful smell of fresh game cooking over an open fire wafted through the air enticing their appetites.

While breakfast was cooking, Drew reviewed the day's agenda, starting with a visit to the Stone of Destiny, then entry into the chamber beneath the Mound of Hostages and retrieval of the blue crystals from their resting place.

"What do we do once we have the crystals?" asked Patrick as he rotated the spit. "To my knowledge, no one has addressed that part of the journey."

"If you'll remember, Dagda said we would get further instructions in the chamber," said Drew.

"I remember that, but instructions from whom?" asked Patrick.

"I guess we'll find out once we're in there," said Chelli. "They don't like to give us too much information in advance, which is probably a good thing."

"I think you're right, Chelli. I am sure that if they had given us more information about the Cave of Damnation, none of us would have gone in there!" said Aube with a shiver.

Everyone nodded and murmured in agreement.

"That sure was a hair-raising experience; the scariest one in my lifetime, that's for sure," said Gar. "Or...," he hesitated tapping his finger tips on his chin, "maybe it was the thought of leaving linear time. That was certainly memorable."

They all laughed.

"Honorable light travelers of Tara, your breakfast is served," announced Patrick as he and Penzil bowed to their anxiously awaiting guests.

Within no time the wild game, mushrooms and some of the nuts had been devoured. The larva tummies had been satisfied, as their dear Bezen would say.

"Look!" said Drew pointing to the northeast. "The winter solstice sun has risen over Red Mountain."

The horizon was a blaze of color.

By late morning, the light travelers had packed up their campsite, doused their campfire with a bladder of water and were making their way through the tall grasses and hazel trees to the Mound of Hostages on the summit.

"According to our instructions, we must first visit the Stone of Destiny," said Drew. "It's at Tara's north cardinal point, next to the mound."

"You've seen the stone before, haven't you, Drew?" inquired Penzil.

"Yes, it was one of the gifts from the Tuatha dé Danann. It was moved to the top of the King's Seat in the center of the earthworks in 1798 to honor the fallen of the Battle of Tara. It's not far now."

As the light travelers approached the entrance of the Mound of Hostages, the Stone of Destiny could be glimpsed behind it. The large phallic–shaped stone gleamed in the sunlight. Drew gasped with surprise at its height.

"The stone in our Earth time is only about five feet in height and the other half is buried in the soil," said Drew.

"Well, if its ten feet in total length, about eight feet of it is sticking out of the ground in 3107 BCE," remarked Gar.

They were dwarfed by its size as the teens formed a circle around the stone.

"Light travelers, begin your centering, grounding and vibrational breathing, NOW!" commanded Drew.

Their rhythmic cadence chant began to play in their heads. Minutes later, feeling the powerful combined vibrations of her team, Drew instructed them to set their intent to draw stored energy and light through their feet from their army of light in their current Earth time. They all focused; their vibrating bodies began to radiate with light.

Feeling the upsurge of energy in her own body, Drew instructed her team to send their vibrations into the stone with the intent to draw on its wisdom and knowledge. Within seconds the stone vibrated, releasing wave after wave of energy through their glowing bodies. A profundity of archaic images and information filled their minds and bodies. They were aware of that same information being transferred to the DNA of their army of light. Moisture leaked from their eyes at the sacredness of the ancient wisdom and knowledge being gifted. After several minutes Drew sent out the command to power down slightly and maintain and to move into the mound.

Unlike Newgrange's seventy-nine-foot passage, the passage of the Mound of Hostages was only thirteen feet in length, with only one elaborately carved orthostat positioned on the left side of the passage. With their bodies still glowing, the light travelers placed their hands on the archaic symbols on the orthostat to activate the decoding sequence. Once the symbols were standing inches out from the orthostat, Drew instructed her team to prepare for the six directions. Facing their assigned cardinal points with their backs to one another, they formed a tight circle in the small passage.

"Send out your intent to connect us with the six directions, NOW!" Drew commanded.

Their laser beams of light shot out from them even more powerfully than before. The light travelers knew they were becoming stronger, more focused, more intense. Each was aware of their iridescent grid lines filled with multicolored beads of light rapidly tracing the grids.

"Power down and maintain," Drew commanded. "We are connected."

The teens heard the sound of a heavy rock moving just ahead of them in the passage and felt the ground vibrate under their feet. Their hearts were pounding and their minds were racing as an orthostat on the right of the passage rotated open to reveal a staircase curving downward into the earth. Quickly, they moved down the rough stone steps into the darkness below. The orthostat could be heard rotating back into place. They were entombed!

This time there was no light at the end of a tunnel. There was no tunnel. Just dark space illuminated by their radiant bodies. Their eyes were on Drew. With complete trust in the Tuatha dé Danann, the Regions and Eittod, Drew calmly felt around on the wall, searching for some means of escape – a knob, a notch or a handle – but none could be found. She turned to her fellow travelers.

"Let's put our hands on the wall and energize it with our intent to open the chamber of the blue crystals. It has to be right in front of us," she said with conviction.

The light travelers trusted Drew completely. They knew she was intuitively connected to Eittod, the Regions and the gods of Erin. She had proven herself competent and capable time after time, and her team followed her directions without question.

As Drew had instructed, they splayed their hands against the wall and set their intent for passage. Within seconds, rays of light appeared around their hands and the rough stone wall turned into solid, etched golden gates that slowly swung open. They were in awe.

There before them was a large circular chamber. Torches in ornate gold and bejeweled brackets came ablaze one by one around the chamber. The chamber walls appeared as if Michelangelo had just completed his work. Rich colors, angelic faces and surreal scenes illuminated out of the dark. In the center of the chamber was a breathtaking, handsomely carved, closed wooden chest on a stone pedestal, flanked by two luminous angelic beings who stared down at them.

"Come closer, dear children of the Earth, but remember, do not touch the chest. We have been expecting you," said one of the Angelics.

"The blue crystals that you seek, light travelers, are not of your Earth, but are living beings from afar, here to assist mankind. The Regions Authority placed them in various parts of the Earth while it was still forming. Humanity had been gifted the crystals once before, but they fought over their power. Hence, the Regions hid them for a later time when mankind was truly ready for peace," said the other Angelic.

"Once your North Portal – the portal of wisdom and love – is cleared, the Regions will return the crystal beings to the safety of Tara. This land is sacred, chosen, holy. Erin is the keeper of the North Portal for the children of Mother Earth," said the first Angelic as she smiled lovingly down at them.

The teens could feel the Angelics' compassion and love for mankind as they spoke.

Suddenly without warning, the earth quaked. The chamber shifted, and the chest containing the blue crystals began to topple from its pedestal. The teens reached out to brace each other, except for Gar, who reached up to keep the chest from falling. The wooden chest pressed hard against his torso and hands as he pushed it back into place. Gar and Aube's screams reverberated throughout the chamber. They were thrown like rag dolls through the air, hitting hard against the stone floor many feet away from the pedestal.

Alarmed and concerned, their fellow light travelers gathered around them. Gar's chest and hands were severely burned and raw. He wept in pain. A large, gaping laceration bled profusely just over Aube's left eye. His skull bone could be glimpsed. He appeared dazed and he was not responding. His eyes were glassed over. Patrick elevated the twins' feet with their survival packs as Drew instructed. Penzil called on his ancestors' wisdom and healing knowledge and placed the palms of his hands just inches from Gar's burnt chest and hands. Light from Penzil's hands radiated deep into Gar's wounds. From her survival pack, Drew quickly withdrew clean bandages and applied them with pressure to the laceration on Aube's forehead. Chelli held her hands just over Drew's hand on Aube's brow, and set her intention for healing. A radiant protective mist encircled the light travelers and their wounded comrades.

Patrick spoke gently to Aube, reassuring him that they were caring for Gar. Drew gently reassured Gar that Aube was shaken but okay, and that Penzil and Chelli were administering hands-on healing to their wounds.

The Angelics stood in silent observation with their magnificent wings and arms spread wide. Their posture resembled that of Bezen and Mingo when the teens were dealing with Eittod's revelation of man's inhumanity to man.

Drew leaned closer to Gar to hear what he was whispering.

"Please, Gar, lie still," she begged. "I know you are concerned, but Aube will be fine. We're taking good care of him. He took a jolt, but he's not burned," said Drew in a soft, reassuring voice. "Penzil is tending to your burns. We know you are in great pain. Are you hurting anywhere else in your body?" she asked.

"I don't kno…" whispered Gar. His voice trailed off as he passed out from the intense pain.

Stunned at what was happening before them, tears eased down their fearful faces as they cared for their fellow light travelers. How could this have happened? They were so close to receiving the blue crystals, so close to clearing the portal. So close!

Drew glanced around at the twins' bodies for any signs of other injuries, but none were obvious. She continued to apply pressure to Aube's forehead and spoke softly into Aube and Gar's ears, uncertain if they could hear her. Tense moments passed. Then Aube and Gar began to stir.

"Gar's burns are healing," said Penzil softly in amazement.

Drew slowly eased the bandage from Aube's head.

"Aube's bleeding has stopped and the wound is closing," cried Chelli.

"The laceration is knitting itself together right before our eyes as if a master surgeon were at work here," said Drew excitedly.

They gently drew back their hands and watched as the wound on Aube's head slowly healed. Gar's severe burns stopped seeping, and new flesh began to appear.

"Gar, can you hear me? Are you okay? I love you, Gar. Please be okay," pleaded Aube, now more alert.

"I'll be fine, Aube," whispered Gar. "I am so sorry for hurting you."

"That's okay, Gar. You were just following your instinct to save the chest," said Aube. "I understand and I forgive you."

"Just take it easy now, guys. You're both going to be alright," said Patrick in a comforting tone. "Give yourselves some time. We're right here for you."

All stood in silent wonder, watching Gar and Aube heal. They became aware of the protective mist that had formed around them. They could feel Eittod, Bezen and Mingo close at hand. Soon Gar's wounds and pain were gone and healthy pink skin covered his chest and hands. There were no signs of scarring. Gar reached out for Aube's hand, and it was there.

"Thanks, everyone. Sorry for the drama," said Gar as he and Aube slowly moved into a sitting position with help from Patrick and Penzil.

With Drew and Gar's eyes locked upon each other, Drew backed away slowly.

"Gar, had you and Aube not been in an immortal state, I believe the jolt of current from the wooden chest would have killed you both instantly," said Drew with tears still easing down her beautiful face.

"You are correct, Drew Megan Campbell," said the first Angelic. "The Regions Authority placed strong energy around the chest to protect the blue crystal beings. The abundance of genuine love, caring and healing from your team filled this chamber and added to the rapid healing of Auben and Garcia's wounds."

Looking into Gar's eyes, the second Angelic spoke, "You are a fine young man, Garcia Gou-Drah Perez, and your courage, intelligence and bravery have served your Earth and its people. It was your selfless act to save the chest that has given you and your fellow light travelers the rite of passage to touch the crystals. It was the final test of your commitment to this journey and to each other," she said, now looking into the faces of all the light travelers.

Gar's head was reeling. The Angelic had just repeated Eittod's words – the words that Gar had repeated to himself so many times since that first night at the outpost, but never truly believed. Gar realized that Eittod knew he would be the one to save the chest and the journey. Gar now felt the truth of Eittod's words in his heart and soul. He *never was* just a tag along. And he knew he would never be the same. Gar was humbled.

CHAPTER THIRTY-ONE:
North Portal Battle of Light and Dark

"Rest, children of the Earth. You need time together," said the first Angelic.

The light travelers sat on the stone floor of the chamber and pulled their water pouches from their packs. Chelli passed the remaining hazelnuts around the circle, and they continued to check on Aube and Gar's healed wounds.

"You doing okay, mates?" asked Penzil, concerned for his new brothers.

"Not as weak as I had been," said Gar "I never want to feel like that again. And if I have to, I pray our light travelers are beside us. Again, thank you for your loving care and concern."

"I know you were more concerned for me than for yourself, Gar," said Aube.

"I never want you to suffer because of me," said Gar. "If a time ever comes, brother, where your life is threatened because of me, please, Aube, cut me loose."

Everyone was stunned by Gar's words.

"Same goes for me, brother. If ever my lack of health threatens your life, cut yourself free. Let's promise on that one," said Aube, reaching out to lock thumbs with his brother.

"Hey, guys, this is very serious talk," said Patrick, placing a hand on Aube's shoulder.

"Where better than in the presence of two angels," laughed Gar. "Let's clear this North Portal!" he said with gusto.

The teens were on their feet and ready for action.

As the Angelics placed their hands over the chest, it slowly opened. Brilliant light radiated out, and an indescribably beautiful sound filled the chamber. The sound vibrated every cell of the teens' immortal bodies. Again the light travelers were aware of their DNA. It mesmerized them. An overwhelming presence of love surrounded and infused them. The Angelics reached into the chest and drew forth clear crystals pulsating with aquamarine light and life. They gently placed them into each set of eager, outstretched hands.

The teens felt the pulsations of the blue beings filling their bodies; it was like a heartbeat, and it synchronized with their own heartbeats. Although they were solid stone, the crystal beings felt weightless and soft and warm in their hands. The aquamarine glow from the crystals lit up their faces and radiated into their auras. The light travelers felt a sacred connection with the beautiful beings from another world. They were awestruck.

"Light travelers, you and your army of light bearers are the chosen *'absorbers of the darkness of mankind.'* Mankind's hatred, rage, greed, fears and pain block the light of the ONE, the ABSOLUTE, from Mother Earth and her children. Remember no matter what happens, you are not alone. Stay strong, and know you have protectors. We honor you and bow to your courage and your love of humanity. You are connected, light travelers!" said the Angelics in unison.

As the Angelics glided upward, the stone ceiling of the chamber dissolved. The light travelers were lifted toward the heavens. Three spirals slowly drew them up into the North Portal which hovered high above the Hill of Tara.

Hundreds of Tuatha dé Danann, the race of the gods of Danu, surrounded them; their swords of deep blue laser light were raised high in commitment to the light travelers and mankind. The Regions Authority and the Angelics flanked them. Bezen and Mingo stood firm with their hands out to the side, sending rays of light and protective energy toward their teens. The light travelers could feel Eittod's presence envelope them, and Gypsy's fragrance filled the air. All their teachers and protectors were ready for battle.

Images of their army of light bearers shimmered around them. The faces of all the children of the Earth who walk beside them for peace and love in their world stood strong, committed, determined. All nationalities, all races, all countries and all belief systems were represented.

"Light travelers, set your intent to restore the portal of Wisdom and Love," instructed Drew. She waited as if listening to an invisible force directing her. Her presence was electric, vibrant and vital.

"Our time has come, children of the Earth, to claim the light, the peace and the love of the ONE, the ABSOLUTE, for all the children of the world, and for Mother Earth. Lift the crystal beings high, and set your intent to draw the darkness of mankind into their aquamarine light and through your immortal bodies, into the core of the Earth for neutralizing.

"Our battle of love begins, NOW!" Drew commanded.

Intense aquamarine light was thrust forth from the crystal beings, shattering the intense darkness of the portal into billions of fragments of ugliness. As the vibrating crystals absorbed the fragments, they sent out a deafening sound that echoed through the light travelers' bodies like a war cry – like the trumpet that sounded at Jericho.

Wave after wave of the darkness, violence and ugliness of mankind impacted them. Images of the atrocities of the wars of the recent centuries flew toward them and through them. Frightening, ghostly images of unthinkable war crimes and their innocent victims were drawn from the portal into the crystal beings, through the light travelers and into the Earth's core. The teens could feel the light and power of their army of light bearers sustaining them.

Horrific storms raged. Thunder cracked like a lion tamer's whip, and lightning bolts flashed all around them as the skies took part in the battle of love.

Century after century regurgitated its vile acts of greed, abuse, fear, terrorism and bullying, revealing man's inhumanity to man. Millions upon millions of men, women and children had paid the price for others' gluttonous appetites for notoriety, power, land and wealth.

Tears streamed from the teens' eyes in disbelief – mankind's violent rage, anger, fear and pain bore through them like javelins. But they did not falter. They held strong, determined to clear the portal – determined to bring peace and love to their world. The light travelers continually drew on their army of light.

Their protectors corralled the darkness, keeping it from escaping back into the world – into the consciousness of man, or into the other portals of the Earth. There was no escape for the wretched energy of the wicked and depraved.

Drew could feel the depth of pain her team was enduring.

"Eittod, I don't know that we can continue to bear this pain that we feel. It is so hard on the heart to care so deeply, so ruefully," Drew silently cried from the depths of her soul, painfully aware of the intensity that clutched at her heart and the hearts of her team.

The light travelers sensed Eittod's presence surround them and heard his voice vibrate in every cell of their being.

"Dear ones, it is easier to numb yourselves of all feeling as so many people of the Earth have done for too long, turning a blind eye and ignoring what needs to be done for the sake of all. You are the *CHOSEN!* The Earth and its people have waited eons for your depth of love, caring and commitment. You *must* be strong, dear ones. *You must!* All your protectors are here to assist you, but it is up to you, children of the Earth, to clear this portal. *Now, complete your assignment.*" His voice faded.

Drew looked around at her team; they nodded to reassure her that they had the strength and the courage to continue the battle. She looked toward their protectors. The faces of the protectors were intense, committed and looking to her for leadership.

Drew glared into the remaining darkness of the portal readying herself for the next onslaught. Her vibrant green eyes flashed with determination and renewed vigor.

There staring back at her from the depths of the portal was a galloping army of ghostly horsemen, some bearing bows and arrows, others wielding curved-blade swords, all screaming with insane rage. Their faces were contorted and their hands were smeared with the blood of thousands. Their leader, a large brute of a man, was covered in matted black hair. Hatred and greed flashed in his large piercing dark eyes. He was heading right for her. Drew grabbed a deep breath, but showed no weakness to her enemy. Her team flanked her. Their protectors moved closer.

Of Mongolian heritage, Attila the Hun drew his mammoth black steed to a sharp halt right in front of her; its nostrils were flared and steaming. Attila raised his sword in challenge. His army readied to strike at his command.

Face to face with evil, Drew realized she was holding a double-edged sword in her right hand, unaware of who had thrust it there.

She was armed!

With uncontrollable rage, Drew raised the sword, returning his challenge. She tightly gripped the crystal being in her left hand. It responded with penetrating warmth and sound.

A pleased expression crossed the Hun's filthy, ruddy face, followed by a growling mouth-curling sneer. Drew sneered back. She felt overwhelming hatred for what he represented race through her body. Never in her whole life had Drew Megan Campbell felt this depth of loathing and contempt. Her feelings frightened her.

The Regions' multi-toned voice spoke in the heads of the light travelers.

"A sword is double-edged – good and evil. Will you, Drew Megan Campbell, be the slayer of darkness and fear or the slayer of light and peace? It's your choice – you are a creator, dear child of the Earth. The choice is always yours. Once you have raised the sword, it must be lowered. But the blood must still flow within the two. Choose wisely, dear one." Their voices faded, yet still echoed in Drew's head.

She quickly put the riddle to memory, for she knew she was to hear it but once. Rage still possessed her – eating at her flesh – demanding retribution, demanding to be heard and freed. Her body was rigid, her mind was manic.

Drew looked around, knowing it was her choice and hers alone. She knew the others would follow her lead. They were waiting for her sign.

The words placed upon her by the Regions raced through her mind, *...slayer of darkness and fear or slayer of light and peace? A slayer* *of darkness and fear, of course,* she thought. *But…how? What is the answer to this riddle? Think, Drew, think!* she commanded herself.

Every fiber of her being – body, mind and spirit – wanted to lash out. *PAYBACK!* She clenched her teeth hard and focused. She could feel the fury in her hand as it tightened around the sword's hilt. Her blood boiled.

Suddenly without warning, Drew felt the overwhelming power of Attila racing through her own veins. It was an evil, hellacious power, yet exhilarating and intoxicating. Was she as evil as he? Had she allowed her rage to overtake her compassion?

Then as if Eittod were whispering directly into her ear, she remembered his words. *"One single act of love and forgiveness in a sea of rage and hate can turn the strongest tide."*

Drawing in a deep breath, Drew straightened her spine. Standing tall with every muscle in her body on fire, the choice was clear. All stood motionless as the sword in Drew's hand began to slowly move. With a slight flick of his sword, Attila readied his army for battle. He sneered at her with a victorious grin on his ugly, ghost-like face.

Penzil's chest pounded so hard it felt like it would erupt; yet he felt frozen as if in a time warp. He will follow Drew whatever her choice, but deep in his heart he wanted peace and compassion. Aube and Gar stood ready, expressionless and motionless as beads of sweat oozed from every pore and seeped into their amber eyes. Gar screamed from inside himself, "Destroy him. He deserves to suffer. He deserves to feel pain." Aube pleaded for forgiveness and mercy. Chelli could feel her Grand-Papá and felt his desire for love and brotherhood in the world. Patrick pleaded for wisdom and guidance for his great-granddaughter.

Drew felt them all in her heart. She knew their wishes and felt their anguish and rage. And she was aware of their compassion and desire for peace.

Finally, she had the answer to the riddle. Drew began to turn the broad side of the blade *down*. It gleamed in the lights of the flashing storm as it slowly turned. Mid-way down, the sword became suspended as she chose not to spill blood, but to allow the blood to flow within the two of them in peace and forgiveness.

"Connect with the six-directions, NOW!" Drew quickly commanded.

The light of unconditional love and forgiveness flew from the light travelers' bodies in all directions. The whole of the North Portal filled with the radiant love and forgiveness of thousands upon thousands of Earth children. Within seconds the battle was over. Drew released the sword from her hand, and it hovered as if frozen for all-time.

A shocked expression crossed the leader's ghostly face as the light travelers and their army of light impacted him. The Great Attila the Hun and his army had been defeated by love and forgiveness. An aquamarine blaze engulfed the portal as Attila and his horsemen faded into the flames. The blaze receded into the crystal beings, into the light travelers and into the depths of the Earth. And the wonderful smell of fresh earth after a storm was left in its wake.

"Power down light travelers. Our assignment here is complete!" said Drew.

CHAPTER THIRTY-TWO:
Palace of the Gods, AD 1725

Drew's hovering sword quivered and glistened. Stars formed around it as it lifted into the heavens toward its master. All watched in wonder as the sword took its rightful place in the scabbard hanging from the walker god's three-starred belt.

The Angelics approached the light travelers.

"Children of the Earth, you are so brave. Humanity and Mother Earth have just stepped into a new era in planet Earth's history. The Era of Love, Compassion and *TRUTH* has dawned. There is still much to do, but it's an amazing start. The crystal beings are proud to have served mankind with you," said the first Angelic as they both reached for the glowing stones. "The Regions will return them to their rightful place at Tara."

As the teens raised the stones toward the Angelics, the crystal beings filled the light travelers with incredible warmth, and the indescribably beautiful sound filled them once again. They felt the love of the crystals vibrate through their every cell.

Concerned for the crystal beings, Drew quickly spoke.

"Dear Angelics, what if man finds the chamber of the blue stones? I know that in my Earth time there is much speculation and excavation at Tara in search of a chamber and a chest."

"My dear Drew, the chamber of the blue crystals is not of your three-dimensional world, but of a dimension far beyond that of your 21st century perception. Humanity, in its growth and understanding, will eventually reach that dimension of compassion and genuine love. When that will happen is up to Earth's children," answered the second Angelic.

"Nothing is predestined," said the first Angelic. "Always remember, light travelers, time is not linear as your three-dimensional world believes. Rather it is circular, as your Outpost teachers have taught you, and as you have experienced. There is no beginning, there is no end and all is changeable; anything is possible. Your current Earth's scientists and physicists are awakening to many new *TRUTHS* in their fields of study. As mankind grows in compassion, love and peace, more *TRUTHS* will be revealed to them by the ONE, the ABSOLUTE."

A deafening sound erupted. Startled, the light travelers turned ready for battle. But to their amazement, they saw and heard their protectors applauding them and expressing gratitude for their overwhelming courage. The teens thanked their protectors with heart-felt gratitude. Overcome with joy and relief, the teens formed a huddle and nurtured each other.

"Great job, team! Let's go home!" said familiar voices.

They turned to see Bezen and Mingo coming toward them. The teens enveloped their beloved teachers in a big hug.

"Set your intent to travel, and repeat with me," said Bezen, joyfully.

Taking one last look, the light travelers glanced back at the brilliant, shimmering light now streaming from the North Portal. They felt closure and completion, and smiled lovingly at each other and their protectors. They then prepared to travel.

"'Gypsy, this is Copper Rings,' shouted Drew.
The other light travelers followed suit.
'The Elder,' shouted Patrick, 'Little Bear,' shouted Chelli,
'Roo, From the Land Beneath,' shouted Penzil,
'The Two-in-One,' shouted Aube and Gar, 'Mingo' and
'Bezen.'
Hear our petition for transport to Outpost Gypsy Tree!
NOW!"

Once again the light travelers felt a slight tingling and vibrational pull at the top of their heads, and the great rush of cold air pressed in on them. The familiar green florescent geometric shapes and symbols collided with their vibrating bodies as spiral after spiral drew them upward. Within seconds they felt their bodies compress and ease through the small slit in Gypsy's tree rings.

They were home.

Eittod was eagerly awaiting them. They rushed into his open arms. Joyful tears eased from his crystal-blue eyes, and overwhelming pride showed in his colorful, ancient face. Bezen and Mingo joined in the celebration.

"Light travelers, you were magnificent. I couldn't believe Attila and his men actually confronted you like that, but you showed those Huns your stuff! Your loving, compassionate, forgiving stuff, that is. And Drew! How amazing you were! We all owe you a debt of gratitude for the courage, strength, love and compassion you demonstrated in the portal. Leader to leader, Attila was no match for you. Bravo!" said Eittod.

Everyone applauded her.

She blushed.

"I owe so much gratitude to all of you for your support, trust and belief in me and our journey. Thank you!" said Drew humbly.

"Sounds like a pageant speech to me, Drew, but you forgot 'world peace,'" snorted Gar.

"You're incorrigible, Gar," said Chelli.

Everyone was bent over laughing, including Drew.

"Eittod, I have a question," said Chelli.

"What is that, Little Bear?" he asked.

"When and where is our next assignment?" she eagerly asked.

"Oh! Be patient, my dear Chelli. Be patient," he replied "All in due time!"

"I believe a victory celebration is in order, my dear Bee," announced Eittod.

Within seconds Bezen had created a homecoming feast for Outpost Gypsy Tree's triumphant warriors of peace. Streamers and confetti swirled through the snuggery. And fireworks exploded throughout the outpost. There were hugs, "way to go's," back slaps, high-fives and accolades all around. Gypsy also chimed in with a melodious welcome home.

The light travelers had been so revved up and tensed up in the portal that their bodies, minds and spirits needed this celebration and welcomed release.

They all feasted and eagerly shared their stories of the palace of the gods and the journey to the other world. They recounted their unforgettable challenges in the Cave of Damnation, the campsite and their playful camaraderie at the Hill of Tara. They told of the tragedy in the chamber of the blue crystals and the amazing battle for the North Portal. More laughter and jubilation erupted.

Unexpectedly, the breathtaking, opalescent presence of the Regions Authority appeared in the snuggery. Everyone's attention turned to the shimmering holographic image. The dedicated, compassionate overseers and protectors of all worlds, seen and unseen within the Milky Way Galaxy, had come to visit.

Eittod stood and gently bowed his head.

"Dear Regions, it's an honor to see you. How can we be of service?" asked Eittod, reverently placing his fist to his heart.

"We have come to thank your most capable light traveler team, their leader and their teachers. Great courage and compassion were displayed this day in the North Portal. Congratulations, everyone!" they said in unison in their deep harmonic voice.

"Now, moving on, we are sure the light travelers are anxious to know of their next assignment. Is that correct?" asked the Regions.

The teens were on their feet. They bowed respectfully and placed their fists to their hearts. All the light travelers started talking excitedly at once. The Regions laughed to hear their excitement and genuine commitment to the Earth and its people.

"Light travelers, you have proven your courage, worthiness and commitment to mankind and the Earth, and we are deeply grateful.

As we are sure you have already guessed by now, your next assignment will be to clear the South Portal."

The teens jumped up and down with excitement. Chelli punched the air. Many questions rolled off their tongues in rapid-fire succession.

"All your questions will eventually be answered, we promise," laughed the Regions. "But for now, we leave you in the capable hands of your beloved teachers." The Regions' hologram faded from the snuggery.

All eyes were now on Eittod.

"Yes, dear ones, your next assignment will be the South Portal. Actually, Peru will be your destination," he said.

Shock and elation filled Aube and Gar's faces.

"Can you believe it, brother? Peru!" said Gar, slapping a high-five with Aube.

"I'll get to see your home country!" said Penzil to his new brothers.

"Where in Peru, Eittod?" asked Aube.

"All in good time, everyone. Bezen, Mingo and I have much work ahead of us to prepare for your next journey. And you, dear light travelers, need to connect with your linear lives."

Mixed emotions ran through the teens. Going home means reconnecting with family, normalcy and – *mortality*. And it means saying goodbye to their beloved teachers and each other. They looked around at the faces that had meant home and family to them for months and at the surroundings that nurtured them. Nostalgia set in. Bezen could feel their mixed emotions.

"I think we need some sunshine and seawater, don't you, Mingo?" she queried.

"Absolutely!" said Mingo, fast on the uptake. Your Cetacean family has missed you, and Nudges has been moping around since you've been gone, Penzil."

The light travelers' faces lit up as they headed for Gypsy's large door. With quick nods, they were out and on their way to the ocean, bathing attire popping on from out of nowhere as they made their way to the water's edge.

There to greet them where the dolphins, the whales and...Lancelot who was watching from the sand dunes.

Penzil was the first one in the waves, and Nudges was right there pushing against him. Penzil's face lit up with joy.

Early the following morning all the teens were gathered in the snuggery.

"The reason I have asked all of you here this morning is of great importance. Drew and Patrick have one more assignment to complete," said Eittod.

"Why can't we all go, Eittod?" asked Gar. "We're a team, Sir."

The others chimed in with their requests to accompany Drew and Patrick.

"I understand that you are a team, and quite an amazing team at that. But this is for the Campbells to complete. It's their task, and their task alone. I have already informed Drew and Patrick of their assignment, and they understand why they must go without you," Eittod explained. "When you witness their journey, you will understand the importance of it being only for the Campbells."

"Have they already gone on their assignment?" asked Chelli, alarmed.

"No! No! Drew and Patrick are in the costuming station with Bezen and Mingo and will be along most anytime now."

The other light travelers sat with deep disappointment etched on their faces. They grumbled among themselves. Chelli was punching a pillow.

"Come, come now! You will be able to view their every move, I promise you. Now we must give them a cheerful send off," said Eittod.

Soon Bezen, Mingo, Patrick and Drew entered the snuggery.

"Wow! Drew, you look so beautiful!" said Chelli, now on her feet checking out Drew's costume. "You look like you're going to a ball."

"Our very own Cinderella!" said Gar.

"That's for sure!" said Aube. "Wow!"

"Drew, you look angelic-like!" whispered Penzil with a reverent tone in his voice.

"Thank you, everyone," said Drew as she blushed and did a graceful curtsy.

"And who is escorting our Cinderella to the ball at the palace? Her great-grandfather! Pathetic!" said Gar, disgruntled. "

Everyone laughed.

"Gypsy is waiting," said Bezen.

Drew and Patrick eagerly stepped onto the tree rings. Standing behind Drew, Patrick placed his hands on her shoulders.

"Ready?" asked Drew.

"Ready!" said Patrick.

> *"Gypsy, this is Drew Megan Campbell*
> *and Patrick Charles Campbell.*

Hear our petition for transport to the Central Chamber of the palace of the gods, Winter Solstice, Earth AD 1725! NOW!"

After the usual departure and the spiral journey down into linear time, Drew and Patrick found themselves in total darkness. They reached out for each other's hands.

"Begin our centering, grounding and vibrational breathing, NOW!" commanded Drew.

The rhythmic cadence chant began to play in Drew and Patrick's heads. Minutes later, feeling their powerful combined vibrations, Drew instructed Patrick to set his intent to draw stored energy and light through his feet, from their army of light in their current Earth time. They focused. Their vibrating bodies radiated with light. As their bodies glowed, they became aware of standing right next to the small obelisk with its pyramidal top. They were saddened to see that it was no longer colorful. All its beauty had faded with time.

As their eyes adjusted to the dim light, they saw heavy debris scattered throughout the chambers. Gnarled, thick tree roots had found their way into the sacred space, crept down the orthostats and chewed their way into the earthen floor. Their beloved palace of the gods had been desecrated by the ravages of time and neglect.

They were not alone. Several Tuatha dé Danann gods joined them. Dagda, Bóinne and Aonghus encircled them with their blue laser swords raised. Alarmed, Drew and Patrick stood frozen in place, unsure if the gods had come in peace and support, or to stop them from completing their mission.

Back in the snuggery, Eittod had summoned the revolving crystal from the rafters as Drew and Patrick left for AD 1725. The remaining light travelers and their teachers watched as Drew and

Patrick reached the dark chamber of the palace of the gods. They were also saddened by the condition of the palace and stunned at the appearance and stance of the gods.

"Eittod, they're in trouble! We must go to them," shouted Penzil, his body in motion. All the teens were on their feet in fear for their colleagues. Pillow piles were in shambles in their wake.

Eittod put his hands up to halt them as they made moves toward the time rings. Bezen and Mingo immediately blocked their path.

"Your colleagues are fine," Eittod stressed. "Please! Please, light travelers, sit down and just witness."

The image of Bóinne was now in the crystal. "Do not be afraid, my dear children of the Earth. We have come to assist you at Eittod's request," she said, looking into Drew and Patrick's faces. "Your assignment is on our behalf, and we are grateful for your assistance."

"Please move back from the obelisk," requested Dagda in his deep voice.

Still concerned, Drew and Patrick carefully stepped around the scattered debris and tangled tree roots to the back recess and stood alongside the triple spiral carving on the orthostat. Their eyes were glued to the three raised blue laser swords.

Dagda, Bóinne and Aonghus closed in on the obelisk; their swords were pointed directly at it.

Drew and Patrick looked at each other with confusion.

The gods' facial expressions were severe; their eyes were focused on the four-sided stone's center. A split second later blinding streaks of blue laser light penetrated the hard stone; the obelisk hummed. But the sound was very different from the sound that emanated from it when Drew had placed her triple spiral stone on its pinnacle in 3107 BCE.

"Our job here is done," said Dagda, "but we will stay close for your protection."

Aonghus looked deep into Drew's eyes as he took his place next to his mother and Dagda. Still unaware of their intentions, Drew was non-responsive to Aonghus' stare.

Drew and Patrick moved back into the central chamber, still leery and unsure of what had just happened with the obelisk.

"I will walk with you to just inside the entrance, Drew," said Patrick, nervously looking from Drew to the gods and back.

The great-granddaughter and great-grandfather walked slowly along the cluttered, root-laden passage toward the entrance. The palace of the gods was no longer the living, breathing creation that they had come to know and interact with. The orthostats leaned in at dangerous angles. There were no fragrant evergreens covered in white flowers nor red berries lining the sides of the passage. In fact, the air was stagnant and putrid. Heaviness surrounded them. The deep colorful carvings that had once radiated inches out from the orthostats, sharing their sacred information and archaic codes, were now shallow, colorless and silent.

Patrick stopped as they neared the end of the passage. "You're on your own, Drew. I'll wait for you here," he said in a whisper. "Holler if you need me."

"I am concerned, Grand. The energy of the gods seems different, cautious, troubled even."

"I agree, Drew. It's like they're fearful of something and it's giving me the heebie-jeebies," whispered Patrick.

"The what?" queried Drew amused.

"Never mind, let's just get this assignment done. I sure wish we had our team here," said Patrick.

"Me too!" said Drew. "I could use some Gar humor right about now!"

Again the light travelers at the outpost bombarded Eittod with requests to go to Drew and Patrick's aid. And again he declined their requests.

Alarmed, Drew could hear someone moving about just outside the passageway.

CHAPTER THIRTY-THREE:
Return to Planet Earth

Cautiously Drew moved out through the overgrown and partially obstructed entrance area. Her heart was heavy. The rundown appearance of her beloved Newgrange deeply tore at her. She had seen drawings at the Brú Na Bóinne visitor's center showing its condition in the early seventeen hundreds, but regretted having to see it with her own eyes.

Just yards from the entrance, a young man was digging through a pile of stones. His back was toward her.

Drew approached him

"Good morning!" said Drew in a very soft, loving voice.

The youth turned around, unable to believe the sight before him. He rubbed his eyes and looked again. He was taken aback with fear.

There before him stood a radiant Tuatha dé Danann goddess, glowing in the golden morning light of the winter solstice sun rising over the hill of Red Mountain. She was a beautiful being of light and perfection who had emerged from the passage; her garments, of what appeared to be fine silk, rippled gently in the cold morning breeze. She held a bejeweled scepter of gold and silver in her hand. A diadem of tiny multi-colored moving lights graced her copper-colored hair. And her fair-skinned feet barely touched the ground. Her bright green eyes looked deep into him.

He froze on the spot. His mouth gaped.

Drew spoke. "Are you of Campbell descent?"

After a long pause, he finally found his voice.

"Who...who...are...you?" he asked, his voice quivering, his tone just a whisper.

"Are you of Campbell descent?" Drew asked again in a soft, loving tone.

"Yes, I...I am...I am David...David Campbell. My...my family...*owns* this land," he stammered in a stronger voice, looking around for someone to help him. But he was quite alone with the goddess.

"Good!" Drew softly responded, aware of his dilemma.

"The Tuatha dé Danann are in great need of your family's help. Is the Campbell family willing to serve the gods of this palace, of this land?" Drew asked as she made a sweeping motion toward the land and the river with her gleaming scepter.

The young man fell to his knees and bowed his head slightly, never taking his eyes from Drew's face.

"The powerful gods of Erin need help from *my* family? How can this be?' he asked dumb-founded.

"The Tuatha dé Danann need the Campbell family's help to protect the secrets of this sacred site from those who would exploit it," answered Drew.

Unable to comprehend the situation he found himself in, the young man cautiously considered Drew's plea.

She patiently waited.

After a long pause, David responded.

"How can the Campbell family serve the gods of Ireland?" he asked, continuing to stare at the goddess as he slowly rose to his feet, mesmerized by her beauty.

"Please put out your left hand, David Campbell," asked Drew.

The young man slowly extended his left hand as Drew had requested.

"The Tuatha dé Danann requests your family's protection of this precious stone," said Drew, placing her small white quartz stone engraved with the triple spiral symbol into his left hand.

When the stone came in contact with his skin, the triple spiral symbol began to glow a brilliant aquamarine, and ancient images of the palace of the gods flashed into his mind.

He gasped. "I...just...just saw a magnificent structure covered with...with white quartz stones. It was glistening in the sunlight, and...and there were animals grazing and...and whooper swans covered the hillside. I don't understand what I just saw. And what's with this stone?" he said stunned and bewildered, looking down at the glowing spiral in his hand.

"David Campbell, what you saw is this structure over five thousand years ago in your distant past," said Drew, pointing to the dilapidated mound behind her.

"The stone with the glowing triple spiral symbol has recognized your Campbell heritage and confirmed your right to serve the Tuatha dé Danann.

His eyes widened with disbelief. Again he froze in place, staring at the stone glowing in his left hand. He then stared at the mound in front of him.

Drew explained to the overwhelmed young man that the task laid upon the Campbell family was the protection of the triple spiral stone. The stone and her words were to be passed down from father to son until such time as the *"rightful 'master of the stone' appears in feminine form when the snow flies."* Not until its rightful master holds it, will it glow again.

Drew explained that it will be the *master of the stone's* task, and hers alone, to travel beyond the Earth at great risk in search of peace, love and brotherhood for mankind. The *master of the stone* will be assisted by the bearers of the blue laser swords, the Two-in-One, the Little Bear, The Elder and the Roo, From the Land Beneath. This time will come to pass only when the Earth and its children finally cry out in great numbers for peace and love in their world.

David listened closely to Drew's every word. He knew this was real, this was important. He could feel it in every fiber of his being. The Campbell family had been chosen by the gods of Ireland. And they were charged with the responsibility of protecting the triple spiral stone.

David Charles Campbell promised the Tuatha dé Danann that his family would keep the words of the goddess in their hearts, and would guard the stone with their lives. He realized that if he had heard the goddess correctly, somehow the little stone he held tightly in his left hand would serve a vital role in bringing peace and brotherhood to mankind and the Earth.

Drew thanked the young man, then slowly walked back into the passage, into the womb of the gods, never to be seen again. It was assumed, according to the Campbell Family Myth, that the beautiful goddess was reborn into the other world – the world of the gods of Ireland.

Once back in the passage, Drew and Patrick made their way back to the center chamber.

"Drew, you amaze me. You were so loving and inspiring with the young David. So this is how it all began! I am speechless!" said Patrick.

"How do you think I feel, Grand, knowing I was the one who set this task on our family and us," said Drew in awe. "They were *my* words that our family passed down from father to son – the words that *you* will pass down to *me*."

Drew was overwhelmed by what she had just done. "It's mind-blowing, Grand! Simply mind-blowing!"

Counting on his fingers, Patrick said, "You do realize, Drew, that you probably just spoke to your great-great-great-great-great-great-great-great-grandfather?"

"Is that what you were doing, Grand, while I was outside with David?" Drew asked.

"Well, it gave me something to do while you were busy being a goddess," he said with a big grin.

"You're getting as incorrigible as Gar," she laughed and shook her head.

The gods were waiting for them in the central chamber. The Tuatha dé Danann bowed gratefully to Drew and Patrick and thanked them for their service and the service of the Campbell family. The energy of the gods seemed more relaxed, composed and content.

Dagda stepped forward to speak. "We have one more request of your family," he said, his tone serious again.

"What is your request?" asked Drew.

"We ask that you take the obelisk back with you to Outpost Gypsy Tree for protection. That way both the key to our world and its lock are in safe keeping."

Drew gave Patrick an alarmed look. He understood her concern.

"Dagda, we would like to oblige your request. The Campbell family and Eittod are always at your service. But the weight of the obelisk is too great for us to carry," said Patrick.

Drew nodded in agreement.

"Light travelers, we have already taken care of that for you," said Dagda. "Place your hands on the obelisk."

Drew and Patrick looked at each other, then back at Dagda. Aonghus stepped forward, again looking deep into Drew's greens eyes. Without saying a word he lifted the obelisk with one hand and then put it back in place. They were stunned.

Drew and Patrick reached forward and placed their hands on the four-sided stone. It certainly looked and felt like stone; it was cold and hard. They tried to lift it and were amazed at its feather-light weight.

"How is that possible?" Patrick gasped. "It feels like stone, and it looks like stone, but it's now almost weightless?"

"There are many things that your physicists have not yet embraced as *TRUTH*. There are those on your planet who have already discovered such things, but your mainstream sciences are not ready for such a leap," explained Bóinne. "How do you think we created our palaces throughout your world?" she asked. "Many ancient civilizations have known this *TRUTH*."

"Yes! Of course we will take it with us. I presume Eittod knows that it's coming?" asked Drew.

"Yes! He is expecting it," said Dagda with a grateful smile.

"We will wait until you are safely on your way. And thank you again for your service to the Tuatha dé Danann," said Bóinne.

Aonghus nodded in Drew's direction but did not speak. Drew acknowledged him with a gentle nod and slight smile. His face beamed.

Drew and Patrick stepped into the center of the chamber and placed their hands on opposite sides of the obelisk.

With one last look at the palace of the gods, they recited their travel request.

"Gypsy, this is Drew Megan Campbell,
Patrick Charles Campbell,
And the lock to the world of the gods.
Hear our petition for transport to Outpost Gypsy Tree!
NOW!"

Within seconds, they were being embraced by their anxiously awaiting team. Accolades bombarded them.

"How amazing, Drew, that you were the goddess who put the task on your own family," said Chelli all excited. "It's come full circle! How exciting!" she shouted, punching the air and jumping up and down. "I love this stuff!" she bellowed.

"Hey, mates, awesome stuff for sure," said Penzil. "And the gods changing the weight of the obelisk right before our eyes. Unbelievable! I've heard of folks who have done that. A physics genius in the U.S. built himself a castle with massive coral stones using the same concepts. I think our physicists need to boot Newton to the curb and get on with it! We're missing a few pieces to the physics puzzle."

"More like a few laws of physics!" piped up Gar.

"Look at the obelisk!" cried Patrick, pointing toward Gypsy's tree rings.

There before them was a completely restored, four-sided, three-feet high stone obelisk. Its colorful etchings were carved deep into the stone and radiating out inches from its surface. Drew reached down and touched it, and it hummed. The ravages of time had completely reversed.

"It's alive again!" Drew cried excitedly.

"Ah! Yes, it's in the eternal now! And later you and Patrick are welcome to place it in its new home here at the Outpost," said Eittod.

Drew and Patrick rushed over to Eittod who was anxiously waiting for them. They wrapped their arms tightly around him.

"Thank you, Eittod, for this amazing experience," said Drew. "Never in my whole life have I ever felt such deep connection with my heritage. First to have met Grand, and have the opportunity to really get to know the man I have loved and admired all of my life. And today, to have stepped back into my seventeenth century ancestry to meet and interact with David Campbell! How blessed I feel right about now," she finished, giving Eittod another big hug.

"I second that!" said Patrick, brushing moisture from his eyes. "I am speechless and deeply grateful."

"The Campbell family can be very proud of the dedicated service they afforded to their beloved Ireland, its gods and its precious monuments," said Eittod. "And you, my dear Drew, make a splendid goddess."

"Hear! Hear!" shouted Gar. "Even though she did go to the ball with her great-grandfather. The least you could have done, Patrick, was dress a bit better for the occasion."

"I guess I should get back to costuming and get out of these seventeenth century farm clothes," chuckled Patrick, moving toward Gypsy's transport chamber.

"Wait for me!" called Drew. "I am very ready to put the goddess to rest."

When Drew and Patrick returned to the snuggery, Eittod invited them to place the obelisk in its new home at the outpost.

"But where should we put it, Eittod?" asked Drew.

"The choice is yours. You and Patrick must decide," he said.

"It has been hidden away in that chamber for so long. It deserves to feel the sunlight, Drew," said Patrick.

"You're right, Grand. And I know the exact location for it. Follow me!"

Everyone followed Drew and Patrick as they carried the precious lock to the world of the gods between them.

"Where are we going, Drew?" asked Patrick.

"You'll see! It's a perfect location!" said Drew.

A parade of light travelers and their teachers made their way out through Gypsy's large wooden door, past the crystal-blue river with its turtles sunning on the banks, across the bridge, and then came to a halt. Above them loomed the archways filled with radiant starbursts and covered in strange symbols and ancient writings, illuminated in an eerie fluorescent green.

"This is the spot, Grand," said Drew, "between the archways of the eternal now and linear time. Just as we are caught between the two worlds, so are the lock to the world of the gods and its key."

"Perfect!" said Patrick. "I can't think of a better place than here, Drew."

Everyone was in agreement.

Patrick and Drew set the obelisk down midway between the two archways. As they did, it hummed. Curiously, Drew and Patrick reached to lift it. But as they had suspected, it had returned to its original weight. They smiled.

"Well, my dear light travelers, it's time for you to return to your linear time," said Eittod.

The teens were stunned. They thought they would have much more time to say goodbye.

"Eittod, how can we go home when our heads are so full of wisdom and knowledge, well beyond that of our world? How can we ever be normal and happy again, knowing what we now know as *TRUTH*? To know of the possibilities that exist, and have to live such a limited existence?" queried Drew.

"My dear light travelers, no one knows the secret to putting the genie back into the bottle. No matter how hard or how long one tries, it is impossible. But, dear ones, the *genie* knows how to return to the bottle. The genie, and the genie alone, knows the secret. You are the genie, and you can go home again and be happy. This I promise all of you who have journeyed from your linear time to here," vowed Eittod, laying his fist over his heart.

Bezen walked over to the departure archway. They all gathered around her.

"This is the way home for you, dear ones, and you know the passwords. As Eittod has told you, you will be able to live in your limited world again and be happy," she assured them. "And you will know that you have been here and that you will be called upon again. Take some time to say goodbye for now."

While everyone was busy saying goodbye, Gar privately approached Drew. "Goddess, please put out your left hand," he requested.

Drew looked into his almond-shaped amber eyes and put out her hand. Gar laid a purple flower of magic into her hand and closed it.

"Drew, remember *me*!" said Gar.

They all clustered together, arms around each other, tears easing down their faces, yet smiling at each other.

"Remember, Eittod will call on us again," Drew reminded them. "We will be back together soon. After all, we light travelers have more portals to clear. Three more that we know of. Right?"

"Right!" They all responded.

"So until then, we will hold each other in our hearts, and know that we have more work to do for Mother Earth and her children. But for now, I promised Mum and Dad that I would be home in time for supper."

They all laughed through their parting tears.

"And we have a football game to go to," said Aube.

"Go Peru!" shouted Gar as he punched the air with his fists.

Everyone shouted, "Go Peru! Go Peru!" and punched the air.

"And Uncle Titus is calling me for the next fish run," giggled Chelli. "I love the feel of the wet salmon slapping against my bare legs."

Everyone looked at Penzil.

"Well, mates, I must finish packing my gear. I promised a guy from CERN I'd guide him and his family through the outback for the next month," said Penzil with a very pleased look on his face. "Seems I've got a name for myself in the physics world these days, and I love it."

"As for me," said Patrick, "I need to pay more attention to my Dad's tales of the Campbell Family Myth. The information could come in handy," he finished with a chuckle.

Everyone laughed and slapped Patrick on the back.

Drew gave him a big hug. "See you soon, Grand. I love you."

"I am really going to miss all of you. It's hard being the only youth around here, but I'll see you all soon," said Mingo.

"One last huddle before we go," said Penzil.

The light travelers and their teachers huddled together, hungrily studying each other's faces. Gypsy's fragrance filled their breath, and her melodious sounds filled their hearts.

The teens stepped into the archway together holding hands, and recited their departure passwords:

"A peaceful, loving world is what we seek within our hearts,
And we are willing to clear the way for it to happen.
We are part of the solution.
We are the solution!
We are chosen.
Eittod, this is Drew Megan Campbell,
Patrick Charles Campbell, Chelli 'Little Bear' Freeman,
Penzil Kangaroo,
Auben Juan Perez and Garcia Gou-Drah Perez.
Hear our petition for transport home!
NOW!"

With one last glance back at Gypsy, they were gone.

EPILOGUE

Drew gasped. She could feel her parents' arms embracing her. The sun was setting behind Newgrange, creating an orange glow around the magnificent ancient structure. Disoriented, Drew looked at Meg first and then at Tom.

"Are you alright, Drew?" asked Meg, alarmed.

"What happened, Drewkins? For a split second there was light all around you, then...it was gone. It was like a big flash bulb went off. Are you okay? Did you see that, Meg?" asked Tom, relieved that Drew had not been taken from them.

"I didn't go anywhere?" asked Drew.

"No, dear," said Meg. Her voice lightened. "Like your Dad told you, there was just this big flash of light all around you and then it was gone," said Meg.

"But...but, I am sure I said the transport passwords correctly," said Drew with great disappointment in her voice. "And I have my stone in my hand as Eittod requested."

Drew opened her left hand. To her amazement, there in her hand was a small, very delicate flower. "It's a purple flower of magic," she said in a soft, knowing whisper. "I have been somewhere, and now I am home."

Tom and Meg stared down at the delicate purple flower in Drew's open hand, and both realized she had gone and been safely returned to them.

"Let's go home, Drew. The shuttle bus is still here," said Meg.

Tom waved to Michael. "Please wait! We're coming!" he called joyously.

On the other side of the world, Aube and Gar were looking at each other in the mirror, both aware of a maroon clad soldier standing behind them smiling with great pride in his almond-shaped amber eyes. Beside him stood a beautiful angel. Then they were gone. Disoriented, Aube and Gar just looked at each other.

"What just happened? We did go, didn't we?" asked Aube, now realizing that the joy he felt in his gut was still there.

Gar was expecting to feel those icy fingers gripping at his spine at the sight of the soldier and the angel, but instead he felt such warmth in his heart, and had a distant memory of beautiful soft green eyes looking into his.

"Gar, these aren't the clothes we had on a few minutes ago, are they?" asked Aube.

"You're right," said Gar, "and look at this, Aube." Gar held up the Perez family ring. The star cluster on the black stone glowed.

"Come on, boys," shouted Senor Perez. "We don't want to be late for the big game."

The twins just smiled at each other in the mirror. They both punched the air shouting, "GO PERU! GO!"

ABOUT THE AUTHOR

Still a child at heart, Dr. Dottie Graham lives with her beloved husband and amazing family in Southeastern Virginia. She is currently writing book two of the series, **Outpost Gypsy Tree, The South Portal**.